AS
THE
RAVEN
FLIES

Job Tyler Leach

MILFORD HOUSE

an imprint of Sunbury Press, Inc.
Mechanicsburg, PA USA

MILFORD HOUSE

an imprint of Sunbury Press, Inc.
Mechanicsburg, PA USA

For information about special discounts for bulk purchases, please contact Sunbury Press Orders Dept. at (855) 338-8359 or orders@sunburypress.com.

To request one of our authors for speaking engagements or book signings, please contact Sunbury Press Publicity Dept. at publicity@sunburypress.com.

ISBN: 978-1-62006-838-0 (Trade paperback)

Library of Congress Control Number: 2018963683

FIRST MILFORD HOUSE PRESS EDITION: November 2018

Product of the United States of America
0 1 1 2 3 5 8 13 21 34 55

Set in Bookman Old Style
Designed by Crystal Devine
Cover by Riaan Wilmans
Edited by Erika Hodges

Continue the Enlightenment!

INTRODUCTION

I lifted my head just slightly, my eyes rolling up as far as they could go. I watched my uncle, head bowed, bless the food in between wet intakes of breath. His meaty hands were pressed flat together and his index fingers rested against his forehead. Everyone else also had their head faced down toward the table, except for my little cousin Sammy. He silently rolled a toy dump-truck over the handle of his butter-knife. I looked back at Uncle Pete.

He was gently scratching his nose as he came to the end of his prayer. "And we give the greatest thanks for our good fortune, this food, and the chance for us to get together. In your name, blessed Jesus, we pray. Amen."

I chewed an annoying piece of skin around my fingernail that had been hanging there since I woke up in the morning. I finally nipped it off right as Uncle Pete said amen. As the 'n' hit the tip of his tongue, Uncle Pete picked up the nearest serving-spoon that was buried in the mashed potatoes. It made a little sucking noise when he pulled it out. He stuck it back in the bowl and yanked a big scoop of potatoes, plopping it sloppily onto his plate. He had already stuffed almost half of a roll into his mouth when I wasn't looking.

He exclaimed loudly, "This is one helluva spread here; it's good I'm starving!"

"When aren't you, dear?" said his wife, my Aunt Sarah, sarcastically.

"Hey, I always feel full for at least ten minutes after I eat. I'm not an animal."

"No comment." Aunt Sarah smirked a little and nibbled on some corn.

They constantly exchanged these foolish remarks back and forth like corny sitcom characters. I guess it was supposed to make all of us see how clever they were. Maybe they though it was sweet in some way. What it really amounted to was that both of them were pretty much idiots. Uncle Pete could have whole conversations like that, being very pleased at how goofy and quick-witted he was. Meanwhile, Aunt Sarah was almost always being quite passive aggressive. I could almost like her if she would just eliminate the passive from that equation and just let my uncle have it. She usually brought up something like the table manners, some trait that drives her nuts. If you pay attention, you know it has probably been grating on her for years. My uncle does not pay attention. He is usually clueless to the whole undertone of the conversation, too busy congratulating himself for his wily replies. Of course, Aunt Sarah would always drop it, so she probably hadn't gotten in the last word for about twenty-five years. At least not any word that my uncle was listening to. Aunt Sarah isn't terrible. Uncle Pete is kind of a bastard.

Thanksgiving. Every year we gather at a different household to celebrate the holiday. This year, everyone came to our house. Usually the guests include my parents, Dean and Allison Heller, Uncle Pete and Aunt Sarah Crayton, their three children, and Grandpa Crayton. And me, of course. Grandma Crayton passed away, like, twelve years ago, so I don't remember her all that well. My father's parents had died around the same time, both coming from families with poor genes when it came to longevity. Uncle Pete and Aunt Sarah's two oldest daughters, Katie and Heather, are absent this year. They're both grown up and spending the holidays with their in-laws. They also both live out-of-state. Sammy was the result of a decision by Uncle Pete and Aunt Sarah to try for a baby late in life. He's five now. Uncle Pete was thrilled when his wife finally squeezed out something with a penis that would continue the family name, hopefully inheriting the genes necessary to make him a spectacular football star.

Uncle Pete had your standard head football coach story: high school star, college scholarship, wasn't quite talented enough for the next level, wasn't entirely comfortable admitting that, stayed involved with football to ease the pain of being mediocre, coached a successful high school program, head coach at a junior college, assistant coach at a major university, and now a head coach at Indiana Central University. ICU has a long football tradition, dating back to the 1920s. They send players to the NFL ever year. The school has been consistently nationally-ranked. Oh yea, and some people at the school even go to class.

It's not the school itself that bothers me. It's mostly that Uncle Pete and the most rabid ICU fans make me want to run head first into a defensive line with no helmet on. I like sports on a more reasonable level. I even played, and enjoyed, several sports growing up. I wasn't any good, so I sort of faded out of the sports scene. Regardless, I did like playing them at one point. I still follow them, though not really intensely. So it isn't some deep-seated bitterness I have about sports in general. I'm not some kind of hater who looks down on stuff like that. There is just some weird stuff going on with some fans, especially at the college level. I don't get fans who follow something with a devotion that probably doesn't exist for anything else in their lives. Basing your whole being on something to which you probably don't have any direct connection is just very strange to me. Maybe some have gone to the school they support; I get that a little more. But many are just random people not involved with the school, football program, or anything except buying shirts, hats, sweatshirts, bumper stickers, license plates, and other shit. I can't believe the extent to which people can convince themselves they are passionate about something. And the money that is involved with college football is truly mind-blowing. I can't say I know the exact figure of what Uncle Pete makes, but I know damn well it is not a small amount.

The sound of Uncle Pete whistling snapped me to attention.

"What's up with you, not going to eat on Thanksgiving? I mean, more for me, I guess. Still seems weird."

I looked at my dad. I know he shared my disdain for Uncle Pete. We talked about it all time. Of course, we always waited till Uncle Pete was gone before we did any of this. When he was around, my dad mostly spent time looking at the floor and grinding his teeth. I don't blame him too much for being non-confrontational. Uncle Pete is not one to take shit off of anybody, really. Still, I would love to see my dad just flip out on him someday. I have some vague sense that arguments and disagreements had gone down in the past. My mom, Allison, is Uncle Pete's sister. She's also had her rifts with him. They get along most of the time, though.

"Helloooo!" said Uncle Pete loudly, tilting his head.

I smirked at Uncle Pete and said, "I'm just not interested in having my hand chewed off. You're a little nuts until you have at least three pounds of food shoved down your gizzard." He laughed, oblivious to how little I was kidding.

"You're a riot, but enough jokes, eat something."

I was hungry as hell too. I had momentarily zoned out, forgetting how starved I was. I have a big appetite, huge really. I wouldn't even doubt I could actually eat more than Uncle Pete. Doesn't mean I shovel it in like a slob, but I am a damn bottomless pit.

"Mom, slide that bowl of potatoes over here, please." I smiled genuinely. "Everything looks great," I added politely.

"Thanks, dear." She nudged the bowl over towards me. I took a large helping of those, followed by large helpings of everything else. Same dishes as every year; stuffing, mashed potatoes, green beans, corn, sweet potatoes, and, of course, turkey. Very Norman Rockwell-ian setup.

"So, tell me what's going on with the college thing, Corvus. I'm sure you've been busy looking all the stuff up online and what not. Have you made any decisions?" probed Aunt Sarah.

My entire fall had been spent listening to similar questions from my parents. The truth was that after seeing the estimated cost of college, I had nearly given up on going to college at all. I could not believe the massive number staring back at me on every school website I went to. My parents had told me that I should not worry about it; they would help me figure it out. I didn't really want that kind of money hanging over my and my parents' heads. It seems like such a load of shit. My father is a fifth-grade teacher, and my mother only works part time at her friend's clothing boutique. I know they worry about the money, I'm not brain-dead.

"I'm still trying to figure that stuff out. There's a lot to think about," I said.

"Have you narrowed your choices down?" asked Aunt Sarah.

I hadn't realized the table was going to become a guidance counselor's office. Why couldn't I just keep my planning private? If I thought she had some kind of even remotely constructive advice for me, maybe I wouldn't be so bothered. But no, her probing was just a way to fill up silence at the dinner table. Fuel for Aunt Sarah's small talk. There was pretty much no part of my personal life that I really felt like sharing with her.

I imagined taking the bowl of mashed potatoes and emptying it on her head. Just dump them and leave the table without a word. That is the response I would have preferred to give her. Instead I just took a bite of the potatoes. I swallowed, then replied, "Well, Middenberg University has always been my first choice. I think I mentioned that before."

"How could we forget," Uncle Pete said through a mouthful of meat, "You pick our arch-rival as your damn top choice. You're killing me here!"

I had to restrain myself from making a crack about choosing Middenberg because they had a better football program. ICU had recently undergone some rough years. I don't know exactly what happened. Maybe poor recruiting. Injuries. Bad luck. Some combination of those and more I guess. Regardless, the unfortunate years had made Uncle Pete even more of a shithead than he had ever been. Like avoiding the mashed-potato-over-the-head response, I held back on any smart-ass comments.

"They're supposed to have a really good psychology program. Good campus, I like the distance that it is from home . . .good sports teams too." I couldn't resist at least a small jab.

"As much as I'd like to see you at ICU, it sounds like you really have made a decision. You have always had good grades. You did great on your SAT too, right? I'm sure you wouldn't have trouble getting in there." said Aunt Sarah.

"Yea, I've done pretty well on everything. Actually, I've already been accepted early. Just trying to sort everything out, I guess." I waited for my mother to jump in; she didn't disappoint.

"He's so worried about the cost. We've been telling him over and over that things will work out if he just goes somewhere that makes him happy to do something he cares about and will work hard at. There are all kinds of programs and grants out there. And loans don't have to be paid back 'til after you graduate. We've tried to tell him."

Uncle Pete weighed in, "She's right. You shouldn't worry so much about the money issue right now. It's good and all, knowing the cost. Sometimes, though, you just have to go for it."

That's easier for some in this room to say than others, I thought. Out loud I said: "Can we drop this right now? I said I'll be thinking about it, and I will. Just let it go for now."

Everyone was silent for a little while, except for Uncle Pete breathing loudly out of his nose while he ate. There was some more talk that I didn't really participate in. Discussion about my cousins' new lives, my mom's new rug, a rug Aunt Sarah might want to buy, what plants would be planted next spring, Christmas talk, how my father's class was this year, the importance of marinating a steak just right, compliments about my mom's cooking, fake modesty from my mom, and on, and on, and on. So much talk to not say much.

Eventually, everyone was full. Even Uncle Pete couldn't stomach any more. Aunt Sarah and mom gently argued over who would the dishes, both insisting the other just go relax. Finally, Aunt Sarah prevailed and started collecting all of the dirty dishes. "Peter, why don't you lend me a hand with the dishes. Won't take long, plus that game doesn't start for another . . ." she glanced at her sparkling watch, "twelve minutes."

"Babe, you know I like the pregame. I've already missed most of it. It's a rare day off, c'mon." He didn't wait for an answer, padding off with his athletic socks swiping the ground. Aunt Sarah strained her neck and said loudly:

"If it's a day off, why are you watching football?"

"Bah! This is different, you know that. I'll help you when it's over."

Aunt Sarah turned to me, rolling her eyes. "The man used to tackle 250 pound men trying to run him over and destroy him, can't tackle a sink full of dishes."

I shrugged at her then left to go to the living room myself. Uncle Pete already had the television up to about 9000 on the volume level. I pretended to clean my ears, but the joke was totally lost on Uncle Pete. Dad had already stretched out on the couch with a book. Oddly enough, he was reading a book about the history of the Detroit Lions while he ignoring the game on the television that was actually being played by the Lions. I almost laughed out loud.

I pulled out my phone and prepared a message to my best friend, Jeremy. I wished him and his family a happy Thanksgiving. I sent him another message:

"Detroit"

A minute later my phone shivered. I opened Jeremy's message:

"Oh yeah this is Packers all the way."

I smiled. Our understanding was that every bet was for ten dollars, unless we stated otherwise. We had been trading bets back and forth for the last couple years. Friendly, but we had loyally paid each other at the end of every week since we started. Ten dollars was just enough action to actually tolerate Uncle Pete's inevitable play-by-play commentary and scornful critique of poor coaching decisions. I laid my phone on the end table and eased back into the swollen cushions of our La-Z-Boy to watch the game.

♥ ♣ ♦ ♠

Later, I watched the flat oval skip along the surface of the river, counting the long but low-rising jumps. The small stone sputtered until I couldn't count the skips, finally sinking for good. From beside me, I heard the faint zoom of another stone flying past me. The sinking sun was still bright enough to put a brilliant glare on the slow-flowing dark brown water. When I looked out to try to count the hops of the tiny boulder, I was temporarily blinded by the intense flash of light off of the water.

"Jeremy, you're almost as shitty at skipping stones as you are at picking winners in betting football." I turned back to look at him. He was already looking for another flat stone to throw. He looked up at me briefly, smiling. Then he just laughed and went back to digging through the tiny boulders.

"Hey, at least you're good with your quick responses to insults," I said sarcastically. We both laughed and I started nudging the ground with my toe, looking for my next skipper.

Ever since I was little, I had come down to the banks of the White River. My friends and I would spend hours scooping up crayfish and tadpoles. We'd put them into buckets with a shallow pool of water, having the grandiose idea of starting some kind of aquatic animal farm back at our houses. Of course, none of our parents ever let us bring the muddy buckets anywhere close to the house. Inevitably, the buckets would sit out by our swing-sets, or a shed, or something; ignored. The water would get progressively more dirty and slimy. Leaves would fall into the creature's already cramped domicile. Sometimes mold even grew on parts of the wall. What had been a terrifically exciting project while still at the river would be forgotten. Our obliviousness and poor attention spans would result in a disgusting and wretched home for the creatures. Eventually, the small animals would fade into a slow, tortured little death. Sad, really. On a less gruesome note, we'd also skip rocks at the river.

"So what happened with Stacy the other night?" asked Jeremy.

"Not much, really. We went to the movie. Didn't make out. We got ice cream afterwards at Jimmy Jack's. Didn't make out. I drove her home. Did not make out."

"That sucks. Haven't you gone out like five times or something?"

"Six. I mean, there isn't a number on these things, but c'mon, I think spending most of the money I make landscaping at the golf course deserves a little tongue, man."

Jeremy chuckled. "If I spent that much, I would have hoped her tongue would have been in a couple different places by this point!" He threw a stone and let out a grunt that punctuated his sentence.

"She's okay. I probably won't go out with her again. We got along decent at first, but now she is already starting to annoy me. We'll be friends and all. I don't think it's going anywhere though."

"You're not even going to try to bang her? I bet if you just went out a few more times, something could happen."

I had heard this plenty of times from Jeremy. He's had sex with one girl but acts like he's some kind of gigolo. Don't get me wrong, Stacy was hot as hell. I was lucky to even go out on a date with her. I would love to take it further with her like Jeremy was suggesting. Still, I just didn't feel like going through so much bullshit. I chucked a small pebble half-heartedly, knowing it was too round to skip.

"I just don't want to bother with it. There are other girls I'd rather go out with anyway."

The truth was that I was a virgin. I had fumbled around a few times with a couple different girls. But never the whole way. It was something I would dance around when talking with my friends. I know that a lot of what comes out of their mouths is probably bullshit anyway. Jeremy knew I had never had sex. Most other friends though, I sort of hid it from them.

I took a break between stones to rest my arm. I stared hard at my barely visible reflection on the murky mirror of the river surface. My features weren't sharp in the rippling water, and my nest of curly brown hair looked even sloppier in my reflection than it did in real life. I'd needed a haircut for weeks but kept putting it off for no real reason. The distortion of my image made my spindly arms look a little bigger, so I subtly flexed one bicep when I knew Jeremy wasn't looking. I let my arm flop down when I could feel him again looking at me. I gazed out at a small island near the middle of the river, not wanting to seem too confrontational, and added, "Plus, you know it's not really like that. There's no guarantee that she's gonna rip her clothes off and go wild because we hit a certain number of dates. You know it's not that simple." I knew if I said something like that he'd stop pushing me about it so he wouldn't seem creepy.

"I know, I know. I don't mean it that way. You do what you think is best, man." Quickly changing the topic he asked, "You have to answer a bunch of questions about college at Thanksgiving?"

"Well, they asked 'em, but I didn't really give too many answers."

"Good, screw that douche uncle of yours." Jeremy flicked away an ant crawling on his forearm.

"Aw, you've never liked him since he didn't give you that award for best defensive player at that football camp in seventh grade."

It was true, too. Jeremy had been badmouthing my uncle at every opportunity since that summer. Not that I cared, I didn't like him any more than Jeremy did. It was just funny; Jeremy had quit football forever after that. He had started as soon as you could at eight years old. It was a pretty big thing in our town, which is a place in Indiana called Jennings, by the way. He played right on through his elementary school years, seemed to love it. I remember he got so wrapped up in trying to win that stupid little ribbon that summer. He was pretty good, too. Maybe the best overall player at the camp. Anyway, the kid that ended up getting the prize had parents who were great friends with Uncle Pete. Old high school teammates, fellow all-stars, probably shared jock straps. Real beautiful friendship. I guess it was pretty clear that even if Jeremy didn't win, that kid sure as hell shouldn't have. Most didn't really pay attention, but it burned Jeremy up. As soon as he got home, he disappointed his parents by declaring that he wouldn't be playing football in the fall. They were a little mad, mostly because they couldn't get the money back that they had paid for him to join the team, though. They were okay though and didn't bust his balls about it too much.

"You know he's a dick, don't act like I'm the only one that thinks so." Jeremy picked up a volleyball-sized rock with two hands. With a big heave he launched it into the water, sending up a splash that looked like a toddler doing a cannonball.

"I won't argue that." I said, turning away from the splash.

Without another word we started walking away from the river, silently agreeing that it was too damn cold to spend any more time there.

CHAPTER 1

Senior year had passed quickly. Some fun moments here and there, but pretty boring for the most part. Nothing exciting enough to make me disappointed at the arrival of graduation.

I scanned the sea of bodies around the gymnasium, stopping here and there to squint my eyes. It really cracked me up. The district superintendent droned on and on. Most of the time I could guess who was next without looking at the line of students waiting to accept their diplomas. I had an unusually good knack for remembering the order of people's last names in my class. I would either think of the person who was next, or check and see. Then I would scan the crowd, trying to place who their family might be. Of course, I knew some people's parents already. Those I just skipped over. It was such a large crowd that I wasn't able to match too many, but the few that I did were funny. You could tell when it was their kid because they would either light up a little bit or clap even though they weren't supposed to. They would also start whispering in each other's ears; no doubt saying how they were about to cry, or how grown-up the kid looked, or how this was the first day of the rest of the kid's life, or something like that. Anyway, it was a good little activity to pass the time.

Take Ashley Aschroft. She's a pretty snotty little bitch with a never-ending supply of fashionable clothes and vicious remarks. She isn't all that intelligent, but smarts aren't always needed when you can rely on pure cruelty. I looked around for any guy that looked like he was either on his way to make a tee-time, or fresh off of the eighteenth hole. Maybe both, depending on how much is wife annoyed him. Almost assuredly, he would have a cell-phone clipped to his belt or something. Mr. Ashcroft's peach polo shirt really gave him away. I got that one.

And Johnny Everly. He's a decent dude. The one and only time I smoked weed, it had come from him. Some sad looking leaves and stems wrapped in wax paper. And stapled. Stapled for God's sake. Needless to say, he wasn't exactly running a large operation. Not exactly a kingpin. Other than that I haven't really spent time with him. We had history together in tenth grade. Maybe science freshman year, I don't remember. He always wore band shirts. Most of the time it was his tried and true Metallica garb. I had a strong feeling his father would have some kind of steel-wool-thick goatee with some gray streaks in it. I also had my eye out for some acid-washed jeans and maybe a do-rag or bandana on his head. I found him quick too. And it didn't take me long to confirm, either. Johnny's father put two fingers in his mouth and let out an insanely piercing whistle. This prompted an announcement:

"IN THE INTEREST OF TIME, PLEASE REFRAIN FROM CELEBRATING INDIVIDUAL STUDENTS. WE HAVE A LONG CEREMONY TO GET THROUGH. ALSO, OTHER PARENTS MAY MISS HEARING THEIR OWN CHILD'S NAME BEING CALLED. PLEASE RESPECT EVERYONE ON THIS SPECIAL DAY."

Johnny's father threw up both arms and held them out wide, signaling his disagreement with the policy. He didn't have any kind of head-covering, but he did have a chain-wallet hanging from a pair of 80s looking, thoroughly-bleached jeans. He had also broken out his black button-up for the semi-formal occasion. Sleeveless, but in a tasteful way; not a single long fray hanging off of it. He had really gone all out, trim job on the shoulders and everything. Anyway, another match.

I also succeeded at guessing Jaron Haver's parents, only, he was one of three black kids in my class, and I actually had a one out of two shot because I knew that the only female black girl in the school had been adopted by white parents. I don't remember who told me that, but if I took them seriously enough to remember that, it must have been a pretty reliable source. Anyway, it's a real diverse institution they have. The amount of black students (or "coloreds," as my grandfather would say) had gone up 300% in the last fifty years. You do the math.

Outside the gymnasium, I posed for a memory card's worth of pictures. I held my diploma up proudly and smiled till my face hurt.

CHAPTER 2

On a cracked street, the evening is turning into night. The place is one that many people think about like a setting for a fairy tale. Like a fairy tale in that one has a vague sense it could exist. But lacking in magic. There are words and stories that say it exists, but nobody seems to really believe those who claim to have been there.

A tickle of a cockroach on bare skin in the dark.

Profuse sweat in summer, uncontrollable shaking during the winter.

A stink that can't be pinpointed.

Bottles with an inch of beer and spit inside, sitting awkwardly in the middle of the sidewalk.

Stores with ugly tan and brown mosaics of cheap floor tiles, generic foods, lurking cameras.

An overriding sense of isolation that grows hands that choke and kill.

♥ ♣ ♦ ♠

But in this place there are lights that shine. Burning beacons that have refused to have their switch flipped off. In this place, there is at least one house, actually one half of a duplex, that offers something. Inside there is a television on, excited voices almost drowning out the drone of it. A voice rises above the rest, firmly shutting everyone up. Finally, all the voices are silent. The television hollers:

> *We have one heck of a young man with us here. He has had an excellent career and there is no doubt he will be missed at his high school. As captain, he led his team to the Illinois state championship the last two years. This young man's back has graciously carried the load of his whole team when they needed him most. He racked up an astounding 5,197 rushing yards, 1430 receiving yards, and 59 touchdowns. Four-time*

league all-star, four-time team MVP, and captain three years. We're proud to introduce Mr. James Raven! Without further ado, let's hear his choice straight from the young man himself! What's it going to be James?

A young African American with a freshly trimmed haircut close to his scalp grabs the microphone with a confident smile and a small humble nod of appreciation to the announcer.

This is a big day for me and my family. I've been waiting to make this official for a while. I'm crazy excited for what is to come in the future. I have high hopes for great things, and I want those great things to happen at . . . Middenberg!

The young man wiggles a dark blue cap onto his head. The cap has a large, calligraphy-style "M" stitched on the front of it. He shoots another radiant grin at the camera while his proud mother grasps him around both of his shoulders.

Far away, inside the half-house, there's hooting and hollering. Those who can whistle let out a series of ear-splitting blasts that sail out into the darkening sky. A cork from a bottle of cheap champagne pops. It's a small party, really. Maybe nobody else gives a shit. But they're making one hell of a racket.

CHAPTER 3

My parents threw me a graduation party right after the commencement ceremonies. It was mostly a bunch of family members and friends of the family; an odd mix of people who I either hadn't seen in years or had never met at all. Even though it was my graduation party, there were very few attendees I particularly cared about. A few decent ones here and there, I guess. The thing was, most of my friends either had graduation parties of their own or were just spending time with their families and stuff.

The sun shone brightly on our manicured back lawn. Mom and Dad had spent weeks trimming trees, snipping the bushes, and pulling weeds in preparation for the party. Mom's flowers were sprouting up in several different areas, purples and pinks and blues and yellows popping out from the other green plants. Even the vegetable garden looked pretty. Most of the plants were still too young to be producing anything, but the zucchini was already turning into a monster of green tentacles like it did every summer. The herbs were still infantile but stood up stiffly like pipe cleaners. My favorites were the tomato plants, which wouldn't pop out edible tomatoes for another few weeks, maybe even a month. They were still tame, but they always grew quickly and became wild bouquets of leaves and tiny yellow flowers. Mom and Dad would fight with them all summer, trying to keep stems clipped and dead leaves removed. Dad would whisper curses while tying and wiring and staking the erratic arms of the plants. The yard really did look great though, they had really done a lot of work to get it as nice as it was.

"Corvus!" I heard my mom's voice from a few yards away, behind me.

"What's up, mom?" I responded pleasantly before turning around.

"Make sure you see Jerry and Nancy before they leave. They have to go early because they are off to Myrtle Beach for their family's annual summer vacation. I don't want you to miss them.

They gave you a really nice card with fifty bucks in it. Really nice of them. They didn't even need to do that."

"What do you mean . . . did you open the card? I didn't even see it yet."

"Well, I knew they were leaving so I opened it while they weren't looking. I figured I'd let you know what was in it so you could make sure to thank them before they get going."

"You just stay out of my cards, nosy," I smiled at her playfully and added, "I think that's a federal offense."

"Oh, shut it and go find them."

I started walking to the other side of the yard. I hadn't seen Jerry and Nancy at all, so I figured they had their big asses in their foldable lawn chairs specially made with extra padding and special support for large behinds. The kind with three cup holders and a roof and maybe a built in TV or something. Although some people were milling around, nearly everybody had brought chairs and had set them up underneath the portable pop-up roof that my dad had put up in the one corner the yard. Of course, once everybody had their chairs up there wasn't enough room to move at all.

I looked around for Jerry and Nancy, occasionally catching the glance of one of the other guests at the party. I gave obligatory smiles and nods to most of them, some "hellos" and "heys" when somebody spoke to me first. I spotted Jerry and Nancy by the drink cooler. Jerry was holding two paper plates with big piles of food on them while Nancy dug through the ice for the drink of her choice. Probably a Diet Coke to go with her seven pound plate of food. They both saw me at the same time and cheesed some big smiles at me while they squinted into the sun. Jerry forgot what he was doing, and when he slid a hand out to shake mine, one of his two cheeseburgers slid off of his plate. It flipped in mid-air, the top bun fell off, and it landed with the sticky ketchup and mustard side face down.

"Ah, shit . . ." he quickly corrected himself, ". . . I mean shoot! Ugh, forget it. You're pretty much an adult now. I guess I can stop worrying about cursing around you, ha ha!"

I replied, failing to hide my sarcasm: "Hey, I have to learn those no-no words sometime, right?"

He laughed but didn't seem to know exactly how to take what I said. I changed the topic to try to squelch the awkwardness.

"Hey, thanks so much for the gift. I'll make sure to put it to good use!"

He seemed relieved, "No problem buddy! You've been such a good kid over the years. Since we don't have any kids of our own, we really like to watch kids from the neighborhood grow into mature adults. . . ."

The whole time he was talking, all I could think about was the spelling of awkwardness, and how it was funny that the word is spelled kind of awkwardly. I mean, there can't be that many words in the English language that have 'wkw" in a row like that. So weird. I was catching most of Jerry's heartfelt speech even though I couldn't stop thinking about that damn spelling.

". . . and we're happy to give a little something on the big day today."

"Well, I really appreciate it. I'm going to go grab a plate of food; seeing your plates got me really hungry. Thanks for coming to the party."

Actually, he must have already downed a burger and the dried ketchup hanging from his light brown mustache was really grossing me out and I had to leave immediately. I gave a quick wave goodbye and started over to the food tables.

On my way through the yard, I stepped on a small spot of bare ground amongst the thick, healthy grass. When I was a kid, some of the kids in the area would come over to play kickball in our yard. We always used a Nerf ball so that we could kick barefoot without hurting our toes. We used the same pink and neon-yellow one for years until it was so torn up it was barely recognizable as a ball. It didn't even roll at the end of its life. My dad hated when the ball smacked the siding or the air-conditioning unit, so if you hit them on a kick it was an automatic out. House rules. When we first began, we used old cushions from our deck furniture for bases. We always forgot to put them away and they eventually wore all of the grass underneath them away. It got to the point that the shallow muddy craters were visible enough that we didn't even need to use the pillows. The tiny bare portion I had stepped on was what was left of second base. After playing a bunch of games, we would call it quits. We'd finish almost every kickball marathon by going to the outside spigot to fill our dried out mouths with cool water from the garden hose. I loved the taste of the water till I realized the distinct taste was mostly coming from residual mold and mildew growing on the inside of the hose.

Making my way towards the food, I saw my aunt and uncle coming around the side of the house, both talking loudly to each other. It didn't seem like they were fighting, but they definitely weren't having a casual, pleasant conversation. To be honest, it really just seemed like they weren't even really paying attention, just competing to see who was louder.

My uncle always showed up to things like this a little toasted, but he wasn't an alcoholic by any means. Although an asshole, I can't say being a problem drinker was one of his issues. Still, at things like weddings and picnics, it was always obvious he had gotten a jump on the celebrations a little earlier than everybody else.

There are two things annoying about that. First, he often can't make it to family stuff at all with his busy schedule, yet he can't even tolerate a few minutes with everybody without getting wasted. Second, and this is even worse, friends and some family members gushed at how much fun Uncle Pete always was when he could fit us into his schedule. Some just weren't smart enough to realize he was probably at least a six-pack deep by the time he showed up; others just didn't care and kissed his ass no matter what.

♥ ♣ ♦ ♠

As I was picking up the last potato chip off my foam plate, I caught my uncle out of the corner of my eye. He had a silver beer can in one hand, and he was signaling for me to come over with the same hand. I crunched down on the last chip, folded the plate in half, and tossed it in a nearby garbage can.

Uncle Pete was slugging the last of the beer he was holding as I approached him. He let out a satisfied breath that was saturated with the distinct, wheaty odor of beer. I turned away from his rude exhale, snorting loudly in disgust.

"How's it going, Corvus?" He didn't wait for an answer. "What's on your schedule tomorrow?"

I shrugged, not really remembering if I was supposed to do anything.

"Well, what the hell. Are you doing anything or not? Simple question, my man."

"I'm almost positive I'm not doing anything. Why, what's up?" I asked, turning my head to the side a little suspiciously. We weren't exactly good buddies who hung out on the weekends too often.

"I was just gonna see if you were interested in helping me with a little yard work tomorrow. We got some weeds getting a little out of hand. Probably have you mow the grass. Our regular guy has been on vacation for a while. I keep forgetting to line something else up. You interested? I'll pay ya good for your time. Figured you might need a little extra money."

There was just a little hint of nastiness in his last remark, although he was right. I didn't feel like being anywhere near him or his giant, tacky house, but I really wanted some extra money. I still hesitated.

"What the shit, take it or leave it. If you aren't doing anything, I'm sure you could use twelve bucks an hour. Besides, I have a little something I'd like to discuss with you, man to man."

"What's it about?"

"Don't worry about it now. Just come on over and do that work for me. I'll have cash for ya. We'll discuss the other thing when you're done."

"Alright, whatever. What time should I come over?"

"I have an early meeting from 7:00 to 9:00. Let's shoot for 9:45."

"I'll be there."

He cracked another beer open loudly, tiny explosions of foam flying around his wrist. He jokingly offered me the can, laughing loudly before he stuck it into his favorite "ICU is #1" foam beer can holder. I ignored him and mingled with a few more people I didn't really care about talking with.

CHAPTER 4

"Call," I said simply, pushing in fifteen dollars of chips.

Anthony, after me, pushed in fifteen $1.00 chips with one hand. With the other, he slid two stacks of blue chips into the area in front of him. Two stacks of five, with the blue chips being worth five dollars each. I went over the hand in my head. Benny had made it a total of six dollars to see the first three cards. Anthony and I had called. Charlie, the shittiest player at the table, also called. Charlie's call didn't mean much, he would call with just about anything early in the hand. The other players had folded.

"What the fuck!" Charlie belted out, in response to Anthony's fifty dollar raise. He started to throw his cards in the muck, but then pulled them upright and looked at them again. Finally, he tossed them into the middle with the other folded cards. He was the type who could barely contain himself; he felt he had to see all of the cards before he could possibly surrender his hand.

The action went back to Benny who had bet the original fifteen dollars that Anthony had raised. He quickly flicked away his cards to fold them. I resumed the replay of the hand in my head. Anthony wasn't crazy in most circumstances. He was pretty careful with what hands he played. Careful also meant that he would drop marginal hands if he had any pressure. He had hit a few full houses and flushes against Charlie earlier. He was sitting behind a $350 stack that he wasn't used to playing with. Usually it was only Joey and I who had large stacks at the table. I looked again at my hand, although it was largely irrelevant. The only thing I had to decide was if I could get Anthony to let go of his cards. He definitely had me beat, but he was nervous. I was guessing he had a jack in his hand that matched the jack of clubs showing on the board. He probably had an ace or a king to go along with it. He was smart to make the raise he did with a hand like that. A decent play, but he always gave himself away with raises like that. Didn't mix up his maneuvers nearly enough.

I also assumed that he hadn't really considered what I had, that he probably thought, or hoped, that the raise would go uncontested and he could just scoop what was already in the middle. If I raised back, he would definitely be flustered. Thoughts would start running through his mind. He'd convince himself that my quiet calls through the first part of the hand were suspicious. That I had a big hand and was sneaking around. Usually I was really active and aggressive with my play.

"140." I counted out the appropriate amount of chips and slid them gently towards the center of the table.

"Oh shit!" said Joey loudly, which was really the only way he ever talked. He got excited over action, even when he wasn't actually involved.

Anthony thought for about two minutes. Finally, he threw the king of spades and the jack away, conceding the hand. I slid my two cards underneath all of the other cards. I didn't want to show Anthony a bluff. Charlie would start calling me every hand, no matter what. That would be great if I got some great hands, dangerous if I didn't really see anything. I'd never be able to make any moves. More importantly, I liked Anthony and he really hated to look stupid. He would take it in stride, wouldn't be a sore loser if I showed him a worse hand than his, but he'd still be embarrassed. He was much more concerned with not looking like a chump than actually winning the game. Which isn't really an effective way to play poker. Still, he was a good dude, so the inferior cards went in face down and got mixed around in the next shuffle.

We had a pretty regular group of guys who played poker at Joey's house. Most of us were pretty good friends, but there were a couple that we pretended to like because they always had money and were always ready for a card game where a decent amount of money exchanged hands. It had become kind of funny, the stakes that our games had risen to. Each person had their own little story of where their money came from.

Joey had parents that were pretty loaded. Years of getting more allowance money than any kid deserved and collecting money on Christmas and birthdays had left him with a nice little bundle of money. He also did some course maintenance at a local country club. He mostly did that so he could play the course on Mondays with the caddies and kitchen staff. He didn't really need the extra money, but I'm sure he didn't turn it down.

Jeremy was obviously my best friend out of the whole group. He washed dishes at the local family restaurant a couple days a week. His grandfather fixed small engines as a convenient part-time job in retirement. He taught Jeremy how to fix different yard and power tools from a pretty young age. Jeremy made some extra money helping him out.

Ethan worked at a local buffet as a host. He also sold alcohol to kids in our high school. He would get it from an older guy that had graduated a few years ago. They got to know each other from playing basketball at the local outdoor courts. They also had similar personalities and Ethan looked at him as something of an idol. Probably not the best role model, but knowing him did provide Ethan with a way to earn some extra money on the side with the little alcohol operation.

Harrison worked at a local butcher shop. He got paid shitty wages to clean up in the rendering plant, pushing nauseating blood and guts around with brooms and strong cleaning chemicals. He wanted to be an accountant since he was a little kid, and it seemed very possible since he was really good with money. Even though he didn't make much, he always had money because he saved it instead of spending it on bullshit. Of course, he gambled with his money, but usually played carefully and would profit or lose only a small amount.

Benny's father owned a successful pizza shop in the next town over. They were full-blooded Italians, and were pretty wealthy. Everybody always made comments about the possibility that there might be more sources of their wealth than just a pizza business, being Italian and all. Nobody really knew for sure. Benny had been working in his parents shop for years, so he always had some ammo for our poker games.

Anthony did yard work and odd jobs for Joey's parents. Because their families had been friends for years, they overpaid him for what he did. He made way more doing stuff for them than he could have possibly made at a crappy minimum wage job like some of the others.

Seth collected scrap metal in his parent's basement. He had started small, but eventually had taken over the whole basement with what he collected scrapping people's trash appliances, cleaning up stray wire for a local electrician, and gathering soda and beer cans. He also shared a sports collectible stand with an older gentleman at a flea market.

Daniel was a numbers guy, sort of like Harrison. He was a cashier at a department store, but made most of his money in small investments. He had started investing in stocks when he was only twelve with the help of his grandfather, and had made a decent sum of money in a just a few years.

Nate was a really good soccer player, and had been involved with several different teams and leagues around the area. He spent any extra time he had refereeing games for a community youth soccer league. He didn't make much doing it, and never played for much money in our games, but he was fun and liked playing for the little bit of money that he had.

Charlie and Corey were two of the regulars that weren't really close friends with all of the others. They were stupid, annoying, and as shady as they could get away with. Both sold weed and the occasional other drug they could get their hands on. Personally, I wouldn't ever think of buying from them because they'd probably rip me off somehow. Both were also known to steal, including from people's houses during parties and card games. One night, Joey's father had come down to our poker game with a worried look on his face. He quietly asked Joey where one of his expensive guitars was; Joey didn't know. Turned out the guitar was missing. It just so happened that Charlie and Corey had left the poker game early after getting stomped for a lot of money. Corey had gone upstairs to go to the bathroom while Charlie stayed in the basement waiting for Corey to drive him home. The guitar was never found, and nobody ever got in trouble for stealing it. Joey's family couldn't say for sure that the guitar was stolen during the poker game that night, so they couldn't actually prove Corey was guilty. We all highly suspected he was, though. Anyway, Charlie and Corey's methods of getting money were pretty sketchy, but they sucked at poker and always lost so nobody inquired too much. We just watched them close. And somebody always went with them when they left the room.

We quit playing cards around one in the morning. Charlie went out to his car and brought back in a bottle of horrible banana-flavored schnapps. Everybody complained about the disgusting liquor even though he was the only one that had brought anything to drink after playing cards. Joey was finally pushed into going to get the two bottles of whiskey he had hidden in his room. They were left over from a huge party he had about a month before when his parents had been away to celebrate their thirtieth anniversary in Switzerland.

Partying (usually about ten of us drinking whatever crappy alcohol we could get our hands on) was done almost exclusively at Joey's household. His parents were lenient about letting our friends drink in their home. They had a huge house, so we were usually downstairs where they couldn't hear us. They often didn't even know if we were drinking, but when they did see the obvious signs, they pretty much let it slide. They had lived for several years in Europe where I think you can drink as young as sixteen in some places. I always thought maybe that had something to do with them letting high schoolers drink and party at their place. I don't really know, but it was never really my problem anyway. If we got in trouble with cops or something, it would be them in serious trouble. I certainly never wished that on them, but that was reality. We had a lot more freedom at the Larsen's than we did anywhere else.

The first time I had ever been drunk was at Ethan's older sister's apartment along Main Street. It was a warm night the summer after I had turned sixteen. I had been to her place before. She and her husband always had the windows open to try to cool the place when it was hot. They sometimes used a box fan too, but turned it off once evening hit. You could always hear cars whooshing by their place. Since it's a small town, the road wasn't terribly busy, but cars seemed to roll by very consistently. If you imagine a slow drip that always seems like it's going to stop but never does, that's what the flow of vehicles was like. Also, their apartment was actually just the top half of a house. Their address number was 825½. I found that strange every time I was there.

That night I drank heavily for the first time, Ethan's sister let us drink any of the booze they had in their refrigerator. They'd just thrown a party and there were a bunch of bottles that only had couple of swigs left in them. If I remember correctly, there was spiced rum, cheap gin, a shot of expensive gin, two kinds of a terrible fruity wine, and a single serving bottle of orange vodka that somebody had given her as a little extra with a twenty-first birthday gift. She told us we could finish any of those bottles that we felt like drinking, along with any of the beer. I learned all about the fucked up results that occur when you mix different kinds of drinks, especially inexpensive but strong liquors.

Ethan drank two beers with me but stopped after that. We played a football video game while I continued to drink. All in all, I had three beers and finished all of the shit that she had given us access to, and the dirt-cheap, banana-flavored wine was the last thing to go. I first passed out, not yet having the sickness punching me in my guts. A few hours later, the war in my stomach hit a serious climax. I explosively vomited on myself and the chair I had been sleeping in, feeling the disgusting burst of acid, alcohol, and supper remnants leaving my body.

I had then decided that my best option was to hop in the shower to clean up, taking with me the pillows that had also caught some stray puke. I was found in her hallway the next morning with just a towel covering my most intimate of areas. I still remember feeling like the most repulsive, impolite asshole that had ever lived. Upon waking up, I had driven to the closest store and gotten every cleaning product I thought I would need to scrub and scour out the mess I had left in Ethan's sister's living room. Just smelling Charlie's banana schnapps had immediately taken me back to that night. It also reminded me that I had vowed to never again drink anything that combined banana flavoring and alcohol.

"Take this." Nate tried to hand me the capless bottle of banana crap.

"Not for me." I said, turning my head and sucking in my breath to avoid a getting any of the vomit-inducing smell in my nostrils. "I will take some of that whiskey, though." I pushed away the bottle still in Nate's hand. Pointing at the whiskey bottle resting on the counter beside Harrison, I said simply, "ere."

Nate grinned at me, snorting out a disgusting tiny whoosh of banana air. "C'mon, ain't you drinkin' tonight!? Since when do you turn down a chance to drink?"

"I just said I wanted to drink the whiskey. We can go shot for shot if you want. Or do you just want to save time and go outside now to throw up in the Larsen's bushes again? You remember the last time you tried to drink whiskey . . . orrr, maybe you don't. Don't worry about me, buddy. Also, don't try to bug me just because you're bitter that you lost seventy bucks to me tonight."

Nate laughed as he was taking a quick swallow and a small dribble of spit crept out of the side of his sticky-looking lips. "Ah, you dick, you won over half of that on lucky draws anyway!" He said with a giggle.

Anthony, always happy to take a shot at Nate, yelled out, "Whatever, Nate. You better take it easy on that banana garbage. You smell like the inside of the condoms you practice with when you steal 'naners from your Mom's fruit basket." They were actually best friends, but loved to make fun of each other.

Everybody laughed except for Nate who tried to keep a straight face and flip off Anthony.

Hours later, after the shots had done their trick of turning the clock hands five times as fast, it was just Jeremy and I hanging out on the Larsen's front porch. Other than Joey, nobody in the Larsen family was home, so we even had free reign of the porch. I smoked a cigarette, Jeremy a small cigar, while we talked about college.

I blew out some smoke and said, "I do want to go to school. I don't think I'm a genius, but I think I'm smart enough that I should actually learn something that might help me get a good job. My parents are definitely for it."

Jeremy made little putt-putt noises with his mouth. Smoke exited his mouth in a syncopated fashion, alternating between long dashes of smoke and short bursts like puffs from a lurching steam engine. "Sounds like you're pretty convinced, so what's the problem?"

"It's so much money, and I'm freaked out that I'll go a couple years and then change my mind or get sick of the place. Lots of people do that. Then they're just stuck with a bill and have to get the same damn job they could have gotten without the couple years of education. Part of the reason I fear going to school is people like my Uncle Pete. People who don't even know him act like he's some kind of savior. I really just want to go to school to learn shit, I don't even care that much about all the school pride stuff."

Jeremy snorted and replied, "Your uncle is no savior, that's for freakin' sure. But that's not important. If you actually want to go to class and take it seriously, I think you're already ahead of the game. Probably 75 percent of the people in our graduating class are going to college. Half of them probably don't give a shit about anything other than being able to drink beers without having to worry about mommy and daddy catching them. And plenty of them are so stupid they wouldn't even be successful if they did apply themselves."

I turned towards Jeremy, stubbing out my third cigarette in the cleanest of the two ashtrays. "You're right."

He squished his cigar butt in the same ashtray. "Hell yeah, man. If you want to do it, you should go for it. The money thing blows, I can't believe how much it costs either. That's why I'm going to community college if I go at all. But you should get your ass to Middenburg if you think that's the place where you need to be."

One of the best things about Jeremy was that he could drink a lot without acting like a jerk. If anything, the conversation probably got better with him as he drank. Also, he smoked cigars like a fifty year old man when he drank, which I found funny. "Thanks, man, I think I needed to hear that to help me make a decision. Not totally committing yet, but I'm leaning towards going."

He tossed the ice, rum, and pop mixture that was left in the bottom of his glass into the yard. "Nice. Now let's go drink a couple more things that we'll regret in the morning."

CHAPTER 5

A young man is at the bottom of large crater in the earth, heaving heavy rocks towards the lip of the hole. His arms are sinewy and strong, with just the hint of sweat starting to layer them in the early morning sun. It's hot, but not quite dreadful like it will be around noon and the mid-afternoon. His power is very evident, but there are still child-like features about him that give away his youth.

For a portion of his summer, this young gentleman travels each day of the week with three other friends to the suburban areas that skirt the city that they call home. In these neighborhoods they use their vigor working for a local pool company. As the temperatures rise, so does the demand for backyards to be turned into little oases with cool, sapphire lagoons. This increased demand requires the speedy work of young men with fresh backs and eager stamina. For this, somebody who's never had more than a hundred dollars to his name can earn nearly that much in one day. It's honest, hard work that, at some points, might even feel like a privilege. With every cruddy stone slung out of the freshly scooped bowl, the young man grimaces. Despite the signs of exertion, he doesn't slow down and works steadily through the morning until lunch.

Under the shade of a tree in the yard they're working in, the entire crew uses the break to eat, rest, and chat. The young man had sat on the grass a few feet from the rest, preferring to relax and listen to the others talk. As if naturally drawn to him, the crew shifts and moves and surround him by mid-break. The older supervisor appears to have taken a particular interest in him, and asks him directly, "So what's up with the football?"

While the young man doesn't seek out attention, his comfortable response makes it evident that he's been asked similar questions before. "Well, Coach Q helped me out a lot. I met him in seventh grade, and he's been guiding me ever since. Kept me away from bullshit and trained me the whole way through high school ball. I played pretty good, and I was lucky enough to attract attention from colleges. I'll be playing D-1 for Middenburg this fall. In fact, I leave next week for camp. Hopin' to make the starting squad right and blow 'em away at ESPN." He grinned after the last comment, throwing off just enough charm to make up for his playful lack of humility.

The mention of football started several conversations and arguments amongst the crew, varying from college teams to pro teams to people's favorite players. The young man takes a more relaxed sitting position with his elbows in the grass, returning to the more familiar position of listener instead of speaker.

CHAPTER 6

I rested one hand on the grass while I spread the jet-black mulch with the other hand. The rake did the trick for most of the flower-bed, but I needed to do it by hand around the bases of the plants. I was three minutes in and drops of sweat were already escaping my face onto the little chunks of dyed wood. Here and there I had to tug out little weeds that had begun to sneak through the old mulch. Whoever my uncle usually had landscape used some kind of weed spray, so there weren't many. They were still a pain though, because it's hard to get a tiny little weed out by the roots.

I had to admit, although I wouldn't said it to my uncle, I sort of enjoyed doing yardwork. I liked the idea of getting a little dirty, being outside, and even making stuff look nice. It was a little hotter than I would have liked it to be, but I still didn't mind the work that much. If I told Uncle Pete that he'd probably try to give me half of what he was paying me. Or not pay me at all, or something.

I even considered trying to find a regular job landscaping in place of going to college. My one friend's brother worked summers in high school, then eventually got a regular job with the same company right after he graduated. Now he makes something like 55 or 60 grand a year just running a couple of crews for that same place. He gets to be outside all the time, he stays in shape from the hard work, and he gets some of the winter months off every year. I don't even know if I care too much about getting a degree. It really does seem like such bullshit sometimes, this long process to try to impress other people. I could skip all that and just get a job right away . . . no debt, no waiting to have a regular life. I could work hard and just enjoy life at night, jump right into my life without a four year or more transition period.

Sounds decent, right? Wrong, I guess. My parents spent hours one night convincing me otherwise. They did make some good points, so I pretty much dropped the landscaping idea. Haven't totally forgotten it though.

I stood up for a second, bending backwards and forwards to stretch my back. I swiped my hands against each other, removing as much debris as possible. I took a long gulp of water from a spring water bottle I had brought from home, letting some of the cool clear fluid drip down my chin and seep into the collar of my tee shirt. I held the bottle against my temples, closed my eyes and faced my head up towards the sun, taking an odd pleasure in roasting my cheeks and forehead temporarily. I could feel that the area where my shirt touched my shoulder blades was saturated with sweat.

"I figured this would be the quality of work I'd get from you!" My uncle followed up his lame joke with an overly-boisterous laugh that ended in a wet cough and a sigh.

I didn't turn around before I answered back, "You really should quit this football garbage and go into comedy. I think you have a bright future."

"Too bad being a smartass isn't a career, then you wouldn't have to worry going to college. You're already damn good at that. Speaking of the college thing, that's kind of what I wanted to talk about. You're still a little torn about the financial issue, am I right?"

Finally turning around, I nodded my head.

"All right, well I may have thought of a way to help you help yourself. I think there is a way that I could provide you some funding to get a nice little jump on paying for school, maybe even enough to cover close to tuition for a semester. Sound good?"

"Sounds like you need to tell me more about it before I can say how it sounds, 'cause it sounds like it's either going to require too much of my time or it's too good to be true. What are we talking about here?"

"To be honest, I can't give you any details right now. I'm still working out some of the logistics of it, so I'll have to wait to explain anything to you. You'll understand, when I finally do explain it, why I had to wait. All I can say is that it won't take up a bunch of your time and it won't get in the way of your schoolwork. I just want you to really think about how important going to college is to you, and how nice it would be to have a head start on paying for it. I need to hear from you that you're willing to make a commitment to make it happen. This could potentially help both you and me if we can trust each other."

"But how am I supposed to know if I really want to do it if you don't even tell me what you want me to do? That's weird."

"I just really want you to think about how important the money issue is to you, and if you care enough to work with me. Like I said, you'll get why I didn't tell you right away what we're going to do. And all the details are not totally worked out yet. Just think about it, and if you think you'd be willing to make a big commitment, we'll talk again and get a little more figured out."

I played with the rubber handle on the end of the rake I was using to steady myself. A little piece fell off into the grass and I didn't bother to pick it up. "So when should we talk again?"

My uncle reached into his pocket and pulled out his money clip. He handed me a folded fifty dollar bill, saying simply, "For today's work." He put the clip back into his pocket and pulled out a can of chew, popped the top off and dug two fingers into the dark brown bits of minty-smelling tobacco. He said, "You can come over and do some more yardwork next week, I'll tell you more then. And do me a favor, don't tell your parents anything about this. Let's just keep it between you and me for now."

That seemed odd, but then again, so did everything else he was saying. I shrugged my shoulders and said, "Whatever."

"That's the spirit. Now get back to work, Juan, those weeds aren't going to pull themselves!" He let out another laugh, wet cough, and a sigh.

"Mexican landscaper jokes, real classy," I said quietly, not sure if he could even hear me.

He didn't say anything, but poked at a little piece of tobacco that was hanging out of the corner of his mouth, then turned around and walked towards the house.

CHAPTER 7

The deep wood grain walls of the office are adorned with a vast array of items like pictures, award certificates with calligraphy writing on them, and plaques. There are large shelves that hold a few books and old trophies with an almost symbolic thin layer of dust. The room reeks with the scent of desperate pride; the type of pride that seesaws back and forth between innocent and haughty.

"4-8? That's fucking unacceptable, Pete. Hovering around .500 is not a tradition we intend to start at this institution, and you know that. You're making it awfully goddamn hard for me to keep defending you here. You can't honestly say we haven't given you the resources to make it happen. We've gathered some of the best scouts and recruiters around, paid who we needed to, and made the effort to seek out high-caliber volunteers. I've personally made moves so that more and more money was allocated in the budget for things you need, whether it be equipment, facilities, or coaches. The bottom line is, you're losing your step, Pete. You're missing something that you used to have."

"These players just aren't responding to me like they once did, Bill. I'm busting my tail like I always have. I belong in this position, this is where I belong right now. I don't intend to be leaving anytime soon."

"Well that might not end up being your decision. In fact, I can guarantee you won't have any say at all if you keep up the same type of shit that's been going on the last few years. We still have credibility at this place, credibility built on a football program that has won twelve national championships. None of those have been won by you, I might add. We will be willing to make drastic personnel changes if it becomes necessary. Heads will roll before we let this program become a joke. Now, don't get me wrong, we are still committed to you for the time being. You were selected for a reason and we know you have it in you to motivate these players and get this team back on track. It's just a matter of you making it happen."

"You're goddamn right I was selected for a reason, and I've given every bit of myself to this job since I began. Just like I gave 1000% at every position I've had. I do what it takes to win, but the pieces just haven't been coming together."

"Let me tell you, I'm speaking out of some anger today, but I'm also speaking in absolute truths. We, including everybody from our alumni to the president of our fine institution, need this garbage to stop by whatever means necessary. I'm tired of sub-.500 records, tired of seeing sinking enrollment, and tired of being blasted on SportsCenter and every damn sports website out there! One thing I am definitely tired of is losing to Middenburg like we have the last six years. This is our rival and we've barely been putting up a fight lately! I am most definitely sick and fucking tired of that, Pete. Just remember that when you're preparing for that game in this upcoming season. Remember that it could be your ass on the line. I'm telling you this so you can help yourself, Pete. Okay, we're done."

And with those words, a large-shouldered man with a full head of salt and pepper hair shrinks into an obedient, frightened child. His mind is overcome with the desperation of a creature backed into a corner. He storms out of the office, trying to mask his fear with anger. After the loud slam of the heavy door, the only sound in the hallway is the slap of his leather loafers on the hard floor.

CHAPTER 8

"U COMIN OR WHAT?"

The vibration of my phone shook the entire coffee table and the repeating bell noise became annoying enough that I woke up. According to the phone, it was 10:45 a.m. and I told my uncle I'd be at his house at 10:30. We played poker again at the Larsens', this time drinking even more afterwards. We had multiple cases of beer. It was cheap stuff, but any beer was better than gross liquor that made you half sick after the first shot. I drank till about 3:30 a.m. before passing out. Everybody had left or fell asleep around one or two except for Ethan and me. We were betting twenty dollars a game on ping-pong because we had won $125 and $90 respectively. I had finally quit, down one game, because I was too drunk and too tired to be awake anymore so I fell asleep on the sectional couch in the Larsen's living room. I answered my uncle's text and said that I would be over in about a half hour. I needed to stop at my house and change my clothes, maybe grab something to eat.

♥ ♣ ♦ ♠

Pulling into Uncle Pete's driveway, I noticed that one of the garage doors was up and my aunt's Lexus SUV wasn't inside. Whatever my uncle was scheming up was apparently going to be a "man-to-man" thing. I preferred to have her there whenever I was over because it meant Uncle Pete talked to me less, which was always a good thing, even if it did mean I'd have to listen to them have their foolish arguments with him acting rude and uncaring and her being passive aggressive.

I pulled into the parking spot underneath their aging basketball hoop. I had to admit, I was really interested to hear what my uncle had to say to me about earning a big chunk of money to put towards my college education. Everyone had been discussing their college plans at the poker game, so it got me thinking about my own situation. I had procrastinated in getting back to Middenburg about attending. It was extremely late at this point, but my parents had called and talked to some kind of counselor or adviser, and she had said that I could still start in the fall semester if I responded by the end of the month.

The damn money issue was still freaking me out. My parents were insistent that I shouldn't worry about it, but the numbers were enough to block out any reassurance that they were giving. I knew that they wanted me to go bad enough that they would keep on a positive face no matter what kind of money it was going to require. I just wasn't buying the nice little lines they were feeding me. I was driving all of us crazy trying to make a decision about going to school, or working, or making some kind of plan for at least the immediate future, if not the distant. As weird as it felt, maybe Uncle Pete had some kind of answer that would help push me along in making a decision.

The sun was still a little irritating to my eyes, and the morning heat was making me uncomfortable in my nagging little hangover. I stepped up to their front door and rang the doorbell several times. Nobody opened the door and I didn't hear any yelling from inside so I hit the bell three more times. Still no answer.

I walked around to the back. I didn't see my uncle doing work in the yard or sitting on the patio. I pulled out my phone and was about to call him when I heard the sound of his voice urging their dog to go out to the yard with him.

"Hey, sorry, I was taking a shit and couldn't yell loud enough for you to hear me."

"Thanks for sharing; you really know how to charm people."

"Aw, relax, everybody does it. I remember your parents even had that *Everyone Poops* book that should have taught you that. You better study it again, it must not have sunk in." He laughed. "You'll have to improve your reading comprehension if you're going to make it in college. Speaking of which, let's just get right into what I started talking about last week when you were here."

I nodded. "So you don't want me to do any work or anything before we start talking about that? That's all right with me, but if I'm going to do work, I'd like it to be before the sun gets really hot, if possible."

"Don't worry about doing much work today. I might have you mow the grass inside the pool fence or something, but it won't be hard or time-consuming. Our discussion might take a little while. I'm guessing you're going to have some questions."

"Okay." I said, plopping down into one of their deck chairs.

I guess I should have found it strange the way my uncle was presenting his idea to me; his mysterious approach should have been some kind of a red flag. For some reason, I didn't really think anything of it. I suppose I just thought it was going to be some kind of regular kind of job that he just didn't want to tell me about until he was sure he could give it to me, or had to get permission to give to me, or something. Being that he and I are virtually never functioning on the same wavelength, I just filed his ambiguous proposal into the 'Shit I don't get about my goofy uncle' part of my brain.

CHAPTER 9

Uncle Pete unscrewed the cap on top of his beer bottle and threw it into a plastic can beside the door that led into the backside of the garage. He put a can of Coke in front of me. "Okay, here's the deal; it's no secret that my team has been struggling the last couple of years. I'm sure you know that. Frankly, it fucking sucks."

Uncle Pete had been swearing in front of me for years, but I had never heard him say "fuck" when he knew I was within earshot. Just hearing him say the word, I immediately knew it was going to be a serious conversation.

"Sometimes in life, you do some shit to get to your destination. Getting anywhere requires you to get dirty and make things happen. I've worked my way up to get to the level I'm at by doing whatever it takes to get there." I furrowed my brow and looked into his eyes. I had heard speeches before about the work he had done to attain a coaching position at a major football university, but this dialogue had an entirely different tone. Usually it was just a prideful spewing of clichés, but now he seemed much more direct. Weird. He continued, "I know you're idealistic and shit, being young and all, but the truth is that life can get messy sometimes. If you don't take what you want, somebody else will get it, believe me."

The introduction was getting on my nerves, and I didn't much feel like listening to his philosophies about life any longer. "You're just avoiding telling me whatever it is you're going to eventually say." As usual, I could barely control my annoyance with him. I normally wouldn't take such a rude tone with an older person, but I just couldn't help myself with Uncle Pete. In my most easygoing voice I added, "Go ahead and let it out."

"You're right, and if we do what I'm about to propose, we're going to have to have a little more trust in each other."

"I'll have to hear it before I can make that promise."

"Understandable. As I said, the team has really been in bad shape the last few years, and my job and reputation are in serious jeopardy. Even though I've worked my ass off, things haven't quite panned out in the wins and losses column, and, quite bluntly, that's the only god damn thing that really matters."

"I still don't get what that has to do with my situation."

"Just relax, I'll get to it, but I need to completely explain everything. I'm gonna give it to you straight, but it's sorta complicated, so bear with me."

I nodded, resigning myself to just sitting back and taking in what he had to say.

"Anyway, I've actually had conversations with the powers-that-be at the ICU athletic department, and they've made it clear that I'm on the hot seat. ESPN has been saying it since last season, but hearing it from these sources actually matters. It isn't just a talking point for an afternoon TV show with a bunch of asshole analysts. ICU expects certain things from their football program, and if the coach doesn't deliver, he's on the chopping block." As he spoke, he was becoming visibly uncomfortable. He turned his head to the side, wiped the sweat from between his eyebrows, and scratched the back of his neck. "If we don't do better next year, I'm definitely going to lose my job. No doubt about it. Now, our staff is doing everything possible to alter our game plans, recruit, and motivate our guys. Unfortunately, I still worry that it isn't going to be enough. We've worked hard every year and we've still fallen short in recent years."

While I was trying to concentrate, I was secretly taking some satisfaction in seeing his discomfort regarding his circumstances. I kept silent, still wanting to hear how I was going to be involved in helping him in his plight.

"One imperative thing that needs to happen next year would be to beat Middenburg. As you know, we have a long-standing rivalry with Middenburg, and they have been man-handling our team for the last decade or so. Well, I not only want to beat them, I want to take it a step further. I want to be all but guaranteed to have a better record than them. They are, by far, the best team in our conference. If they have a worse record, we're pretty much set up to win the conference. Nobody else is going to put up much of a challenge in that regard if we can get our team rolling with some confidence."

Up in one of the statuesque pine trees that surrounded Uncle Pete's property, a crow cawed loudly. We both looked away from each other and stared up at the tops of the trees. Uncle Pete seemed to need a break after speaking so openly to me about his problem, and he sat in silence, taking short sips from his beer every ten or fifteen seconds. I looked around the yard, noting that there was absolutely no work that needed to be done today and Uncle Pete had definitely just had me over for the purpose of talking and nothing else. The small feeling of glee over his vulnerability had passed, and now I was just becoming very curious about the direction he was taking.

The back patio door slid open and Aunt Sarah popped out, closing the door quickly. "Stupid flies are a big pain this year," she said, offering an unnecessary explanation for closing the door so fast. She squeaked and squished in flip-flops, making her way across the grass towards the table we were at. She rested one hand on Uncle Pete's shoulder, not saying anything.

Uncle Pete looked up at her with a smile. "We didn't even hear you pull in. How was the market this morning?"

"Oh it was pretty good. I got some good cheeses for next week when we have the Jensens over for dinner. Should go good with the wine we already have, so we don't need to pick any up yet. Produce looked really good, but I just got some cherries today. We still have some bananas and grapefruit that we haven't finished yet."

"Great. Could you please grab me another beer from the garage fridge? I'm all out."

She didn't say anything, but went into the garage. After some clinking and clanking, she came out with a fresh beer, the top already popped off. "Do you need a new Coke, Corvus?"

"Nope, no thanks." I said, shaking my head side-to-side at the same time.

She sat the fresh beer in front of my uncle, laying her hand on his shoulder again. It was the most cordial I had seen them act towards each other in a long while. She stretched backwards, yawning at the same time, and turned back towards the patio door. She said over her shoulder, "I'll leave you fellas to your serious conversation," obviously sensing that she wasn't entirely welcome to stay.

"Thanks for the drink, dear, we won't be too much longer. I know you wanted to get to the winery early for the concert tonight."

She said simply, "Yup," and entered the house, opening and closing the door in one swift motion.

I zoned out for a few moments, staring at the perfectly green, fresh looking grass. I thought about the kickball and wiffleball games that we'd had in the yard at my parent's house. The only really good memory I had of my uncle's yard was of the one and only time my cousins and I had played wiffleball during a Memorial Day picnic. Uncle Pete had thrown us pitches for over an hour, displaying a patience and selflessness that I pretty much never saw again from him. He giggled while throwing the weightless ball so it curved like a banana, taking light-hearted delight while the maize-colored bat whooshed and swished through the air from our desperate cuts. Really, he had us all laughing at each other, too. After a few misses, he even helped each of us until we hit at least one of his curveballs. There was something in the guy that was human, and I had seen it. But that was a long time ago.

While finishing a swallow of beer, my uncle said "Like I said, try not to ask too many questions or interrupt until I give you all the details. Just keep an open mind until I'm completely done, then you can ask me whatever you want or just leave and we'll never speak of it again."

I gave a short nod, encouraging him to move on and showing that I was going to give him a fair chance to talk.

"I'm gonna say this early so you know I'm not wasting your time. I'm prepared to give you $8,000 at the start of the first semester if you agree to help me out with what I have planned. If the plan works out, I'll provide you with another seven grand. Now there are going to be some details that aren't quite worked out yet, it's going to be something that is going to require us to work and adapt on the fly a little bit, when we have to."

I think Uncle Pete read the look on my face immediately, seeing that I was taken aback by the numbers he was presenting to me. He held up his hand a few inches off the table as if to pause my reaction.

"Now, I know these are some mighty big numbers to a young man just coming out of high school. It's also a stupid amount of money to hand to an eighteen-year-old who isn't used to it. Frankly, I see that you're a pretty level-headed kid. We don't always see eye-to-eye, but I do have some trust in you - we're family after all. I want to be taken seriously and I think this is a fair amount to really have your attention."

I tapped my fingers lightly on the table in a quick rhythm. I said in a serious tone, "That is certainly something that will get my attention. Honestly, with my part-time jobs for the last few years I don't think I've even made five grand total, much less eight."

"I understand that, and I'm not throwing them out there to make you uncomfortable, and I'm not bullshitting either. But forget those dollar amounts for the time being; I know, I know, easier said than done. But make sure to keep your attention on exactly what I'm about to explain."

CHAPTER 10

It is quite plausible that the sin and general despondency that murmurs in the mind of the grown human being, and shrieks in some, is completely rooted in one primitive yearning: the impossible desire to return to youth. Some may not be able to recognize this, others may deny it, but it is entirely possible that this, as a general explanation, sums up our more base behaviors.

The hand that grabs somebody else's property, when not done in desperation for raw survival, is spurred on by the desire to have something without an equal exchange of some kind. That very well could be an impetuous need to somehow return to that childlike state where one is given things with no expectation of compensation.

The fingers reach for chemical potions that provide an adequate excuse to let the inhibitions slip further and slide away and eventually disappear. Childlike selfishness is a delicious thing obtained when in the throes of a wide-open binge. To ingest a dose of immaturity can be delectable, but the fountain of youth is only available in extremely finite amounts.

The fingertips tingle with the selfish satisfaction of carnal pleasure without concern for consequences. Adult-like desire executed in the most child-like ways imaginable.

A child takes the well-being of the world for granted because of forgivable innocence and naivety. The adult does so because of laziness, insensitivity, and carelessness.

Much is done under the guise of being, or trying to be, a better grown-up, but is really just a reeling attempt to be a grown-up child. Grace keeps us reasonable, but things turn ugly when it's on hiatus.

CHAPTER 11

"And that's the general idea how we can help each other out. We both have needs and we might be able to kill two birds with one stone."

I had to physically shake my head after hearing what my uncle had proposed to me. The general idea was that I was, in theory, going to help my uncle set up one or two important Middenburg football players to get in major trouble right before their game with ICU. Their matchup was on October 27th, the tenth game of the year for both teams. The thought was that if drugs were planted in the residence of the players, they would likely face immediate consequences from their coach, the cops, the NCAA, or all three. In my uncle's estimation, they could very possibly face an immediate suspension and miss the ICU game, if everything was timed correctly. The set-up would be made easier by the fact that Middenburg was going to be playing at ICU's home field, so they would be gone a few days before the game.

My job, while starting my freshman year of college, would be to casually stalk the targeted players and find out where they lived and what their normal routine consisted of; basically figure out any details that would help us pull off the set-up without suspicion. My uncle and I would figure out how and when we could break in to their residence to do the deed. He assured me that college students are both unbelievably trusting and incredibly careless when it comes to keeping their dorms and apartments secure, so it would probably be easier than I might think. My uncle would be at ICU preparing for the game, so I'd be the one doing pretty much all of the dirty work.

If I was successful at getting into the dorm or apartment, I would stash the drugs in a way that they seemed hidden. The stash would consist of a variety of different drugs, all weighed and packaged in small amounts. This would obviously give the impression that they were small time dealers, not just consumers of the drugs. This would attract more police and media attention, and also give more plausibility to the idea that such a large stash was in the possession of a Division 1 college football player. Most people know that these players are frequently tested for narcotics and performance-enhancing drugs, so it might draw suspicion if the drugs were just planted in a way that made them look like addicts or drug-takers of the non-casual variety. Anything to throw people off the scent of our scheme would be a good thing.

My uncle's thought, of course, was that if Middenburg lost important players at the last minute, this would put them at a serious disadvantage during the game. He would even secretly develop a game plan beforehand that would make the players' absences hurt even more. While a high-profile team might be able to lose a couple players and still have the talent to seal the holes, the fact that there would be almost no recovery time would make that a near-impossible task. Losing players would also rock the psyche of the entire team with no time to right the ship. My uncle figured that the likely win over Middenburg would not just be important in and of itself, it'd also jump start the ICU team and propel them into the last portion of the season with some swagger.

I definitely felt some disgust towards my uncle, but I had to give him credit for drawing up the plan. Though deviant and obviously risky, I had to admit he had me convinced it would work.

On my end, I'd tell my parents that I'd decided, finally, to go to school. I could just have them help me apply for financial aid and loans in a completely normal way, and they'd have no idea that I'd be sitting on a sum of money from my uncle. The money, while not being enough to cover very much of my schooling, would at least give me some comfort about financing it. I could even just let it collect interest or even invest it somehow to make money on it while I was in school.

Uncle Pete eyed me calmly while I digested everything he'd said.

I finally spoke, asking, "How can we be sure the police, or campus security, or whoever, will get to the house that morning. Actually, how do we know they'll ever check the apartment?"

"Good question. I actually know somebody at the Middenburg Police Department. He's a friend of a very close friend. He knows nothing of the plan, except that he's getting a thousand bucks to make absolutely certain the police enter that apartment that morning. He said he actually prefers it that way. The less he knows, the better. That means he won't know your name or your relationship to me at all. He'll have no connection to you whatsoever, and vice versa. He assured me it won't be a problem to get into the apartment. He'll figure out some way to get the landlord to open the door for them. A fake complaint that somebody walking by smells weed, some kind of paraphernalia near their door, or maybe say that a known drug user was seen leaving their apartment at a strange hour. I don't know what he'll dream up, but he'll think of something. He knows there's an extra grand in it for him if everything works as planned once the cops enter the apartment."

With that question answered, all I could think about was my conversation with Jeremy about going to college. If I was going to go, $8000, would be one hell of a financial boost. $15,000 would be even better.

CHAPTER 12

I was roused from my sleep by my mom throwing a *Time* magazine at me from the door of my room. She and my dad had just arrived home from church, and this was her normal routine of waking me up to invite me along to eat lunch with her and my dad. I went about half the time. I was definitely planning to go this time because I wanted to announce to them that I was going to answer my acceptance letter to Middenburg with a yes. Obviously, they wouldn't know the entire reason for my decision to go to school, and hopefully never would.

My mom stood halfway in the door, halfway out, watching me wriggle around in my blanket. Seeing that I was mostly awake, she said, "You coming along with us today? We're thinking of going to that new sub shop that went in over in Brunston; we've heard good things."

I picked out eye-crust with the pinky on my right hand and reached for the bottled water that I had set on my nightstand the night before. "Yea, I'm definitely going. What time are you leaving?"

"Soon as possible: your dad needs to pick up a new pair of boots and the store closes at one o'clock. We can get going as soon as you're ready."

I knew this wasn't true. Every time my parents said they were ready to go on a Sunday, they always had something else they wanted to do before leaving. I was pretty sure my dad was sitting in his chair reading the Sunday Newspaper with his slippers on, totally not ready to leave. My mom would probably have to wash some dishes or load the washing machine before we got going. Since my dad wanted to get boots I wouldn't take forever, but I wasn't going to rush either. I looked at the clock and it read 11:33, so I decided to stay in bed for another two minutes and get up at 11:35.

♥♣♦♠

I waited till we were seated before I let on that I wanted to tell them anything. I had ordered a smoked turkey sub with provolone cheese. I took a big bite and chewed it slowly, thinking one last time about what I was planning to say before I actually went through with it. The bite went down and I followed it with a gulp of iced tea. I figured the only way to go about it was to just jump right into it, "I made a decision about school." I didn't say anything else and watched their reactions. When what I had said finally sunk in, they both looked at me with cautious smiles.

My dad was the first to speak: "Well, that's good. We've certainly been waiting to hear what you want to do, but we didn't want to pressure you too much about it. So, what's the big decision?"

I opened my mouth, but before any sound came out, my mom said, "We really do support anything you do, I promise. We're confident you'll make good decisions and be happy no matter what."

I laughed, hearing the same line she had repeated several times a few times a month since the beginning of my senior year. "I know, I know, I believe ya. I've decided to go to Middenburg. Hopefully I'm still good for the fall semester. Now that I've made the decision, I'm actually pretty excited about it."

My dad set down his sandwich and looked at my mom with a gleaming smile and said, "Have to admit, I was really hoping for that decision. You're a smart kid and I think you'll like the college atmosphere; much more conducive to your learning style than high school classrooms. Of course, all the other stuff is pretty darn awesome too!"

I smiled at my mom, who was almost clapping her hands in glee. Something tells me she wouldn't have been clapping her hands in excitement if I had told her I had decided to work at the local dog food plant or something. Anyway, it was still nice to see her happy. She looked at me with an almost sneaky smile and said, "We actually already have the paperwork filled out. We talked to somebody at the school about financing and everything. At this point, you pretty much just need to put your signature on a few lines. Again, we didn't want to stress you out, but we wanted to be totally prepared in the event that you decided to go to Middenburg." She squeaked out, "Oh, we're so happy for you!"

In the corner of my mind, there was a little nuisance thought rattling around that I couldn't totally ignore. I felt a tiny pang of guilt that I was, at this point, planning to be involved in a pretty terrible conspiracy with my uncle just to comfort myself enough to commit to entering college. Even so, the looks on my parents' face certainly helped me push it far enough to the back of my brain to hide any emotions that might make my parents suspicious.

We spent the rest of the day talking about things I would buy for my dorm room, the best websites to buy textbooks (my mom had been getting tips from her friends with kids in college already), and about a million other things that my parents had been bursting to discuss with me. My dad was even so excited that he forgot to buy new boots. He was going on a hike with another teacher friend, so now he'd have to decide between his sneakers or his boat shoes that had ripped toes and one sole that was a scuff away from having a quarter-sized hole in the rubber.

CHAPTER 13

From high above a football field, slightly yellowed from a recent heat wave and ragged from the abuse of young men with size 14 cleats and muscled bodies, a coach taps his chin while thinking alone. While he doesn't like to show much emotion, he can't help but crack a subtle smile. He's spent the last couple weeks watching his football team work together on the practice field. The earliest practices of the year are always interesting with the mix of inexperienced underclassmen and confident upperclassmen. The players all wear matching uniforms and helmets with the same 'M' on them, but it's pretty easy to separate the new from the experienced.

The coach's glee is not from examining the team beginning to develop into a solid unit, but from watching one of his new recruits. Amongst the popping of helmets and pads, growls, and screams, a young man seems to be hovering a few feet higher than everybody else on the field. Every talented freshman arrives with both wild expectations and wild scrutiny from the men who'll be leading them if they earn a spot on the team and are able to keep it.

The young man that's caught the attention of the coach is at physical levels that the coach has never seen in a freshman at camp. He'd checked his clipboard twice, because apparently the freshman had put on at least twenty to twenty-five pounds of pure muscle just since the last time they had collected height and weight information from the members of the freshmen class. It wasn't unusual to see growth in new recruits from hard work or natural maturity, but this was beyond anything the coach had ever seen.

Even more amazing, the young player was using every pound in a positive way. To say he was agile was an understatement. While other players were getting through plays cautiously to avoid getting yelled at, he was attacking every hole from his running-back position with the confidence of an NFL veteran and the spunk of a ten year old. He wants to hide it, but the coach's thoughts were run amuck with altered game strategies and exuberant newspaper headlines in bold type and capital letters.

CHAPTER 14

With a hollow pop, the pink golf ball hit the bottom of the cup and jumped out, trailing off and coming to rest against the bricks that lined the twelfth hole of Captain Jig's Mini-Golf Course. I stared at the ball in silence until I was sure it had stopped

"Oh my God, how does that happen? I've been getting so unlucky all day!"

Somehow, I had found myself in the midst of a putt-putt game with Morgan Gillis. I was considering bashing myself to death with the bright blue putter I had selected from the little shed that served as a clubhouse. I remembered that the putter was coated in some kind of rubbery substance that was durable but not quite hard enough to fracture my skull and end the slow torture of playing mini-golf with Morgan Gillis. I had a quick daydream in which I threw my putter into the man-made creek that ran through the course, ripped the scorecard in half, and just ran off into the horizon, leaving Morgan with a confused look. Then, back in reality, I watched her bend over to flick a leaf away from her ball and reconsidered.

I wasn't quite sure how somebody didn't understand that if you putt the golf ball with three times the force necessary to get it in the hole, even if it is straight at the cup, the ball is not going to stay in the cup. You really don't have to be a golf-pro to understand this basic theory. I could accept her repeated failure at executing a reasonable putt, which was due to the fact that she just physically couldn't swing a putter with consistency. What I couldn't wrap my head around was her assumption that she was somehow getting "unlucky" on every hole. "Unlucky" doesn't get you an average score of seven on every hole.

I put on the best fake sympathetic face I could and said, "Yea, that totally sucks. It's almost like something is wrong with the cups or something. They should replace them with something newer that doesn't spit the ball out like that. Stupid."

She seemed satisfied with that response and nodded in agreement. I tapped my own ball in for a two, feeling relieved that the discussion about her bad luck wasn't going to go any further, at least until the next hole. She swung her arms awkwardly, jabbing the putter at the ball. Somehow, the ball swirled around the rim and dropped inside. We gave each other a high-five to celebrate her six and moved on the next hole.

♥ ♣ ♦ ♠

In all honesty, Morgan was an okay girl, but I definitely wouldn't be taking her mini-golfing again. I had met her in a study period at the end of my junior year, using the fact that I was a year older than her to boost my confidence. We had talked everyday instead of doing any work, often being told sternly by the teacher in charge that we were to be silently studying or reading. I had found her attractive right away, with special affection for her ass in short jean shorts and her full head of curly brown hair. By the second to last week of school we had traded phone numbers and texted occasionally. I had driven her home a few times because she didn't drive and didn't feel like taking the bus. She didn't need rides anymore when she got her license and a brand new Honda Civic from her parents. We had also kissed several times, a couple of those resulting in an all-out make-out sessions after school dances, but never any further than that.

The decision to go to college had me thinking a lot more about leaving my hometown, and the date was a result of some of that thinking. I wasn't kidding myself, I knew going to college a few hours away wasn't exactly the same as going to the other side of the world or something. Still, Morgan was one of just a couple girls that I had ever had any kind of relationship with, even if it was just something stupid. We had never actually gone on a date, even though I had made plans to do so in my own mind. For one reason or another, nothing had ever happened and I was feeling some foolish regret about it.

Morgan walked to the next hole with her putter upside down in her hand like a cane. She used the grip to scratch at a bump just under the hem of her shorts from a mosquito bite. We had to wait for the players in front of us so we sat on a small bench a few yards away. For a few minutes we sat in silence, but I could feel that she didn't like waiting without engaging in conversation. She smiled at me and asked, "Doing anything special over the summer?"

I looked up to the sky like I was thinking, but I knew I didn't really have any big plans. I responded, "Not really. I'll probably just do some landscaping work for my uncle. I'm sure I'll play a ton of poker and maybe party a little bit when I can."

She perked up. "How do you play poker? I've never really played except for some dumb game on my phone. Even then I didn't really know what I was doing."

"We play Texas Hold'em. Like other poker games, the goal is to eventually make a poker hand like pairs, straights, and flushes. Each hand starts with two people putting a small amount of money in the pot before the cards are dealt to start the betting. That's called the small and big blind. They're called small and big because one is generally half the size of the other. If the blinds are one dollar and two dollars, people usually call it a 'one-two game'. Once the blinds are out, you're dealt two cards and you bet on how good you think your starting cards are compared to everybody else's. After that, the dealer puts three cards face up on the table, which is called the 'flop.' Everybody uses them, combined with their personal cards, to make a hand. You bet again depending on the strength of your hand. The dealer flips another card that's called the 'turn.' That is followed by another round of betting. Finally, the last card, or the 'river,' is dealt. That is all the cards you get, seven total, to make the best five card hand that you can. You bet one last time and whoever stays in flips their cards to see who wins. Of course, there's a lot of strategy and bluffing that happens."

She actually seemed to be paying attention to my explanation, which was nice. I instantly felt bad that I wasn't more patient about her crappy miniature golf game. She replied, "Wow, that was a lot. Maybe I'll come over and watch you play sometime. I'll probably understand it better if I see it happening."

I nodded. "Yeah, it would probably make a lot more sense if you watch people play. I'll text you sometime when we're playing. There'll be plenty of opportunities before I leave for school." We both stood up and made our way to the next hole, now clear of any people.

"Oh yeahhh . . . are you excited for Middenburg? I heard it's not that easy to get in there. Are you nervous about going?"

I threw my golf ball down hard against the astro-turf and the concrete underneath sent it flying up to shoulder height. I swiped my hand like a cat and caught it, enjoying the little smack sound it made when it hit my palm. I sort of wished I could just stand in the same spot and keep bouncing the ball and listening to it hit my hand.

I turned my attention back to Morgan and said, "I don't get too worked up about things like that, I'm just ready to move on from high school."

She looked back at me and smiled, then turned around and hit her ball. While she was swinging she said, "I don't believe you, I think you're at least a little nervous about the change. I know you."

She really didn't know me as well as she thought, but she was right in this case; I was feeling some anxiety. Of course, I wasn't wild about giving her the satisfaction of knowing that. Plus, she really didn't know what my serious anxieties were about. I flipped my head to the side in a goofy manner and replied, "Well, I guess it's true, you really do know everything about me. Why don't I hide you in my dorm room so you can guide me through my first year of college?" I hadn't meant it to sound mean, but there was definitely a sharp bite to the comment that didn't sit very well with Morgan. It was a bad attempt at a joke, but she didn't even give me a courtesy laugh.

"Well, you'll have to wait a year, but Middenburg is one of the schools I was thinking about applying to, so you might have to put up with me."

I silently lined up my putt, took two practice strokes, and missed the putt by an inch. I let out a frustrated "Bahh!" and walked up to my ball to tap in the two-footer. Morgan walked behind me and I heard her making clicking sounds with her tongue to show me her annoyance. She spoke again in a more agitated tone, "Jeez, don't be so excited at the possibility of having me at the same college as you; you can barely contain your joy."

"Oh, c'mon, of course I would love that. Truth is, you're right, I do worry about things, so I guess that's why I'm a little weird about the whole thing."

She smiled, but a little tension remained. I didn't know what else to say, so we finished the round with almost no more conversation. I tried to let out a few "Whoo" and "Yow" cheers when she made putts, but she only twirled her putter sarcastically in the air in mock celebration. She declined my offer to have ice cream at the snack bar, saying that she had to get home to help her mom with something. Appropriately, the date ended with me trying to kiss her like a buffoon while she cheeked me and I planted a peck on a thin layer of blush and cakey foundation. My last smooth move was an awkward pat on the back before she got in her car. I'm such a goddamn stud I can barely stand myself.

♥ ♣ ♦ ♠

I didn't want to go home after that debacle, so I was happy to get a text from Anthony. He and a few guys were just driving around hanging out. I didn't know the other guys, Tim and Joel, all that well, but I was really up for anything to avoid watching TV at home while I figured out different ways the date could have gone, most of them ending with Morgan straddling me while I said all the right things to convince her to blow me. I replied to Anthony's text, letting him know that we could meet in fifteen minutes at the park near the little league softball and baseball fields on Park Street.

Even though my mind wasn't totally with the guys, I still had a good time riding around with them. We didn't do anything special, but they were okay guys to waste time with. We got some Italian ice and yelled crazy shit out the window for no reason. Anthony knew I had been out with Morgan because he had been talking to Jeremy earlier. He asked me how it went, looking back at me in the rearview mirror. He wasn't exactly the kind of friend I discussed emotions with, so I knew he meant physically. I looked back at him and said "Oh it was awesome, she let me kiss one whole cheek. It was very sensual." Anthony took the hint and didn't pry anymore. Tim had a fresh pack of cigarettes and I politely asked if I could have one. He nodded in time to the music and handed the whole pack to me along with a brown lighter. I knelt my head down behind the seat to avoid the wind coming in the open windows and lit one of the menthols. When I brought my head up, Anthony flicked on the car lights against the approaching dusk. When the lights popped on, a thought passed through my mind. It wasn't any kind of brilliant revelation, just a recurring thought that I'd been having for several weeks. I had this sinking feeling that I'd never see any of these guys ever again. Not because I was going to die or something; just that our paths would never cross again. It was kind of silly; chances were that I'd at least see them in passing at some point. The thought still lingered and made me irrationally sad. I blew smoke out the window and stared at the last of the departing sun, feeling better when I saw Joel's hand out the passenger window, riding up and down on the gusts of wind passing by the car.

CHAPTER 15

It is one of the small tragedies of life when you move on from a friend or group of friends. Goodbyes deemed temporary are accompanied by all the familiar pleasantries and informal plans to hang out again, start annual traditions that guarantee a yearly reunion, or even once again be in the same direct realm someday.

It is quite an odd feeling to have the little rock form down in the stomach. That little rock, growing into a nuisance, is the sense that you may never see or talk to a person ever again. When a person who was once an important, or at least consistently present, cast member in the play of your life is slinking offstage for good, it can be very peculiar and very uncomfortable.

One of the rites of passage is the acceptance that we will be separated from people by the ebbs and flows of life, leaving one to consider if this or that relationship should have been worked on to make it last longer. Friends from youth move away, find other social circles, or, in the most regrettable circumstances, terminate a friendship because of ill feelings.

Adolescence, for even the most reluctant participant, is a period in which to gather as many acquaintances as possible—both positive and negative. So soon, the difficult filtering process begins for a young adult. As quickly as they are collected, the bodies depart. Sometimes it's the same to just let bodies leave and keep the memory, because sometimes, even when the body's still around, you're only friends with the memory anyway.

Consolation can be taken in the few that remain, and the few important ones added here and there. But the ultimate realization is that there are far more goodbyes; goodbyes that leave you wondering, in a selfish little mourning, why anything in your world has to be altered without your permission.

CHAPTER 16

Before I was to leave for school, I had to meet my uncle for a final discussion about our plan. Naturally, I was growing very anxious as the start of the school year was approaching. Not only did I have the regular concerns of an incoming freshman, I also had the deal with my uncle. He still hadn't made a decision as to who we would be targeting with his crazy scheme, which was probably better anyway. If, over the summer, I had been aware of who would be bearing the potentially life-ruining consequences of our set-up, I might have been more inclined to end my involvement. My uncle kept telling me that he was still trying to figure out who would be best. With the upcoming season he was busy with his normal duties, and he kept reminding me that he had to choose the perfect player or players. I certainly wasn't going to rush him. In fact, a part of me definitely just wanted him to scrap the whole thing altogether, even if it meant losing the money. But the show was still slated to go on, which included a meeting a week before I was to start classes.

"Okay, we can make this pretty quick. I have a meeting with some of my assistant coaches that I have to be at in a half hour or so. First off, here's this before your aunt gets home. Take it to your car or shove it in your pockets now." He handed me two tightly packed stacks of money. For how much money it was and what it represented to me, the stacks were almost comically small, fitting easily into my two front pockets without even bulging noticeably. Still, it might as well have been two bricks in my pants as far as my nerves were concerned. This exchange was, without a doubt, a signal that we had crossed into a more serious area that wasn't just some far-off hypothetical thing. We both knew it. "I'm still not decided on who it's gonna be. Definitely have it narrowed down, though."

I couldn't help but wonder how many times my uncle had been involved in things like this. He seemed pretty relaxed, although I didn't really picture him ever letting on if he was feeling scared or doubtful. He was never one to outwardly question his own actions, as it would show weakness. He had still been awfully casual throughout the whole planning process. It was good in a way because it made up for my nervousness. Nobody, it seemed, had any kind of clue that we were up to anything because Uncle Pete had done such a good job covering our little meetings by having me do yard work. He had even cut his regular landscaper's hours in half so that there'd be things for me to do when I was over at his house. I had only had to follow along. My parents found it funny that he and I were getting along so well, but not to the point that they were suspicious. I assumed that they just thought I was happy to make some good money before I left for school, even if it meant spending time with him.

I said to my uncle, trying to seem confident, "So classes start in a week and I'll be living in Roth Hall on the southern end of the campus near the gym. On Monday, Wednesday, and Friday, I have three classes during the day. I'll be on campus from eight in the morning until about three in the afternoon. I'll have lunch and some non-class time in there, but I'll probably be doing work or be too busy to talk on the phone. Tuesday and Thursday I have a morning class that ends at 10:30. I also have an evening class from six to nine on Tuesdays. Just thought you should know my schedule in case you're looking for a good time to call."

He didn't seem too interested in my schedule, but he didn't give any kind of smartass remark about being too detailed or anything. When I was finished he said, "Okay, I'll keep that in mind, but my schedule is pretty crazy. If I have to get a hold of you, I'm gonna call when I have any free time. You don't have to answer if it's not convenient; I'll always leave a voicemail and let you know if it's important to call me back. But I'll never leave any message about what we're doing. And no texts about anything, don't forget that."

"Gotcha. I'll pretty much wait to talk to you until you contact me, unless I have something urgent to say."

My uncle's butt-chin went up and down quickly, his way of showing agreement. "I'm gonna let you get settled in and everything, so I won't be bothering you for the first week or two. But once I decide on the player and get everything we need to make it happen, it's gonna be game on. I'll be relying on you to be watching the player regularly so I can concentrate on my coaching responsibilities."

While I had a twinge of annoyance at the way he was talking to me, I knew it would be stupid to cause any tension at this point. I replied in my most obedient manner, "Understood. I'll talk to you in a few weeks and we can finish up with the last few details."

"Sounds good. You can mow the lawn and trim around the shed and garage. Also, there are a few weeds in the landscape bed around the front door; yank them and that should be it for today."

As I was walking away towards the shed where the mower was stored, I heard my uncle say one last thing: "Just remember, you can pull out of this at any point. If you're feeling too much pressure, I'd rather have you return the money and forget about the whole thing. I think you realize by now that I'm in a spot here. I'm desperate enough to do something drastic because I can't afford to fuck this season up, but I can't afford you slipping up when it comes to what we're doing here." He didn't wait for an answer and spun around towards the house, his sneakers squeaking on the long blades of grass.

By the time I was done with my work, my uncle had left for his meeting and my aunt hadn't arrived home yet. Before setting off for my own home, I needed to stash the money somewhere so my parents wouldn't accidentally see it. I knew they'd be home, so I would just wait to take it to my room until they left to get groceries or something. I didn't want to deposit the cash at the bank. The bank still sent paper statements and sometimes my mom opened mine thinking it was her and my dad's statement. I decided to stick the money in the spare tire reservoir underneath the carpet in the trunk of my '94 Nissan Maxima, even putting it underneath the tire for good measure.

CHAPTER 17

Move-in Day! Something about those words just annoyed the shit out of me. Probably the exclamation point. The pictures on the pamphlet of silly parents carrying their silly kid's shit around are also pretty nauseating. It doesn't seem accurate for a dad to have a giant grin on his face when he's lugging around an old mini-fridge or TV while getting lost in dorm room hallways. I don't understand why everything has to be such a phony celebration.

I had stopped in the student union to buy a drink after the three hour drive to the campus. Looking through the couple of singles I knew I had in my pocket, I found the crumpled pamphlet about "Move-in Day!" I had kept it to check what time I would be allowed to move my belongings into my dorm room. I had also written the time on my palm, so the pamphlet was unnecessary now. I glanced one last time at the proud father in the pictures and took another look at the mom carrying a lamp with a fake football for a base. I tossed the pamphlet in the nearest garbage can. It didn't have a bag in it yet, but I figured it was better than throwing it on the floor or sidewalk or something. At least maybe a janitor would find it when they got around to putting trash bags in the cans.

I specifically asked my parents not to come on "Move-in Day!" The thought of my family being featured in next year's pamphlet made me sick. Those pictures were staged anyway, but why risk it? I just didn't find it necessary to have the corny moving and goodbyes and stuff. My parents reluctantly agreed to just let me use their mini-van but not come along. I didn't look down on the kids who were moving things in with the help of their parents. I wasn't exactly excited to carry a van-load of crap to my room by myself, but I wouldn't be able to handle the conversation about being excited on the 'big day.' I couldn't withstand the questions about my apprehensions and subtle remarks about which girls were cute. These would inevitably accompany the help my parents would give me. Also, I would have had to skip the smoke break that I'd probably like to take at some point during the trips to and from the van. They still didn't know I smoked, and I just didn't feel like having them find out yet. It was stupid, but I couldn't bring myself to smoke in front of them.

I had to admit, I did feel bad about not having my parents come help. My mom, especially. I knew the big-ass envelope of brightly-colored pamphlets had gotten her wound up about the whole process. They had just given me a headache. Call me crazy, but I don't think they need to be making high-gloss, multi-colored pamphlets with high resolution photos of goofballs for ridiculous things like "Move-in Day!" For every single one of the estimated 15,278 incoming freshman, no less. Couldn't they just send a black and white copy with the date, time, and details on it? "Move-in Day!" was just one of seventeen pamphlets that had been included in my welcome package.

The student union was oddly deserted. I found the lineup of soda and drink machines and tapped a rhythm on the front of each one, deciding what to have. I settled on a root beer.

CHAPTER 18

Still sipping my root beer, I entered the dorm room that was my new home with a loud exhale and set down the duffel bag I was carrying.

"Hey man! Nice to see you, finally!"

A tall guy with a clean smile and a messy head of blond hair was reaching his hand out to me. I put my own hand out and when they met, he squeezed tight and pulled me in for a friendly hug. I laughed, a bit uncomfortable, but not hating that he at least seemed like a decent guy. I pulled back and looked up so our eyes met.

"Nice to meet you too, Josh." I had kept looking at the paperwork the entire ride up so I wouldn't forget it when we met. I felt a ridiculous sense of pride that I hadn't messed up my first goal. "Guess this is our new home for a little while. Not too bad I guess."

"Not exactly a mansion, but I'll feel right at home once I get my Mickey and Minnie Mouse posters hung on my side of the room." He pointed to the painted cinder block walls with his index finger. It took me a while to process what he said, but finally I reacted with a confused look on my face.

He was obviously waiting for the reaction and immediately burst out in a loud, high-pitched laugh. "I'm just playing with you dude, we don't have to have any Disneyworld merchandise as decorations." He giggled again. "Unless you're into that!"

I put on my best mock-serious face and said, "Shit, I guess it would be weird to have this life-size cardboard cutout of Goofy in the corner beside my bed, then. I'll have to burn it once I get my clothes unpacked." It felt pretty good to get a hearty laugh in response to my joke, and I actually felt some good feelings about the guy that I'd be sharing my living space with.

Meeting Josh had immediately made me think of Jeremy. I had gotten the chance to see him one more time during the last week before I left. He planned to stay with his parents, get a job, and possibly enroll in community college. Before our senior year ended, he and I had talked like it would be the greatest summer of our lives. We, along with all of our other friends, had expected that we'd be hanging out constantly before we'd be dealing with the distance that going to college would put between us. In reality, pretty much everybody had been busy with summer jobs, girlfriends, or vacations with their families. We had a decent amount of time to just mess around, but it was nothing like we thought it would be.

I wondered if Josh would become an important part of my life at all. Maybe he'd just be some dude that I lived with for a while. Or maybe he and I would become best friends and Jeremy would go by the wayside. I really didn't want that to happen, but who knows how I'd feel in a month or so. It already felt weird that Jeremy and I hadn't spent as much time together during the summer as we had every other summer since we were little kids.

"I pretty much have all my stuff in here already, do you need any help getting your shit in from your car?"

I hesitated a little bit, but he seemed like he was genuinely okay with giving me a hand. "That would be awesome man, I don't have a whole lot but it would make it go faster."

"Lead the way."

I made a mental note to first grab the duffel bag of clothes that also held the packs of money that I'd gotten from my uncle. I'd taken them from my trunk while my parents were at church and hid them in the duffel bag in my closet. I didn't expect Josh to open anything without asking, but it would obviously be best if the bag was in my hands at all times.

CHAPTER 19

After Josh had helped me carry all my stuff up from my parents' van, we went to a meeting for our dorm floor. It was held in the social area, a great big open space with a bunch of furniture that all looked the same, a few vending machines, and a 55" flat screen. I knew it was 55" because it still had a sticker on the bottom right corner that nobody had ever peeled off. The meeting was just about boring stuff, mostly common sense rules and warnings about the consequences of using drugs and alcohol in the dorms.

I spent most of the meeting concerned with the sticker on the TV. Jeremy's family had a television exactly like it that they had bought three years ago, so I knew it wasn't a brand new set. So, for a few years, nobody had peeled off the damn sticker on this TV. I don't know if that meant nobody hung out in this area or something, but it bugged me that the bright blue and yellow sticker was still stuck on there. I made a mental note to peel it off when nobody was around.

I had sent my mom a text message earlier in the day letting her know that I had gotten to the school safely and was doing fine and that I would give her and Dad a call later. After the meeting I went outside to give them a ring and smoke a cigarette. I found a walled-in corridor area and, leaning against one of the drab gray walls, tried to get my lighter going. Even with the walls, there was a slight breeze sailing through, so I cupped my hand around the lighter and cigarette and finally got it lit. Holding the cigarette in my mouth, I found my phone in my pocket and hit send, knowing my mom's number was the last one I had called. Or I thought so, anyway.

It turned out that the last number I had called was Uncle Pete's home phone. Before I had left for school, my parents had asked me to return a dish that they had left at my parents' house at some point over the summer. I had called them first to make sure that one of them was home before I stopped by their house. Aunt Sarah had been the only one home because Uncle Pete was watching game film and jerking off an alumni booster or something. I was glad that he wasn't there, and actually had a nice time drinking orange juice and saying goodbye to my aunt.

I hadn't even realized I dialed the wrong number until Uncle Pete picked up the phone and startled me with the sound of his booming baritone "Hello." I dropped my cigarette on the ground and stumbled after it with my phone cradled on my shoulder.

I sputtered out, "Uh, hey what's goin' on?"

"Not too much. I know I'd said that we wouldn't talk for the first couple weeks, but I kinda thought you might want to chat earlier than that. Wasn't expecting it at this time of night, though." His words were followed by a brief pause, and I could picture him straightening out his arm then bringing his Rolex back to his face.

"Yea, I actually meant to call my parents. I accidentally dialed the wrong number and got you."

"Well, don't be so happy to talk to me."

I let out a half-hearted "Nah," but he interrupted me.

"We should have a chat, though, since it seems you have the time. Your aunt is in the bath but she's gettin' out soon. Let me give you a call from the garage once she falls asleep so we can talk without her listening in."

"That would work better anyway, I should call my parents as soon as I can."

I could tell he hadn't listened to me. He made a hasty reply that I couldn't quite make out, and then hung up quickly.

CHAPTER 20

"Hey bud!"

My father's greeting was loud and cheerful, and I could hear my mom saying "Hellooo!" in the background at the same time because it was on speakerphone. I held my phone away from my ear and turned the volume down two notches, then switched it to my other ear. Even though they couldn't actually see me, I put on a giant cheesy grin before answering, "Heyyyy, it's Bill and Cathy, right? Do I have those names correct? I can't quite remember . . . I vaguely recall some older couple I used to live with, but I'm not sure I'm getting those names right."

My dad picked up on my joke and said, "Yes, you got them right. And your name is Andy, yes? Cathy was going to send a box of fresh cookies and snacks for someone named Corvus, but I guess we have that wrong . . . we'll just send them to Andy." I heard my mom shout in the background, "Why'd you tell him?!" My dad laughed and my mom yelled again, "and Corvus, don't even make jokes about forgetting us like that, it's hard enough that you're away . . . and that you asked us to stay at home for Move-in Day!" My dad and I both snickered, our laughs sounding remarkably similar.

"Mom, you know I'm teasing, and the Move-in Day thing wasn't personal, I just wanted some space. I really think it helped me get adjusted quicker to move my stuff in and get started on my own. My roommate seems like a really cool guy, by the way." I wasn't sure yet if Josh was really as great as I made him sound, but he was nice, and I knew my mom would love to hear that I was getting along with my roommate.

"Well that's great, but we want to meet him ourselves soon. We're coming out to visit as soon as we can."

"Of course, mom."

I heard a shuffling noise and I could tell she had picked up the phone and took it off speakerphone. "How is the food? For the money they charge for board, it better be decent."

I laughed and replied, "I've been here one day; the cafeteria wasn't even open yet. They had free pizza in the common room area on my floor. I just grabbed some of that for both meals. I had the banana and granola bar you gave me for breakfast."

"Okay, but maybe you should eat more than just pizza."

I remembered that I still had a lit cigarette, and I took a small puff with my mouth away from the phone. "Just one day, mom. I promise I won't become a pizzaholic." I flicked the spent cigarette away. "But seriously, everything went fine so far."

"Sounds good! We didn't really talk about money before you left. Do you need a little cash to get started? We can put a few bucks in your account. I know you were thinking of getting a job, but we don't want you to rush into that."

"Nah, it's okay. You don't have to do that."

She answered with a mixture of confusion and surprise, "Really? I can't imagine you made *that* much doing yardwork for your uncle."

I instantly got nervous. I realized that, to somebody who didn't know I'd gotten an eight-thousand-dollar advance from my uncle, turning down money was a kind of strange. Even though I wasn't one to drain my parents of money, it probably looked a bit odd for me to so casually pass on the offer. I collected myself and said, "Actually, that would be great. You know I don't like to take money from you guys any more than I have to, but I could use it."

"It's no problem, we put aside a little extra this summer to give you when school started. We weren't able to give you much at your graduation party, so we felt like this would help you out. We'll deposit $250 into your account tomorrow."

I felt an immediate pang of sadness at the thought of them saving a few dollars a week while I had the equivalent of a few months of my dad's salary still hidden in the spare tire area of my car. "That's awesome, thanks so much! That will get me a ton of pizza!"

My mom finally giggled and said, "Alright, honey, we don't want to hold you up any more, so we'll let you go for now. Dean, do you want to say anything else to your son?" I heard the familiar click of my dad's recliner going forward, and pictured him sitting forward with his hands circled around his mouth to shout,

"Hey, love you Corvus! Do well, have fun, and let us know if you need anything."

I said, "I will," and I heard my mom relay the message. "Love you both!"

"We love you, too. Talk to you again soon hopefully!"

We exchanged goodbyes and I heard the other end of the phone go silent. Pulling out my key card, I let out a long breath, relieved that the phone call was over. It wasn't that I especially disliked conversations with my parents, I just hated talking on the phone.

I was so glad to be off the phone that I nearly forgot that I'd told my uncle I'd wait for his phone call. I even went to the door and dipped my key card before I remembered I had to talk to him. I needed to stay outside to talk because I didn't want anybody to hear our conversation, even if it was only my side. Better safe than sorry. It was rare that I smoked two cigarettes so closely together, but I didn't want to look weird standing outside waiting for my phone to ring, so I popped another cigarette from the pack I had. Lighting it was a struggle again, but it finally sparked and caught properly on the fourth try.

I didn't have to wait too long for my uncle. My phone started wriggling around just a few minutes after I hung up with my parents. I answered on the third buzz, "Hello."

"Hey Corvus, how was moving day?"

I honestly didn't expect him to wait for an answer, and the silence became awkward when neither one of us talked. I finally said back, "It was good, no problems at all. My roommate seems like a real decent dude. I didn't bring too much, so I got all my stuff moved in real quick with his help. Monday is the first day of classes."

"Sounds good, glad to hear it." He was clearly in a business-like mood, so I knew we were not going to be having much more small talk. I'd never complain about that. "Alright, here's what I've been thinking about. Not sure if you've followed anything with college football and Middenburg's team, but there's a true fresh-man coming up who is a monster. He's a running back, and he's already moved beyond the point of just competing for the start-ing job with Allen, the junior back. This new player, Raven, will be the guy for them this year. He was freakin' amazing in high school, and he's gotten bigger and stronger just in the last couple months. For a kid from the 'hood, he actually seems to be pretty smart too. Still, he's from the freakin' hood, so making him our guy would make sense."

I cringed at my uncle's last sentence, even though I knew it might be true. For being around a lot of inner city kids, many of whom were black, my uncle's view of them was not exactly compassionate. It's not that he was blatantly racist, but I'd heard him speak of "ghetto kids" and "homeboys" in not-very-nice ways. He'd had close relationships with some of his past players who came from rough areas, but it was almost like he gave himself credit for changing them into proper men, and only respected them after he put his stamp on them. It was weird.

My uncle continued, "Frankly, I wanted the motherfucker on my team, and I didn't get him. I have to admit, that's another reason I don't mind picking him. But that doesn't even really matter, he's just going to be the right choice, anyway. That side bullshit will just be a bonus for me. I'm banking on the fact that he's going to become immensely important to their offensive schemes as a whole."

I finally spoke up, asking, "What's his name again?"

"James Raven. You can even see stuff about him on SportsCenter and whatnot."

When he said it, the name was vaguely familiar, although I didn't know anything about him in particular. I tried to recall any of the ESPN stories I'd half listened to while eating my mid-morning cereal over the summer.

My uncle cleared his throat and asked, "Do you have a piece of paper and something to write with?"

I poked around in my pocket, my hand pushing past my keys, key card, cigarettes, and lighter. Finally I came to the receipt I had from the convenience store that I'd stopped at on the drive to school. As luck had it, I also had a pen in my other pocket, still in there from filling out a couple of forms that our R.A. had given to us. "I do, actually. Do you really have information on the dude already?"

"Damn right. Listen, I can't say it enough, I'm dead-freakin'-serious about doing this. I didn't give you eight grand for shits and giggles. If we keep going with this, expect that I'm going to do it right, and I expect the same from you."

"I understand, that's the last time you have to say it to me. What info do you want to give me tonight?"

My uncle seemed satisfied with my blunt response, and he replied with a quick "Alright," seeming content to continue on with business. "I have the address he's living at. He was lucky enough to get an exception from the school to live in an apartment with an older friend of his from his hometown. The friend, Jamal Figuero, is a starting cornerback on the team. He's a good player too. Although Raven is our main target, we're going to hope Figuero gets hit a little bit in the process. If we can make it look like they're working together, which shouldn't be hard with them living in the same place, it would be even more of a boost for us."

Again, it was almost surreal to hear my uncle speak in the manner he was. While I'd thought he was an ass for years, I never expected him to be so conniving, vicious, and blasé about potentially ruining another person's life. Then again, I couldn't say much. At this point, I was going right along with the whole thing.

"I guess it's hard to argue with that choice if you can get a two-for-one deal. Give me the information you got, I want to get to bed soon. Plus I don't want anybody to pass by and hear us talking."

"I got no problem with that. He also has a car, a real beater. I'll give you the make and model of that, too. Ready?"

I clicked the pen and said, "Go ahead."

"619 Russian Street, apartment nine. There are only twelve apartments in the complex and not much else around. It's on the edge of town so it's pretty quiet. He drives a scuffed up 1993 Buick LeSabre with a bunch of missing paint, but the paint that's left is green. No doubt a present from his friendly neighborhood crack dealer, hoping Raven doesn't forget him when he makes the pros."

I'd written down everything quickly, careful to get as much as I could. I read it back to him, doing my best not to speak too loudly. When he confirmed all the details, I jammed the paper into my left pocket and put the pen on the right hand side with everything else.

My uncle quipped, "Get your beauty sleep, dear. I'll talk to you in a few weeks. Don't forget, the important game is October 27th. Bye." He didn't wait for my response, and I checked my phone to see that the call was over. I took a very deep breath and exhaled with a low moan, happy again to be off the phone.

CHAPTER 21

Set amidst the wonderfully expansive landscape of Middenburg, this campus boasts historically significant structures
from the nineteenth century, numerous grassy terraces with
mature trees, and the famous Horowitz Pond. On the north
side of the university property, one can see gorgeous views
of the nearby agricultural fields. The south side opens up
into the downtown area of Middenburg, where one can find
plenty of restaurants and interesting shops. Those details
complement the impressive thirty-seven educational buildings, fourteen residence halls, and vast array of athletic
facilities that can be found at on campus. Please use this
convenient map to navigate everything that Middenburg
University has to offer!

After reading the description on the front of the pamphlet, I
unfolded the entire thing to reveal the illustrated campus map
inside. I used my hand and thigh to iron out the nine rectangle
sections so that it would be flatter. My thigh was too bony to
work very well, but I finally got the map smoothed out enough to
comfortably read it.

Since it was closest to my dorm, I checked out the gym where
my phys ed class would be held. It was easy to find because it
was right beside the massive arena where basketball games were
played. The arena was an incredible sight to see. It had a large
cornerstone on the front side that had '2015' chiseled into it, so
it was pretty new. Above the front doors there was a huge banner
with the Middenburg logo on it. On the sides there were stadium-
height banners that featured the likenesses of former Middenburg
basketball stars. The arena looked like it could hold tens of thou-
sands of people and it also looked like it cost a shitload of money.
The smaller gym where my class would be held looked comically
small compared to the basketball complex. It was in pretty good
shape, but it looked more like it should be the shed where they

stored the basketballs instead of the place where classes took place.

None of the other buildings were as exciting as the arena. My English class would be held in one of several buildings that looked like old churches in a clump. They all had some kind of steeple or bell-tower thing. They were pretty cool, but they all needed masonry work in some area or another. On the other side of campus, there was a small creek that marked the edge of university property. Extended along that creek was a long one-story brick building that looked like it was built in the seventies. It had a flat roof and a seemingly endless row of windows. Both my psychology and history classes would be in this building. Near the center of campus and the student union was the multi-story building where I'd go for math class. It was clean and modern, but not particularly distinctive in any way. It did have an awesome piece of modern art out front that looked like a giant see-saw.

After seeing each building and making my way towards Horowitz Pond, I still held the map in my left hand. It flapped like an awkward stiff flag in the breeze. I sorta felt like smoking a cigarette, but I'd seen signs all over campus marking places as prohibited areas for smoking. I didn't bother to light one. I didn't really feel like getting yelled at by a security guard my first week on campus. With my map still in hand, I noticed a cute girl walking towards me. Her skin was a shade darker than iced tea and she had a magnificent mane of hair that was curled and stretched past her shoulder blades. A lot of volume, I guess you'd say. She was a little chubby but still very striking. She had on a Middenburg hoodie and bright green shorts. It was a little too warm for a hoodie yet, but I guessed that she'd probably just bought it and was anxious to wear it.

She pointed at my map with her own rolled up one and smiled, saying, "Looking for your buildings too?"

I clumsily folded my map in half and answered, "Um, yeah, I just want to make sure I can find everything on the first day. Even though I've seen it before the campus is still so big and confusing. Think I'm getting the hang of it, though."

"I know, right? I've circled everything two times and it's still intimidating. What's your major?"

"Psychology."

"Oh, that's cool! Are you living on campus?"

"Yep, Roth Hall over near the big gym."

"Nice!" There was a long pause between us, then she said warmly, "Well, good luck getting started!"

She started walking and I replied dorkily, "You too, hopefully you get more comfortable on the third time around!" She laughed and smiled while waving goodbye with her map. I suddenly realized that the long pause in the conversation was her allowing me to ask her things like her major, where she lived, or maybe her name. I instantly felt flush and embarrassed even though she wasn't even there anymore. She seemed incredibly nice and pleasant, but I secretly hoped I'd never run into her again because of my awkwardness.

I found Horowitz Pond and sat on the grassy bank, careful not to sit in any of the goose or duck shit that was everywhere. Beside the pond there was a hand-written sign that said "PLEASE DON'T FEED BREAD TO THE GOOSE OR DUCKS" on it. I think I'd heard once that the bread wasn't good for their stomach, or something. I wondered what food was okay to feed the birds, if any. I also wondered if whoever made the sign was only worried about bread specifically, or if they didn't want people feeding the birds at all. I sat for a while, enjoying the quiet and rest after walking all around campus. Not too long later I stood up and stumbled a little bit since my feet had fallen asleep. I noticed a full piece of stale bread sitting right near the handmade sign. I picked it up, did my civic duty by throwing it in the trash, and then started making my way back to my dorm.

CHAPTER 22

I was excited for my first day of classes. While there was a lot of bullshit that came along with the whole college thing, and, of course, the uncle thing, I was actually looking forward to the academics. All of the books that I'd ordered online had shown up on time, so that was one thing that I didn't need to worry about. I found it funny that I was a psychology major and only had one psychology class. I was definitely interested in a lot of other things, so I wasn't that concerned. It just made me really realize that there would be a lot of general education junk before I'd really be getting into my main interests. I had kind of understood that just by looking through brochures and stuff online, but seeing my schedule in print made it more real.

The early morning sun gave off both a warmth and brightness that was pleasant at first, but became bothersome the longer I was exposed to it. After exiting the heavy metal door at the south end of my dorm hall, I pulled out my trusty campus map. Even though I'd gone around the campus the day before, I wanted to be absolutely sure I was going to the right place.

I still remember when I was in sixth grade and didn't understand the concept of homeroom on my first day of junior high. My homeroom teacher and my first period teacher were the same, so I got confused. When the bell for the completion of homeroom sounded, everybody picked up their backpacks and began to file out of the room. I did the same, moving on to what I thought was my second period class. The class started out pretty good. The teacher, Mrs. Houseal, asked a trivia question. Something about JFK, I think. I got it right and was awarded a piece of raspberry hard candy. More importantly, I thought I had won the respect of my peers by looking smart. After that, I sat patiently listening to Mrs. Houseal call out the list of names of students who were supposed to be in the class. She got past the spot in the alphabet where my name should have been, and I got more and more worried as she went further and further past the S's. She got to the end of the names and asked if anybody was in the class who hadn't heard their name called. I slowly raised my hand. She asked to look at my schedule, motioning with her hand to come to the front of the class. She squinted at the small print, moving her dry, wrinkly finger along each line. "Ah", she said simply, "Looks like you should be here second period. It's only first period. Go back to Miss Cressman's room for Reading class. I'll see you in forty-five minutes."

My sense of pride from earlier took an abrupt turn in the other direction. I felt like a fool who was too child-like to understand a simple junior high schedule. That feeling of being embarrassed in front of an entire classroom had never left me, and since then I'd always been careful to read and re-read my schedules from that point on. College wouldn't be any different. I can still vividly remember the tart, delicious taste of that raspberry hard candy, but the memory of my mistake was even stronger.

My first class was an English Composition class in room 1150 in the Arthur J. Hearst Building. I arrived at 7:59 to a full room. Since most had gotten there before me, I had to take a seat in the front row, which wouldn't have been my first choice. The professor wasn't there yet, so there was a little bit of chatter floating around the room. The class looked to be almost all younger students, so the talking was mostly being done in short, nervous exchanges between people who looked like they already knew each other. There were some older looking students who appeared more comfortable. They were grouped together near the back and were having much more casual conversations. I took a seat beside a fortyish looking woman with a large binder in front of her, already full with folders and composition paper. She had a pencil case that was stuffed full to the point that the zipper looked to be struggling to stay closed.

The professor entered the classroom at about three minutes after eight. She was about the same age as the woman beside me and had a head full of chestnut hair hanging out every which way. She was hopping and buzzing about like she was already flustered. I wondered what she had to be stressed about at eight in the morning on the first day of classes that had her flipping stacks of paper and wiping little beads of sweat off her face. I figured it would be an interesting semester with her; she had me feeling a little antsy before she even said anything to the class.

She began to pass out papers, speaking in a loud voice at the same time:

"Hey guys, as you probably already know, my name is Dr. Cirelli and you should be here for English 1-0-1, English Composition. Basically, this class will give you a good basis in writing solid essay papers that are appropriate for college level course work. Some of what we talk about might be review from high school or other college classes you've had, but even re-learning this stuff is a good thing. We'll be discussing MLA and APA form, developing a little style in your writing, and, of course, working on grammar and sentence structure. Everybody's favorite, I know." She smiled with a mouthful of teeth that looked like tightly packed bowling pins. I felt a little more at ease.

"I'm now passing out the syllabus, which contains all of the information about grading, the general class schedule, my office hours, and so on and so forth. I'm required by the university to go over this, so that's pretty much all we'll be doing today. I'm also passing out the list of all the reading material you're going to need this semester. I apologize that I didn't make these known beforehand, but I have made some changes to my curriculum and made some last minute choices. Don't worry though, the books you'll need for this class can all be easily found in paperback editions. I assure you that you're going to spend way less on my books than you will for other professors. And that's just one reason I'll be your favorite professor ever!" She swung her arm in front of her in a sarcastically cheerful manner while the class laughed tenuously.

She seemed pretty damn cool, and the entire class eventually seemed to loosen up. We went over all the boring stuff, with Dr. Cirelli appearing even more bored than the class. The fifty minute class period came to an end and I shuffled out with the rest of the class after stuffing the syllabus into the green folder that I had written 'ENG 101' on with thick marker. I thought to myself that if I had to have an early morning class on a Monday, this one was a pretty good one.

"What's up dude, you on your way to another class?"

Josh had appeared from behind me, slapping me lightly on the back. I gave him a warm smile. "Yea, man. I just came from my English class." I pointed my thumb back towards the aging brick building behind us. "The professor seems pretty cool, actually. How's your day going so far?"

"I actually haven't had a class yet. I just had to visit the bookstore to pick up my last book for College Algebra. I hit the student union after that and got a breakfast sandwich, shit was pretty bangin', haha! There are a freakin' million hot girls walking around!"

Laughing, I said "I know, it's unbelievable. I think this town has a factory producing robots that look like models. I saw at least a dozen girls as hot as the hottest girl I knew in high school. And it's not even nine o'clock!"

"Craziness. Hey, you said you liked poker, right?"

"Oh yea, I play cards with my buddies back home all the time."

"Awesome! Just wanted to let you know that a few guys told me that they'll be playing a game tonight around eight. It's gonna be in the common room on the floor above us."

"Sounds good man, I'm definitely in. Even if I have a demonic professor who assigns some kind of work the first day, I'm already prepared to start blowing off my responsibilities to play poker."

Josh slapped me on the back again, laughing loudly. "Nice, man. I gotta go a different way, but I'll see you later in the dorm."

My second class was a physical education class with about a hundred students. We quickly went over the syllabus and then ran in circles around the gymnasium. There were so many people that it just became an impromptu game of bumper cars. The professor sat in a folding chair underneath one of the basketball nets and periodically shouted out how many minutes we had "run" so far. I floated along with everybody else, alternating between jogging and walking, trading sarcastic comments with the guy next to me, and hoping that the rest of the semester wouldn't be this boring. After what seemed like hours of foolish jogwalking, the class finally came to an end. Before we left, we had to fill out a sheet with the exercise that we had done. I signed my name and stuck it in the appropriate section of the open filing cabinet in the corner of the professor's office before starting off to the student union for lunch.

After waiting in a long line, I got a sandwich and took it to an area that had a couple of stuffed chairs and a wooden couch with turquoise cushions. There was an outdated big screen television playing SportsCenter with the volume awkwardly loud. Two other guys were in the area, one on the couch copying notes, the other in a chair eating a candy bar staring intently at the television. Biting into the marble rye bread, my teeth hit the lettuce and crunched through three green layers, finally hitting the thick pile of turkey and provolone cheese. It's amazing what a good sandwich can do for the soul; who needs chicken soup? The perfect ratio of lettuce to meat is crucial. Also, if there's mayonnaise, it needs to be just a lightly spread layer on each piece of bread. My first day sandwich pretty much hit all the qualifications, and even had a perfectly chilled pickle on the side. If everything else went wrong at Middenburg, I'd at least be able to say they served an excellent turkey on marble rye.

CHAPTER 23

The guy they were calling Vic appeared to be a little older than everybody else in the room. He had an even tan that disappeared into his socks and shirtsleeves. He had on extremely baggy basketball shorts, a white t-shirt, and sandals with a Nike swoosh adorning the tops and sides. His facial hair rode along his jawline and matched the dark, buzzed bristles on his head.

I didn't know exactly why he was watching us play; I just assumed he had a friend he was waiting for, or something. I wouldn't have really paid particular attention to him but at one point he stood behind me with his hand on the backrest of my chair, about an inch from my shoulder. He didn't seem to notice that he was sort of invading my space as he chatted with everybody at the table. I slid to the other side of the chair, not wanting to draw attention to the fact that I was feeling weird about him hovering over my chair. I didn't know why I felt guilty about leaning away from him. After all, he was the one invading my personal area.

"I am so unlucky at freakin' poker. Damn it."

The girl complaining tossed an ace of clubs and a queen of diamonds into the middle of the table in frustration. She'd had two good cards to start the hand, but she'd also kept calling all of her chips when neither of her cards had paired, and she hadn't made any kind of straight or flush or anything. After the bet that somebody had made on the river, she was left with only two chips that just barely covered the big blind that she would have to put in for the next hand.

By this time, Vic had moved on to another person's chair to hover. I watched the girl in silence until I felt Vic's eyes on me from behind a tiny guy sitting to my left. He smiled as the girl complained, trying not to be too obvious, but clearly trying to attract my attention. Any time you played poker with people who didn't play much, the grumbling and complaining was inevitable. Even when people caused their own problems at the table, it was easy to blame bad cards and shitty luck. Even people who are otherwise intelligent people can become infantile when things don't go their way, assuming that fortune is against them. It's a strange thing with card games and other things that involve a bit of luck; the casual person doesn't generally have a clear gauge of their own skill. This skewed expectation is what often causes the moaning and groaning.

I couldn't help but grin at Vic, but I immediately wiped it off my face, worried that the girl would think I was being mean to her if she saw me. And she did see me. She furrowed her brow and looked past me, then swung her eyes back at mine. I gave my best empathetic shrug as if to say, "What can ya do?" It was a free game in our dorm common room, and the prizes were a mug with the school logo, a hat with the name of a local accounting firm on it, and a card for a free Starbucks coffee. Not exactly life-changing prizes. Needless to say, my empathetic gesture may not have been as sincere-looking as I'd hoped.

I exited pretty early from the poker game, not really caring to spend much more time playing for crappy promotional items. Josh had gone out nearly an hour before me, so I figured I'd head back to the room to hang out with him. I made my way to the bathroom to take a piss. Actually, I first went the whole way down the wrong hallway before I realized the bathrooms were in the opposite direction. When I did find the men's room, I pushed open the thick metal door with my foot. As soon as the door opened, I heard somebody talking loudly. Taking a quick survey, I saw there were no feet underneath any of the stalls, and only one guy was at the line of urinals. The guy was Vic.

He was chatting on his cellphone that he held between his head and shoulder. His left hand was directly in front of him and he was scratching at a piece of chipping paint with the visible hand. I stepped up to a urinal that was two down from Vic's and unzipped my pants, then picked a spot on the wall to focus on while I clenched my mid-section. Vic kept pissing and continued his conversation as if I wasn't even there.

When I was done, I washed my hands at the waist-high porcelain sink and took a healthy clump of paper towels, pulling the lever slowly to avoid making a lot of noise. Of course, background noise probably doesn't matter much to a person who is already taking a leak while they talk on the phone. I finished drying my hands and threw away the paper towels. By the time I was a step out the door, Vic had already quickly washed his hands and was wiping his wet hands on his oversized shorts.

"Hey," he said simply.

"What's up," I said casually. I thought for a second, then continued, "I don't often hear people having long discussions on their cell while they're at the urinal." I grinned at him, instantly hoping he wouldn't take it wrong, or something. I didn't have to wait long to be relieved of my worry when he laughed sincerely at my joke.

"You think that's something, I once wrote an entire two page paper on a laptop while I took a shit!"

I returned a laugh and shot back, "Man, I heard it called a number two, but never a two-pager!"

When we both finally stopped snickering, he took two quick steps so he was right beside me as we padded down the carpeted hallway. For ten seconds or so, we both walked in unison like soldiers.

"You seem like you're okay at playing cards, do you play much?"

"My friends and I back home played all through high school. I've only played a few other games. Mostly only with buddies, although we did have some good games. Other than this dorm shit, I haven't really talked to anybody yet that plays here."

The scratch-pop sound of his flip-flops on the carpet bounced around obnoxiously in the hallway. I looked closely at the doors, all of them with two construction paper fish taped to them, each containing one of the names of the people who had just moved in to the room inside. I don't know if it was the stupid fish or what, but I got a sudden feeling that I shouldn't be in the place. It wasn't just the hallway or the residence hall either, it was everything. It was a hell of a time to get a wave of conflicted emotion, having just moved my shit and started my classes. It wasn't a new feeling, but it was the most potent it had ever been. I was walking down the hall with some near-stranger, actually carrying on decent conversation, and something in the back of my head had to act up.

Vic saw me looking at the paper fish and turned his head to look himself. After a couple of doors, he instantly stopped at one. I instinctively stopped as well, even though he hadn't said anything to me. He reached up with his index finger and thumb and gently peeled off one fish, then the other, with equal precision on both.

He held the two fish, one orange and one purple, with the same index finger and thumb. He was careful not to mess up the tape on either one. We both started walking again, passing two more doors. Vic stopped again at a door that had two fish of the same colors, orange and purple, and peeled them off. When they were off, he put the two he had been holding in the spots where the recent ones had come off, petting them with the side of his hand to make sure they stuck. He slowly jogged back to the previous door, placed the two new fish on it, and jogged back towards me.

"That should be interesting for somebody tomorrow when they come back from class."

We laughed in unison and continued walking.

He continued our conversation from where we'd left off and said, "I play, and I know some games around here. Off campus stuff, mostly. Do you bet sports at all?"

"Yea, here and there." For some reason, I didn't want to say "only with friends" again. Even though I was too young to have played cards or bet money in a casino, it seemed so juvenile to tell him that repeatedly. I didn't want to lie, but I also felt dumb saying "only with friends" to an older person.

"That's cool. Do you bet with friends or do you have someone else who takes your bets?"

"Just friends at this point. My one buddy has placed some bets online, but I haven't."

"Ah, fuck that sketchy internet shit, giving your credit card and all that nonsense. Face to face is where it's at." He pulled out a cigarette and put it, unlit, between his lips. He reached deep in his pocket and pulled out a black Bic. He flipped it to his other hand, then threw it deep in the air, just missing the low ceiling tiles. He ran after it and caught it like a kid imagining he was catching a pass to win the Super Bowl. "I take bets, nothing too crazy, but I'll take your action most any game you wanna bet. I pretty much go by the lines they set in Vegas, unless I think it's shitty for some reason." He didn't say anything else, and seemed to allow time for his words to sink in.

After a few moments, I answered, "I'll definitely remember you if I wanna bet something. Sometimes I want to throw some money on a game and I can't get a hold of my friend, Jeremy, who I usually bet with. I might want to play in some poker games, if you're offering that, too."

"No doubt, I can get you into most of the games I play. I'll give you my phone number. What's your name?"

"Corvus -yours is Vic, right-?"

"Yup, ready for my number?"

I snagged my phone from my pocket and pressed a few buttons. "Go ahead." He talked fast, and I had to have him repeat the string of numbers three times before I was sure I had the right combination. "I'll dial you so my number is in your phone."

"That's cool. I won't bother you unless you get a hold of me first; so you have to call or text if you wanna do something."

I heard his phone vibrate in his pocket when I pressed send, but he didn't reach to pull it out and look at it. We got to a door to the stairs that would take us to the ground floor and he held it open for me. When we got to the bottom of the staircase, I returned the favor by holding the door to the outside open for him.

Once out in the darkness, he turned back towards me while walking backwards. "Nice to meet you, boss, maybe we'll talk again. If not on the phone, maybe I'll see you around." He nodded and spun around, his back to me again.

"I'll get ahold of you." I said after him. He didn't answer, but waved one arm in the air to say goodbye. I lit a cigarette and watched him as he walked away and eventually turned a corner into the darkness.

CHAPTER 24

It's a strange feeling for one to have on a college campus, to perceive the insulation that exists around students in a metaphysical sense, and sometimes even a physical sense in terms of campus property. The insulation from outside society. It's quite odd to see students who actually convince themselves that they're living a real adult life during their time on campus. It's not to say that nobody works hard, or that slivers of real life can't be experienced in theory-based mock set-ups, but colleges and universities seem to be off the mark sometimes.

Among the problems that exist on college campuses, the most troubling might be that the classes, the living situations, and the social life are not of a nature that prepares young adults for real life. Quite the contrary, they often offer a false sense of security and comfort to the most unsuspecting and naïve of young people. For those that recognize it while they're in school, it's troubling enough that it can cause great pains in the gut when observed on a daily basis.

CHAPTER 25

ICU: 1-0, Corvus: $8,000

CHAPTER 26

"We should really keep it down, I'm not trying to get in trouble the first weekend here."

"Relax man, we're not exactly having a huge fucking party in here. Allan told us that he would leave us alone if we don't get out of hand in our rooms. He said he's not looking to confront anybody if they're keeping it respectful."

"That's what I'm saying! Not tryin' to be an ass or anything, I just think we should keep our yelling and shit in check."

"I get it, I get it; no worries man."

I looked on with a beer in my hand, listening to Josh and our neighbor Kevin going back and forth. They were talking about our R.A. who lived in a single-occupant room at the other end of our hallway. Allan really did seem to be a nice guy, and Josh was probably right to not worry. Still, I kinda sided with Kevin about keeping it low-key. I'm not a loud person, so I didn't feel like getting busted because other people couldn't control themselves when they had a few beers in their system.

Josh stood up in front of us and said firmly, "Okay fellas, I already like all of you guys just in the very short time we've known each other, so I think we should get to know each other better. We've gone through some of the orientation bullshit, and some of us have probably done some of the things that they set up so we can 'network with our fellow freshman.' That's fine and all, but I think we all know that crap is not the way that people really get to know each other." He talked with his hands, including lots of finger waving and air quotes when he said 'network with fellow freshman.' He held up a can of beer towards the ceiling, still sober enough that he was careful enough not to spill. "I want to propose a little something. I say we use tonight to share some shit about ourselves, with the help of a little alky-haul of course. I'd like to hear what you guys got goin' on with girlfriends, how much you partied in high school, what you might want to do with your life, who your best friends are from back home, if your parents are divorced, how you like your classes, whatever. I want to hear everything from the dirtiest stuff you feel like sharing to the more basic shit that you might discuss with a guidance counselor or something. Only as much as you want to talk about, don't feel like you need to get personal if you don't want to."

There was only the four of us in the room, which, I suppose, is why Josh felt it would be okay to open up with each other a little bit. I had to admit, I admired Josh's ability to take charge of a situation, and I even kind of liked his idea of getting to know the other guys better. I was a little terrified about talking about myself, being a private person and all. Still, Josh's personality was quite amusing and comforting, and I was on my fourth beer in forty-five minutes, so I wasn't terribly concerned.

Another reason that I respected Josh was because he wasn't just trying to pry into our lives without giving up some things himself. He jumped right into his own little life story, which was pretty similar to most small town people I knew. He had some funny stories about visiting his brother at college that might have looked like bragging until he revealed that he was totally petrified when he went to parties with his brother. He laughed openly while he told us how he would be so intimidated and afraid to turn down drinks that he'd drink half of every drink then go to the bathroom and dump out most of it, leaving just a little bit so he could go back out into the party and finish it while his brother's friends were all looking. He also told us about his one and only hookup during one of his visits to see his brother. At the beginning, this was also a story that seemed like it was going to turn into bragging. Wrong. The last half of the story involved him being so drunk and disoriented that he fondled a mole on the girl's breast, thinking that she just had tiny nipples. The girl got so weirded out by his "mole fetish" that she scurried out the door and completely left the party. He had us laughing so hard at his story that even Kevin stopped caring if Allan heard us giggling like idiots.

Although Josh kicked off the discussion with some funny stories and embarrassing moments, the conversation did turn serious at times, and everyone seemed to be comfortable enough to talk pretty open and honestly. Kevin told us about his frustrations with his parents getting a divorce in the last year, and how he'd had a serious problem with cutting weight to extremes when he wrestled. His wrestling issues ended with him quitting his senior year despite being a team co-captain. He never told anybody how bad he'd gotten with laxatives and fasting, so his departure from the team was mysterious to his coach, teammates, and parents.

The discussion, at times, moved to how we were reacting to starting college, and how our first week had been. It felt good to talk about my fear about money, my thoughts about skipping college to just get a job, and my worry that a college campus wasn't the place for me.

Even though it got kinda intense at times, the talk always moved back into joking around again. Josh had a few more stories, and I had to tell them about my embarrassing first time drinking when I puked all over Eric's sister's house and she found me naked in her hallway. Shane didn't say much, but we did get one story from him about pissing in a sleeping bag at a sleepover for his friend's birthday. He had way too much Mountain Dew when they were playing video games and woke up in the early morning with a soaked bag and freaked out. He had to quietly change his underwear and shorts and stuff the wet stuff in the bottom of his backpack while praying nobody would wake up. He also had to hope that nobody would notice he was wearing different shorts than the ones he'd gone to sleep in. There were two really strange things about his story. First, he was fourteen at the time, not nine or ten like we all expected. Second, and the detail that had us howling, was that he rolled up his sleeping bag like nothing had happened and never told his parents. He threw the bag into their basement when he got home, and his sister used it on a few camping trips throughout the next year without ever washing it. Shane was still unsure if the smell just went away or if his sister just dealt with the odd scent of pee when she tried to fall asleep in the bag. We gave Shane a round of applause, appreciative that he'd made up for his initial lack of talking with a top-notch story.

It got to the point that I even considered telling them about the situation with my uncle, but I dismissed the idea in hurry. Even though it was really the biggest thing weighing me down, I couldn't be stupid and overly trusting of people I hardly knew. But I was able to let all that shit escape my brain and just enjoy the time with them. Thoughts about my uncle came up when the guys started talking about the football team, and how hard it was for freshmen to get season tickets to the games. They discussed going to some games, and we all agreed to go to the same games

if we could get our hands on some cheap tickets. I almost casually mentioned that my uncle was the coach of ICU, but quickly
reminded myself that telling them would open me up to questions
that might make me nervous.

We fit in as much bullshitting as we could until we called it
quits around four in the morning. We laughed a lot, drank everything we had (a 24-pack of beer and half of a fifth of cheap vodka),
and made quick strides towards becoming friends. After the others had left and Josh had fallen asleep, I sent a text to Jeremy to
ask him how he was doing and see what he'd been up to since I'd
left. I wasn't surprised when I didn't get a response, seeing as it
was 4:37 a.m. when I sent the message. I put headphones on and
fell asleep soon after sending it.

CHAPTER 27

"Yo"

It was funny, even after just one word, that I could tell he wasn't totally engaged in the conversation. I could hear some noise in the background and it sounded like he was tapping keys on a computer keyboard and clicking a mouse. Despite the fact that it seemed he wasn't really paying attention, he went on, "If you want, you can to come with me to the game above Coasters on Friday. If you decide to come, you gotta park in the lot on the opposite side of the bar that most people park in . . . you'll see what I mean when you get there. There are wooden steps that lead up to an apartment right above the bar. Nobody actually lives there, they just run games out of it. Occasionally the bar owner lets oldhead regulars sleep off their drunkenness before they drive home in the morning. It's a raked game, so they keep the game running just like a casino would.

I was instantly excited by what he said. I hadn't played any poker since the last game at Joey's house. I'd sent a text message to Vic to tell him that I wanted to play sometime soon if he had a game I could go to. Normally I'd be pretty reserved about even texting a complete stranger, but it felt different with Vic, and it felt different because it was about playing cards. I'd heard about Coasters from a few different people, how it was a bar in downtown Middenburg that was pretty popular with students. Although I'd heard about the bar, nobody had mentioned anything about the game. This was probably due to the fact that running a raked poker game isn't legal. That made me even more excited to now be one of the people aware of the game. It wasn't exactly some kind of huge honor, but it still made my blood pump a little faster.

I quickly muttered "Gotcha" and let him continue.

"The guy who runs the game is the bar-owner's brother, Brad. He's a good guy, and he'll be the one to answer the door unless he isn't there Friday. Speaking of which, you'll go to the only door that's on the second level, which is basically the roof of the bar. Just ring the doorbell. I'll be there already, and I'll tell them I know you."

I realized that he hadn't even waited for me to say I could go before he started giving me details about the game. It was almost like he could sense that I'd definitely clear any plans or change things around to make sure to get to the game. It was weird, but he was totally right. I'd already started to imagine what the place would look like, make guesses about how other players would react to a young college student being at the game, and wonder how I'd actually feel about playing in an illegal game.

"There is a camera at the door, just make sure to let the light shine on your face so we can see who it is. And don't do anything retarded; everyone will be watching you on the little monitor that they have mounted near the table." After a slight pause, he added, "I'd appreciate if you didn't tell anybody about the game, at least not right away. They don't want total strangers showing up and fucking up the game. Also, they take a rake, so it's not exactly legal. You'll be welcome, but just hold off on discussing it with friends or anything for now."

The week dragged while I was looking forward to Friday, but I did eventually get through my classes and arrive at the end of the week. I'd followed Vic's instructions to the letter, and was now standing outside the apartment door, waiting for Brad to open it. Inside, I'd heard a rough voice say "Yeah" as soon as I'd rung the bell, so I waited patiently. After a long couple minutes, the door opened and a tall, husky guy answered the door wearing shorts, a Green Bay Packers jersey, and a bright orange pair of Crocs.

"Welcome." Brad grabbed my hand with his own meaty paw, and grinned cheerfully at me. His teeth were very small, almost childlike, and looked comical in his mouth. He had a large gap between his front two teeth. "Go ahead in, I'll get the door so I can lock it up." I heard the clicking of the lock on the doorknob and the sliding the chain lock as I walked around the table to where Vic was sitting with a pile of red, white, and green chips. He took a peek at the cards in front of him, then slid them gently forward to fold them.

"You caught Brad at a good time, he just sucked out and hit a straight to take down a monster pot. He's not always such a sweetheart."

I nodded at the chips in front of Vic and said, "Looks like you're still okay after taking that hit."

"Oh, it wasn't me. I stopped playing pots with Brad's lucky ass the first night I met him. It was that poor bastard over there." I followed his index finger and it was pointed at a heavy guy with a bulbous nose who was wearing a chef's outfit with a long stain at a 45-degree angle across his chest. He looked at me with a good-hearted, relaxed smile and shook his head. Vic continued, "Max doesn't do much complaining, so I do his share of bitching for him. I can't help it, it just doesn't seem right to let Brad off the hook when he's being stupid and hitting cards."

Brad stepped into the room from the hallway that led to the door and said, "Oh give it a fucking rest, Vic. You know as well as I do that was a coinflip." Brad stood behind Vic's chair while Vic looked up at him and laughed. Without any more words, Vic stuck a fist up in the air and Brad bumped it with his own. Brad had three bills in his hand that was in a fist, one of them a hundred and the two others fifties. He pulled his hand away from Vic's and held the bills over the table. "Max, you want all of this in chips, right?"

"Yep, don't forget to just give me $190 in chips because I owe you ten bucks for the wings you bought downstairs."

"Tell you what," said Brad slowly, fingering the bills, "we'll just call it even on the wings since I took that big-ass pot from you." Max gave him a thumbs-up and leaned back in his chair to wait for his chips.

I felt a tug at my shirtsleeve, and looked down to Vic's smiling face. He was stacking his chips in little piles of fives, then taking those stacks and making larger stacks of twenty. He said, "Hang out with me in the kitchen, I'm gonna have a smoke. By the way, only place you can smoke is in the kitchen because there's exhaust fans in there. Keeps the rest of the place decent."

"Makes sense."

He nodded and stuck an unlit cigarette in his mouth, motioning towards the doorway right behind me. We talked a little bit about our classes, and he seemed genuinely interested in how I was doing getting used to life on campus. He also talked about the players in a low voice so they wouldn't hear him. He gave a brief rundown of each player, and also threw in little jokes about some of the guys. I couldn't help but laugh at his jokes, and every time I did he put a finger up to his own grinning mouth in a 'sh' signal. After we were done with our cigarettes, he held out his hand and asked me what I wanted to buy in to the game. I gave him three $100 bills after I fished them from my pocket. Fingering each bill to make sure there wasn't any sticking to each other, he said, "I can get you chips, Brad doesn't care if I do it. Take any seat but seat seven, that's reserved for a guy that's showing up in ten minutes or so." I took seat five directly across from the dealer and tipped my head as a hello gesture to any of the players who looked at me. I waited with my arms folded on the table, starting to feel anxiety and excitement rising in my guts.

It was kind of silly, but the whole game just seemed so sur-real. I'd played plenty of games with my friends, but this was on another level, with people who weren't screwing around. Nobody was mean or anything, but it was clear that it wasn't the same as a group of close friends exchanging chips back and forth in a basement. It wasn't some crazy high stakes Vegas thing either, but it was definitely different than anything I'd experienced be-fore. I was probably romanticizing it all, I guess.

Since there was a rake, they provided a designated dealer who wasn't involved in playing at all. That was something else I'd never experienced, as I hadn't ever played at an organized game or in a casino. Our dealer was a short Asian guy wearing cargo shorts, a faded polo shirt, and a flat cap that hugged his small bald head. Not the most professional-looking guy, but he snapped the cards around the table like a robot and always paid attention to keep the game going fast, which helped him deal more hands and increase the chance of getting a tip from a large pot. There was really only one guy that ever held the game up, a middle-aged guy who was practically giving his money away, but the dealer made sure even that guy didn't slow down the game too much.

The chips and cards flipped and slid around the table un-der the direction of expert hands. It was fascinating to see how natural most of the players were with the movements of a serious poker game. The simple act of folding a hand could become a micro-drama put on by the person who was letting the cards go. Often, two players would get involved in a hand that didn't seem at all important, carefully mulling over their decisions. These players understood that making an incorrect decision, even at a seemingly safe time early in a hand, could easily be the start of a series of stupid choices.

They talked, sometimes in terms I didn't even understand, about all kinds of stuff like other poker games and sports betting. They also talked about random things other than gambling, and even the occasional anecdote about their personal life, but anything personal ended pretty quickly. It was clear that nobody was at the table to bear their souls to everybody else.

The playful but vicious jokes, the swings, the steely stares, the mischievous grins, and the risk—both calculated and foolish—all felt exhilarating and intoxicating. Along with my excitement came a more realistic understanding of the costs that came with playing the game for many of those seated at the table. You could hear it in their stories about near misses at the track, or see it in the stacks of dead twenty dollar lottery tickets sitting scratched and worthless on top of the trash in the garbage can: they weren't just playing games—they were living a lifestyle—.

I mostly felt like a participant the whole night, not really knowing anybody and not making any crazy moves in the game. By the time I decided to leave at 3:57 a.m. (much later than my original plan to leave at 2:00 a.m.) I had squeaked out a thirty dollar win. It was hardly a big score for that kind of game, but I was at least walking away with some extra money. I'd also been told by Brad that I could come back any time, with or without Vic. I felt like I had passed their test.

CHAPTER 28

ICU: 1-1, Corvus: $8,030

CHAPTER 29

"Nice win that first week." I had convinced myself before the phone call that I was going to be as pleasant as I could with Uncle Pete.

"Thanks, but I think we both know that was a freakin' cupcake team. This week against Wisconsin really exposed our flaws. I can't seem to get this group of seniors motivated like I usually can."

I thought for a moment and said weakly, "Hey, at least you're .500."

He snorted and said in a mildly disgusted tone, "Thanks for the support, but this week reminded me that we might need a little outside help this year. Which is where you come into play, of course. Did you go to either of the first two Middenburg games?"

Middenburg had started off the year with two consecutive home games. Usually teams were only home every other week, but there had been some kind of scheduling conflict. I'd started to read a short article about it on ESPN but hadn't made it very far. I'd asked a couple people if they knew of tickets for sale, but anything that was available cost more money than I felt like paying. I didn't look very hard because I wasn't overly concerned with going. "I didn't go, but I saw some re-caps on TV."

"Raven is an absolute monster already, the prick. In case you didn't see the stats, he has 319 rushing yards and three touchdowns in the first two games. Not only that, he's playing tons of downs and is blocking like a fullback on the downs where he doesn't get touches. Just insane."

"Must be playing cupcake teams," I cracked.

He ignored me and cleared his throat. "You know, I do have a little hesitation about doing this. I can't say enough, I hope you realize that sometimes people have to do questionable things to get where they want to be. This kid's an amazing talent and I think what we do will just be a small roadblock for him once he clears his name."

Uncle Pete seemed sincere, but I wasn't really sure if it was just some kind of show to avoid looking like a total jerk. Regardless, I wasn't going to challenge him about it. "Hey, If I'm involved in this, I'm not innocent either. I feel bad, but I also feel like it's kind of opportunity to get me and my parents ahead a little bit with money."

"I think we understand each other then. Obviously, the point I was making is that Raven is clearly the guy we want to target. He's already an integral part of their offensive schemes. Do you need his address again, or do you remember it from last time?"

I pictured my desk in my room and the drawer where I'd stashed the folded receipt that I'd written his address on the last time I'd been on the phone with my uncle. "I wrote it down, I have it in a safe spot in my dorm room. Do you have any other information about him that might help me?"

"I'm thinking this is where you can take over. I want to keep myself as distanced from Raven as I can. I don't want to be asking other people any questions to arise suspicions. You should start doing a little bit of spying, for lack of a better word. Just start getting a clear idea of his class schedule, if and when he's going to class. Pay attention, because he might go to a few classes and then stop. As you might guess, profs are a little lax with athletes sometimes. We don't want to assume he'll be in class when he stopped going weeks or even months before."

"Right, that makes sense."

"You'll also want to get an idea what he does with his free time. He's probably busy all the time with football, but we want to have all bases covered so we can get a really solid idea when it would be best to plant the shit in his room. You should keep writing things down so you don't forget."

There was an incredibly long stretch of time that neither of us wanted to fill. It seemed we were done with the call.

"Uncle Pete, do you think you would have done something like this earlier on in your coaching career?" I wasn't quite sure if I was assuming he hadn't done something along these lines before, or if I was fishing for some kind of admission about ethical sins he'd committed in the past. I'd let the question out almost subconsciously.

"I'm not really sure, I was really in demand then. When you're young and sought after, you're not directly faced with problems and ethical conflicts in quite the same way. When people are willing to take care of you, they're willing to make those tough decisions for you and deal with the consequences." He paused. I could hear a tapping sound in the background, and I knew it was his hand rapping a desk or table or banister wherever he was standing. I'd seen him rapidly knocking one of his rings on things before when he got uncomfortable. "Of course, I was pretty fuck-in' cutthroat then too. I probably would have made some tough moves if I'd been put in a position where I needed to."

CHAPTER 30

I had this terrible feeling that, even from afar, he would feel a set of eyes trailing him. Any second I expected him to poke his head out a window and yell "Get the hell outta here, ya creep!" or something like that. I'd only been there five minutes, and it already felt like I was sticking out like a sore thumb. Conveniently, there was a small park with a weathered bench that I could sit on. I'd brought along a book that I used to hide my face while my eyes peeked over the top of the pages.

There wasn't a lot of activity at Raven's apartment, which wasn't unexpected for 9:36 a.m. on a Tuesday. I'd walked around the day before in the area where the apartment was located. I'd even checked back a couple times, but I hadn't even seen Raven all day. I was caught up enough in my classes to skip a few, so I'd skipped my Monday gym class and spent nearly three hours shooting hoops at the small park. It gave me a good excuse to spend a chunk of time to try to get a glimpse of Raven's activity. Shooting on the rusty rim sucked because it was bent and missing a net. It ended up being a complete waste of time because I never saw him. A couple walk-bys in the evening also resulted in nothing. If he had a Monday class schedule, it either included very weird times or he wasn't going to them.

At quarter till ten, Raven came out of his apartment in a hooded sweatshirt and baggy sweatpants, a sagging backpack hanging from his back. After he locked his door, he started in the direction of campus while stuffing earbuds into his ears. The other end of the cord disappeared into the large pocket on the front of his sweatshirt. He let his feet slap lazily on the pavement while he slowly moved down the hill that led to campus. I let him get to the point that his head was just barely visible above the horizon before I closed my book and started after him.

It was strange to spend the entire day on campus alone without going to class. I probably could have gone to at least one of my classes, but it was easier to just concentrate on watching Raven dip in-and-out of his classes, talk to friends, and eat lunch. He also spent a lot of time greeting other students who clearly approached him as fans and admirers. The behavior of the student-fans ranged from timid and nervous to loud and boundary-crossing. A couple of girls overtly flirted with him, but he didn't seem overly fazed by the attention. He mostly kept quiet unless approached, and he didn't really do anything to purposely cause a stir. I found myself rolling my eyes to nobody in particular a few times. It was amazing how people went crazy over a football player that was only two games into his college career. You'd think he was the president or something.

I'd been careful to stay as far away from him as possible, so I was very confident he hadn't noticed me at all. I got more comfortable following him and ended up spending the entire day tailing him. It was a little weird, but it had to be done at some point if I was going to get an idea how he spent his days. By the end I realized that all his classes were on Tuesdays and Thursdays. It was a packed schedule but I assumed it was easier to do it that way so his other days were totally free for workouts, watching game film, and going to regular football practices.

CHAPTER 31

ICU: 1-2, Corvus: $7968

CHAPTER 32

"My bad, I didn't get a chance to text you the next morning when you
    texted the other night"
"No problem, man, I sent that at a pretty weird time lol"
"Yea, I noticed haha"
"I was actually hanging out with my roommate and some people from our
    floor"
"Any girls?"
"Nope, 2 other guys"
"Sounds about right lol jk"
"We can't all be like you, I'm sure you're getting all kinds of ass in your
    parents' basement"

I was a little worried that I'd gone too far with my joke. I knew
he was a little sensitive about the fact that he was staying at
home instead of going away to college. I wasn't sure if I imagined
it or not, but there seemed to be a longer pause before a response
came through.

"Damn, that's f-ed up dude lol"
"You know I'm just screwing with you. But seriously, it was a good time just
    hanging out with them . . . good guys. You'd like my roommate, he's cool
    and his brother went here"
"That's cool, I have to get outta here n visit sometime"
"Yea man, whenever you aren't working you're welcome to come up"
"Thanks. You should try 2 come back here sometime soon 2. I might go
    crazy with nobody around"

I immediately thought of Vic and playing poker, and realized
that I probably wouldn't be visiting home anytime soon. In fact, I
was sure it wouldn't be until the first official break that I would go
home, especially because my parents would be showing up in a
few hours for their first visit. Between the poker that I was already
preparing to play, hanging out with Josh and the others, and

even maybe some parties, I was pretty sure I wouldn't squeeze in a visit home. I felt a sad punch of depression and weird guilt because of it. I tried my best to answer Jeremy in a way that didn't convey the truth, but wasn't exactly a lie either.

> "I should man, but I'm not really sure if I'll be able to make it back in the next couple weeks. My classes will keep me pretty busy and stuff"
>
> "Classes haha. U lyin bitch lol. It's cool man, I understand. For Gods sake, at least hit on a couple girls 4 me."
>
> "Haha, you got it man. Hey, sorry to cut you off, but I gotta go for now. My parents are calling me. They're visiting this weekend and I think they're here."
>
> "Alright, have a good time up there and let me know when you finally bring ur ass back home."
>
> "No doubt, you take it easy and don't work too hard."

The call from my mom had gone to voicemail in the time it took me to end the text conversation with Jeremy. I called back and my mom answered before I said anything, saying in a fake stern voice, "Hey! It's about time. I called twice."

"Sorry, I was talking with Jeremy." I didn't add in the fact that we were actually texting, not talking on the phone. I didn't really feel like starting off their visit with an annoying conversation that would kinda drive me crazy for no reason. She would casually say that I could have answered and responded to Jeremy right after the call with her. Then I'd say that I didn't like to interrupt talking to somebody, even while texting, because I'd forget what I was talking about or even forget to answer at all. After that, my mom would say "Oh, for crying out loud." Finally, I'd try to logically explain that going back to a conversation with Jeremy after the call would only interrupt our visit and make her think I was ignoring her. She would passive-aggressively end the conversation by marveling at how much I loved to win arguments, even unimportant ones. It was much easier to avoid it altogether; chalk it up to some new maturity that must have descended upon me since going to college.

"We're at the big student thingy!"

I assumed she was talking about the student union. I laughed and replied, "I think I know where you're talking about. I'll be there in a couple minutes."

On my way to the student union, I had a funky sense of guilt. I suddenly found myself thinking about my relationship with my parents, whom I genuinely consider fine people and good souls. The guilt came from the realization that in a couple weeks' time I had probably not really thought even once about my parents. It was really kinda shitty, but it was also the truth. I was already feeling a separation from them to some degree, but I certainly was not independent from them. Despite the chunk of money I'd secretly been given from my uncle, I was still absolutely dependent on them for many things. Their signatures were still on the loans sending me to college. I still owed them money for the sum that they'd fronted me to help purchase my crappy car (I couldn't pay them with my newfound money and risk arousing suspicion). I'd still be staying at their home on school breaks. After only mere weeks away from them, I already felt an emotional distance from them. It had started before I'd even left home. Still, my guilt seemed to disappear pretty quickly when I justified in my head that most young adults probably do the same thing when they have their first true separation from their parents. It was pretty selfish and I knew it. Hell, even walking towards the student union, I was already kind of ready for the visit to be over.

I saw my parents through the largest window on the east side of the building. My dad stood in front of a rack of the brightly colored pamphlets with topics like jobs on campus, getting a parking pass, and other stuff about the university. My mom seemed to be struggling with her camera phone to try to get a picture. She kept pointing it in the same direction for a few seconds at a time, then staring at the screen while she shook her head in frustration. I wasn't sure if she wasn't happy with any of the pictures she was taking, couldn't get the flash to work, wasn't able to zoom in or out, or wasn't hitting the right thing on the screen to take a picture. I couldn't tell from far away which it was, and I'd seen her do all of those things in the past. They saw me at about the same time. My dad tucked the pamphlet he was reading into his pocket and my mom put her phone into her purse. We exchanged greetings and hugs and I said cheerfully, "Let's take a walk around campus and then go into town for lunch."

CHAPTER 33

We walked along the sidewalk in the "downtown" section of Middenburg, a rather boring collection of two and three-story-buildings, most of them made of crusty red brick. It was nearly all apartment buildings, but there were things like the post office and a laundromat. There were also a few chain restaurants scattered amongst the old structures. I let my parents choose the restaurant for lunch, and they ended up picking Taco John's because there weren't any around home.

As we strolled along the street walking to the restaurant, I watched myself in the large windows that lined the street. I'm not vain by any stretch of the imagination, but I'd always liked watching myself in windows and mirrors. I don't really know why. I'm okay looking, but I definitely didn't look at my reflection to admire myself. It was more like watching my image in a movie or constantly trying to see what I looked like to other people. It's impossible to ever really know what that looks like, but it still seems like maybe you can get close if you keep watching yourself.

After we bought our tacos and burritos, we sat down in a booth near the back of the restaurant. A couple booths away there were three college-age guys discussing the previous night, which apparently involved some partying and some attractive girls. They didn't spare any details, and I cringed as I listened to them. I wasn't even sure if my mom was paying attention enough to hear them, but it was weird anyway.

"Okay, so now we have to hear about your classes so far. What do you like? Which professors seem nice?"

I looked at my mom and she had a small drop of hot sauce hanging from the corner of her mouth. I laughed a little and pointed my index finger at my own mouth to signal that she had something on hers. She let out a little huff in mild embarrassment and dabbed both corners of her mouth with her napkin.

"You got it," I said, before continuing, "My classes seem pretty cool, except the gym class will probably be pretty boring. Seems like we'll just be doing lame exercises instead of playing sports or anything. I really like my English Composition professor so far -she's really relaxed. I'm sure I'm going to like the Intro to Psychology class, but we haven't done a whole lot yet for me to judge. The professor has pretty much just discussed what we'll be doing in very general terms."

"Which is what?" My dad had put his burrito down and spoke up after a long sip from his pop.

"Um, I think we'll start with learning all of the important psychology lingo. After that we'll read about some major studies and point out areas where the lingo and concepts apply. Then we'll document some of our own reactions to the studies. After that, I don't really know."

"That does sound interesting. Have you done anything at all assignment-wise?"

My mom chimed in and added, "Yea, any grades yet? Or anything due soon?"

"Nothing really important in any of my classes except some real basic open book quizzes and really short homework on the class guidelines and rules and whatnot." That wasn't entirely the truth. I actually had my first important reading and reaction paper for my psychology class, and a reading assignment due for my history class that would come with a medium-sized quiz. They were due on Monday and Tuesday, respectively. I hadn't started them yet. It was a silly little lie. My parents would have just made some kind of comments about being responsible, or something. I just didn't feel like revealing my procrastination.

"You'll be getting work soon enough. Can't say enough, college is a whole different ballgame than high school. It's not all going to come easy like it seemed to in high school. Costs money now, too," my dad said seriously. His eyes were leveled right above the burrito he held in his hand, searching my eyes to see if I was listening. I was both annoyed and saddened by his comment. I couldn't help my annoyance, both at the fact that going to college cost so much damn money, and that he was probably going to dwell on that fact the entire time I was in college. I wished I could just tell him that I was going to have nearly all my tuition paid for the first semester if everything worked out with my uncle. Of course, I couldn't do that. I was saddened by the fact that I'd be doing some serious lying to both of my parents within the next couple months. As depressing as that was, the money was still enough for me to justify those lies.

"I know, Dad. I'm taking it seriously."

"Good, I know you are. Are you behaving?" His comment caught me off guard a bit, as he said it in a bit of a playful tone, like he knew something I wasn't telling him. I'd never gotten in trouble for drinking or partying, even though I'd done some in high school. Because I hadn't been caught, we never really had any kind of serious talks about drinking or drugs. I'd never even had any kind of sex talk with either one of my parents, not that I was ever begging to have those awkward conversations. I knew that my dad, when younger, had been a little wilder than the guy I had known all my life. I'd overheard some stories amongst my parents and aunts and uncles that I wasn't supposed to be listening in on. There wasn't anything *too* crazy in his past, but he had drunk his fair share and smoked some pot in college.

"No misbehavior to report." I laughed and my mom eyed me with a mildly suspicious look.

My dad changed the subject, saying, "Well, what groceries are we going to pick up for you at the supermarket after lunch? I'm sure that little fridge won't fit much, but there's gotta be some stuff you need."

After lunch we went to the nearest grocery store and picked up some of the things that I'd listed at lunch. We bought enough groceries to fill the fridge and half my closet then we had ice cream cones at a nearby shop. Afterward, they dropped me off back on campus. My dad had to supervise a 7:00 p.m. PTA meeting at his school. They took the van that I'd brought up on 'Moving Day' and left my car.

Despite having a nice time with my parents, I was ready to say goodbye to them. I still felt a tinge of guilt, but I was relieved that they weren't able to spend more time at the university. When I got back to my dorm room, it was like Josh was reading my mind. He was standing in the middle of the room when I entered, holding two cans of beer.

"Well, the first visit is officially over. Now we can hang out." He grinned, popped one of the can tabs, and handed it to me. I immediately dropped the grocery bags on the floor and accepted the can that had a little foam rising from the top. He fell back lazily onto the new futon he had purchased a few days earlier. "Let's work on this twelve pack together, then we can hit a party over on George Street."

I tried not to sound concerned while asking, "Will I know anybody there?"

"I guess there might be a person or two from our hallway, but probably not many other people you'll know. It'll be mostly upperclassmen. I know a guy and his girlfriend, Adam and Amanda, who'll be there. When he was a freshman, Adam played basketball with my brother. My brother graduated. Adam and Amanda are juniors."

"Cool," I said back simply, "but you and I should drink all this beer before we go."

"That's exactly what I was thinking. Let's watch the end of the Yankees game and then head to the party."

I didn't answer, but leaned back and finished the last of the beer that was in the first can.

CHAPTER 34

Completely unaware how the time had passed, I found myself at a huge party with a shitload of people and noise. The beers I had with Josh were enough that I'd pretty much lost track of time. I also hadn't really paid attention to how we got to the party. I looked at my phone and was surprised to see it was already nearly midnight. It felt like Josh had just handed me the first beer of the night a few minutes ago. Time-wise it felt that way, but my buzz was telling me that I was well past my first drink. I was beginning to feel a little more comfortable being amongst a bunch of strangers, so I figured I'd just go with it.

The hub of the party was in the basement of the house around the continuously flowing keg. Beside the keg, a guy with a backwards baseball cap sat on a tall wooden chair with the tap held firmly in his right hand, his left hand occasionally pumping the keg. There was a steady line of partygoers waiting with their plastic cups in hand like homeless folks at a soup kitchen, ready to put it under the steady flow of golden beer that almost seemed to magically pour from the keg-guard's hand.

Everyone in the dingy, unfinished basement tended to stay close to one of the concrete block walls. One wall held a bold painted mural of a Condor, Middenburg's school mascot. It was really well done and seemed kind of out of place in the gross basement that was obviously not cleaned very often. Beside the painted mascot there was a poster-sized Middenburg football schedule. The first three games were crossed off. My eyes went immediately to the ninth game on the schedule. October 27th @ Indiana Central University. I felt an immediate uneasiness just thinking about it. Before my thoughts started swirling with moral questions and thoughts about my uncle, I turned away from the poster and faced the other half of the room.

There was one old plaid couch and two stained arm chairs full of drunk students, but everybody else either stood or sat on one of the flipped-over buckets or milk crates positioned randomly

around the room. Screams and groans of disappointment ema-
nated from the beer pong game on the netless ping-pong table.
The repeating noise of ping-pong balls whacking plastic cups
sounded like intermittent hail hitting the windows. After filling
two cups, I returned up the rickety wooden steps to meet Josh in
the living room.

♥ ♣ ♦ ♠

Even though I had drank with my friends before, and we had
even had parties and stuff, my first real college party was a completely different environment. There were plenty of decent people
in the crowd, but also a bunch of clamoring dickheads that talked
too loud and walked around not caring who they bumped into or
bothered. Everywhere I looked I saw guys spilling beer down their
necks, thinking they were setting world records in chugging, even
though half of it was ending up on their collar. There were a ton of
hot girls, but almost all of them seemed to be snapping pictures of
themselves with their phones, talking behind their hands to their
friends, or sipping their drinks with their eyes straight up to the
ceiling in a gesture of boredom.

Josh smiled warmly when he saw me approaching, and said,
"Hey Corvus, this is Amanda Winstaff and Adam Binkley, but
everyone calls him Bink. I won't tell you the names they call
Amanda, but you'll figure it out." He said the last part loudly, but
held up a hand like he was telling a secret.

Amanda socked him in the arm with a lot of force, and Josh
nearly dropped the plastic cup in his hand. A little stream of beer
hit his sneaker, but he didn't seem to notice or care. He laughed
and put his head on her shoulder playfully. "Aww, you know I'm
just kiddin', you're just a little ol' sweetheart!"

I felt a little out of place since they seemed to know each other
pretty well. The buzz I had wasn't quite enough to make me a
social butterfly. Josh, Bink, and Amanda kept talking while I took
long sips from my cup of beer and watched other people when
they weren't looking at me.

"Hey!"

I turned and smiled at Josh, who was trying to get my attention.

He poked my shoulder and asked, "D'ya wanna get on the list
to play beer pong?" As he was asking me, several guys in one of
the corners of the room shouted loudly, and a couple girls let out

shrill shrieks. Josh and I both turned to see what the commotion was about, and it didn't take long to see. A muscular young guy in a tank top and camouflage trucker hat had vomited on the cement floor in front of him. He had his hands on his knees and was still breathing heavily, and a string of sticky saliva hung from the corner of his mouth. It was clear he probably hadn't eaten much that evening, because the puddle was quickly spreading due to the fact that it was pretty much entirely beer and some kind of bright red fluid that looked like Hawaiian Punch.

From the wooden steps some guy yelled out, "Ah shit Nick, I was only fucking gone for five minutes." The guy rushed down the steps and grabbed the guy by the arm like he was a misbehaving child. Nick either didn't care about his friend grabbing him, or he didn't have the energy to fight back. People got out of the way so they could go upstairs.

Three guys I didn't know leapt into action like a professional crew and started cleaning up the disgusting liquid on the floor. I had to look away or I might let something fly myself. One guy dashed to a sink and filled up a five gallon bucket with water, the second guy found a mop in the corner and started picking dust off it, and the third guy held his arm out to keep people away from the puke. It was almost comical to watch, and the basement was almost silent while everybody stared at them. The guy with the bucket tossed the water towards the accident area. The water diluted the vomit and the whole mixture started flowing toward s the drain that was in the middle of the floor. The mop guy helped it along and the arm guy was staying strong on crowd control. After another half bucket of water, there wasn't any vomit left. It probably wasn't the most sanitary clean up, but the party was back in full swing seconds after they were done. Mop guy snapped the soiled cleaning tool in half and threw it in a large trash can that was underneath the stairs.

I looked at Josh and the others and quipped, "I guess Nick and his buddy won't be on the beer pong list."

All three laughed, and I felt a silly little warmth from it, happy that I'd said something funny when they were listening. I didn't want to think that I put so much importance on the approval of people that I didn't even know very well, but there was at least a small thing inside of me that was pleased with the attention.

♥ ♣ ♦ ♠

Amidst the vibrating party, I was only able to shed a few layers of my discomfort, but I did have a good time with Josh. Adam and Amanda returned back to us a few times and we chatted pleasantly with them, although Amanda was getting very drunk and increasingly difficult to understand. Josh and I played and lost a single game of beer pong. I'd only played the game one time, but I did my best to act like I was super-experienced. I was a little shaky on some of the rules, but I was able to hide it by observing the others and picking everything up as I went. If somebody started to talk about a rule I didn't know about, I just said, "Oh, is that how you guys play in this house," like I played somewhere else with slightly different regulations.

I watched a bunch of people bong beers, saw an entire cup of beer spilled on the dirty loveseat in the corner of the basement, and got extremely uneasy seeing dirtbag guys making out with hammered, nearly unconscious girls. I also pissed approximately 74,000 times.

After yet another bathroom break, I found Josh sitting on the arm of a puffy easy chair in the living room. I let him know that I was heading back to our dorm room.

"You okay with walking back alone?"

"Yep, I'm drunk but I'll be fine getting back. Thanks for bringing me along tonight." I held out my hand and he instantly swung his towards my flat palm. It made a sharp crack and I gave him a quick smile. I flipped my hand in one more little wave and said goodbye to two girls who were on the couch. I didn't know them, and they didn't know me. They were in the middle of a conversation and both gave quick hummingbird-speed waves with one hand, neither looking to even see who was saying goodbye. It looked more like they were shooing me away than saying goodbye. I laughed to myself as I stepped out the front door and ambled lazily down the walkway that led towards the empty street.

The air was thick and sticky with humidity, not unlike the crowded basement that I'd left just a bit earlier. I was already sweaty, and the dense environment was making my pores leak even more. I was pretty sure I looked like a perspiring, fairly sloppy mess, but I was drunk enough not to care. I reveled in my lack of vanity and floated along the crumbled sidewalk. I pulled my crumpled pack of cigarettes from my pocket and flipped it open, revealing a single cigarette inside with a lighter by its side. I pulled both out and crumpled up the pack. I saw a bulky metal trash can about ten feet away. With a flourish, I popped my wrist and shot the balled-up pack into the sky. I was excited when it hit the opening, looking like it was a successful shot. My self-celebration was cut short when I saw it come to rest on a dirty paper plate that was balanced on the edge of the can. Like slow-motion, I saw the plate shift just enough so that the angle allowed the pack to drop to the ground. I picked it up off the ground and whipped it into the can. I would have slammed it home if the trash can rim wasn't so dirty.

I lit my last cigarette, careful to ignite the tip evenly. I held it out like a torch against the black sky and waved it like a sparkler. My eyes were blurred and I briefly had double vision, which caused the fiery cherry to look like two glowing eyes. I stopped playing and stuck the cigarette back into my mouth. I could hear occasional swells of noise coming from different houses, and saw several groups of two or three kids standing drunkenly in yards and on porches at a few of them. For reasons I wasn't quite sure of, I felt oddly at ease viewing the people and parties from a distance rather than being a part of them. A couple partygoers waved and yelled incoherently at me. I was glad they all seemed to be happy-drunk instead of belligerent. I didn't say anything but waved back to them. My eyes were adjusting back to normal already, so when I lifted my hand to acknowledge the people I was passing, the tip was just a cyclops instead of two orange eyes.

CHAPTER 35

My head hurt a little bit, but it wasn't that terrible. I'd had a fair share of alcohol the night before, but I remembered most of the night clearly. I woke up to a text from Vic. Even though it was already 11:00 a.m., I probably would have slept for another hour if Vic hadn't texted. He asked if I wanted to grab a bite to eat around noon. I liked hanging out with him, even away from the card table, so I told him I'd be there. Of course, it was also probably best to keep a good relationship with him if I wanted to continue going to poker games with him. It was pretty easy since he was a decent guy. I rolled out of bed shortly after and watched forty-five minutes of SportsCenter before dressing and heading to the student union.

♥♣♦♠

I saw him from far away and watched him drink his entire orange juice in one hearty chug. The empty plastic tumbler made a loud popping sound when he returned it to the table. When he saw me, he said, "Hey, over here!"

When I was within a couple tables of the one Vic was at I said, "Hey, what's up, man?"

He remarked, "Damn, I love coffee and orange juice." It wasn't exactly a reply to my greeting. Sometimes, when it was just the two of us, he would say things and I could tell he wasn't actually talking to me. It had already happened a couple times in the short period that I'd known him. He seemed to go into some little trance where he was only vaguely aware that another person was present. I think he just really liked to hear himself talk, but whenever he did it, it did seem like he was almost in a meditative state. After his random exclamation about his drinks, he picked up his coffee and smiled at me in a childish manner.

I sat down and said, "How'd it go at the tables last night. You got enough to quit school yet?"

He sipped, cleared his throat, and answered, "Just down about a hundy. Really didn't play long. I took so many fucking bets on college football that I had to make sure I had everything straight before I went crazy. Over five grand in action, just in yesterday's bets. Nearly fifteen for the week. Fucking bigger bookie might laugh at that, but that's some pretty serious coin changing hands. It's been getting bigger every year it seems. Word of mouth and whatnot."

"That's a good thing, right? Don't you want as much action as you can handle?"

"Yeah, it's always good to have an evenly split crowd when it comes to each wager. Just make money from the juice and not have to lay off any action. The more people I have placing bets with me, the better the chance that sides will be even and I can just safely take my commission. Thing is, I don't know where to cut it off. I try to keep a low profile but people tell their friends and shit. I even ask 'em not to, but guys love to tell their buddies they got a bookie to take action. Also, students are sticking around the area longer. They either take forever to finish like I am, or somehow fall in love with this shitty town and decided to stay after graduating." He sipped his coffee, then grabbed the stirrer between his teeth and chewed on it for a moment. It almost seemed like a sign that he was waiting for me to say something.

I obliged and said, "It's not terrible, I guess, but I don't think I'll be staying here any longer than I have to."

He set his mug down and a single streak of coffee slid down the side. He dabbed his finger on the drop before it reached the bottom. "You're preachin' to the choir on that one, man! I told you before, I'm cool with what I've done here, but I'm ready to bounce. I feel like I might as well stay till I graduate, though. I make better money taking bets than I would make doing anything else, and I know all the gamblers here. Kinda between a rock and a hard place."

I nodded while simultaneously noticing a small tablet with a red cover on the table in front of him. I watched him flip to a page that held a cluster of scrawls and numbers. He also swiped the screen of his phone. The faint sound of a thudding rap beat came from the headphones Vic had laying on the table.

Vic poked the screen to stop the music. He saw me looking at his notebook and said, "Nothin' like writing everything down by hand when it comes to betting. My uncle would always tell me that. Keeps you extra organized if you write it down in addition to storing it in a computer or phone. I use my phone to keep track of stuff, but I always transcribe that shit into my little book, man. Plus, if I would lose my phone or have to ditch it for some reason, I still have a record of things."

"I always handwrite my notes in classes or when somebody tells me something I really wanna remember. Helps it stick in my brain better."

"That's it, you get it. Keeps me sharp. As long as I remember not to take bets when I'm wasted."

"It's pretty crazy, man, all that action. I don't think I could ever deal with that. I like to bet and all, but I wouldn't wanna be responsible for all that."

"You would when it's time to collect," He said, laughing. "Hey man, I almost forgot, do you wanna play a game in a dorm room tonight? Not a serious money game, just kinda hanging out. There's this kid who wants to bet with me and I want to spend some more time with him before I say yes. There'll be a couple girls there and I'm bringing some beer. It'll be fun. I know the girls better than the guy at this point, and they're pretty laid-back."

It actually sounded pretty cool. I hadn't played a truly relaxed game since the night I met Vic at the dorm hall poker game. "Count me in for sure, I don't have plans."

"Nice!" Vic took a last gulp of his coffee and stood up. "Alright dude, I'm outta here. I got a couple things to take care of and then I'm gonna nap before we chill later. I'll text you details and let you in when you get to the hall where the girls live. Later!"

He really could be a strange guy. He'd asked if I wanted to come eat lunch with him, but I hadn't even gone up to the front of the cafeteria and gotten so much as a drink yet. In fact, I was pretty sure he hadn't even eaten as there was no plate or silverware. Not a speck of ketchup, a crumb of bread, or a grain of salt. It was kind of funny, but I guess he just liked to have somebody around. I was glad he remembered to mention the dorm room game. It probably wouldn't be a good game to win any decent money, but I was looking forward to it anyway.

CHAPTER 36

Vic peeked at his cards and threw them into the center of the table with a flick of his wrist. They spun around for a moment before settling amongst the other folded cards. He took a long gulp from his bottle of beer and looked over at Ramona. "Go ahead, Ramona."

Ramona was a good looking sophomore who lived in the dorm hall closest to mine. She had reddish-brown hair that was neatly pulled into two braids that hung over her shoulders. She wore a loose-fitting t-shirt, but I could still tell that she had amazing breasts. Whenever she thought about how to play her hand, she twisted one of the braids around her index finger and it was driving me a little crazy -in a good way. Her shirt was askew and the edge of her purple bra strap peeked out of her collar when she moved her braid.

Vic concentrated on her while she looked at her cards. He grinned and said, "You're gonna yank that goddamn braid out of your head if you think any harder."

She rolled her eyes towards Vic and let the braid fall limply to her shoulder. "Don't make fun of me because I actually think when I play, Vic." While she was playfully ribbing Vic, she tossed her cards beside Vic's discarded ones. "I fold, I wouldn't want to upset Vic by taking any longer."

Waiting for people to play wasn't my favorite thing in the world either, but I was definitely willing to watch Ramona take as long as she wanted. I silently cursed Vic for saying anything about her playing with her braid because now that she realized she did it, she'd probably stop. I also pushed my cards toward the muck pile and said, "Next hand."

Ben, the guy who was interested in betting with Vic, silently gathered the cards and shuffled. While he dealt, I looked around at the five other players' stacks of chips. We weren't playing for much money, but it was actually still competitive. I was sort of surprised, but Ramona really seemed to know how to play well.

Jen, Ramona's friend, was the only one playing who didn't seem to care at all. She had just been bored. Instead of hanging out in the room she shared with Ramona, she tagged along and played for a few dollars. Jen was in my Phys. Ed class, so I was thinking maybe I'd casually bring Ramona up when I saw her on Monday.

It was Ramona's turn to play and she threw in a small handful of chips into the pot, enough to raise it a little bit. She looked at me, waiting to see what I'd do. She said, almost as an afterthought, "Raise to four dollars." She had about the same amount of money as I did. I hadn't played a hand with her for a while, so I figured I'd just call her no matter what cards I had. I looked down and saw a seven of spades and an eight of spades. I called, sliding forward a neat little stack of red chips worth fifty cents each. Everybody else folded and the first three community cards slid from Ben's hands onto the wooden table. The first card was the ace of hearts, next a two of spades, and finally a four of spades.

Ramona looked straight down at the table and bet five dollars. Since it wasn't a huge bet, I was able to call her to see if I could hit a flush. That's exactly what happened when the next card, the jack of spades, hit the table. She checked to me and I did the same. I had a feeling she had paired the ace and was now worried that I had a flush, so I thought I'd throw her off by checking when the spade hit.

Even though she was hot as hell, I wasn't going to play her any differently because of that. We were still playing for real money and I wasn't about to take it easy on her and end up losing. In the little bit of time we played, she seemed to know what she was doing. Plus, she messed with Vic. Her confidence was incredibly attractive to me. But I was still going to make it as hard as possible for her to win.

The last card was a ten of diamonds that couldn't hurt me in any way, so I was very sure that I had the best hand. This time, Ramona made a pretty big bet of seventeen dollars. In other games I played, a bet of this size wouldn't have even caught anybody's attention, but this was getting pretty big for a dorm-room game. I thought for a while and finally threw in enough money to cover Ramona's entire stack. I was certain that she had a hand just slightly worse than mine, so I figured she would have to call and surrender all her money to me.

Vic hadn't spoken up for a while, and he couldn't contain himself anymore. "Jesus, no mercy for the young lady, huh?

You're just heartless aren't you?" He laughed his ass off at his own comments, but I just shrugged my shoulders. I looked at Ramona, whose hazel eyes danced back and forth between the five upturned cards on the table. She pursed her lips and threw her cards away after just a few seconds.

She half-smiled at me and said, "What did ya' have?"

I smirked, not looking at her but pulling the small pile of chips toward me. "Sorry, you have to call to see what I have. It's secret unless you pay to see." I actually wouldn't have minded showing, but it was fun to mess with her. Even though I knew she had probably had a good hand and I got a little lucky to hit the flush, I said nonchalantly, "You didn't have anything anyway, you were probably just trying to bluff me before I came back at you."

"Nuh uh!" She continued defiantly, "I had a good hand to start and I hit top pair! Don't start pulling shit like Vic does!" She was annoyed she lost the hand but I could tell she wasn't really mad that I was playing around with her.

"You should have messed with that braid a little more, this time. Maybe you would have built up the courage to call me at the end."

She laughed, reached over and flicked me as hard as she could on the edge of my ear. It stung and I shouted "Shit!" while rubbing my lobe between my fingers. Even though it really did hurt, a little warmth spread inside my chest from her physical contact. I glanced at Vic and said teasingly, "Damn, dude, I never knew girls were such sore losers when they played poker."

He guffawed and replied back with a dramatically stoic glance into the distance, "I guess you have a lot to learn about the female species then, my man."

Ramona reached across the table and grabbed the bottle of beer that Vic had recently opened. She thumped it lightly on the table directly in front of him, causing a surge of foam to spurt out of the top of the brown glass container. A bunch of it ran onto Vic's lap, causing him to spring up in surprise. It soaked in to his shorts on both of his thighs while he stood shaking his head and chuckling at the same time. Ramona dipped her finger into the spilled beer left on the table and flicked a few drops playfully into my face. In between giggles she said, "You better get some paper towels for your boy over there."

After the game, Ramona walked with me to my dorm since hers was close to mine. We discussed our classes and stuff like our hometowns and families. She apparently lived a few states away and loved the fact that she was able to get away from her hometown. She said she didn't hate it there, but needed to be far enough that she wouldn't feel pressured by friends and family to come home for weekends all the time. She had one brother who was eight years younger than her who she suspected was an accident because her parents were pretty old when they had him, although they hadn't admitted it to her yet.

I, of course, focused on her like I was hanging on every word. I was sincerely listening, but I was also dreaming about lightly biting the purple bra strap that was still peeking out of her shirt. It must have been the poker game that left me capable of actually holding a pleasant conversation with her the entire walk to her dorm room. Poker brought out a friendly confidence in me that I didn't always have when meeting new people. The walk ended far too quickly and I was ecstatic when she asked me if I wanted to come inside and watch a movie.

CHAPTER 37

I sat with my legs splayed open, jutting at awkward angles. I could feel my body shaking mildly. I hooked four fingers onto the headboard tightly, let go, squeezed again, then finally let them rest limply on the wood.

Ramona stared silently into my eyes, aware of the power she held over me. Without a word, she wiggled her tongue over my naked testicles. When her tongue hit the tiny, wispy hairs, it provoked a sensation that ran from the 'V' of my legs up the ticklish nerves on either side of my ribs, and release a series of paralyzing energy bursts in my head. With my mid-section quivering, I can feel sounds and words escaping my throat. Mostly 'Ahh' on the upstrokes of her tongue and curse words on the downstroke.

Ramona reached out with a greedy clawed hand that slowly relaxed as it got closer to me. She replaces her mouth with her hand and runs a finger on the underside of my shaft.

Even through the lavish treatment and waves of pleasure, I couldn't keep a stupid dialogue from starting in my head:

"Will I talk about this later? Brag about it? Discuss the finer points of a blowjob?"

"Shut up!"

"Is this what it's like for most guys? Do most girls go for the balls because it feels so good for guys?"

"Just fucking enjoy it, you jerk!"

"How big am I compared to others she's had in her mouth? Is she silently bored and just being nice? Will she expect me to return the favor?"

"Goddamn it, just stop thinking and enjoy getting blown!"

"But does she like this at all? She seems to, but any realistic guy knows girls fake things sometimes."

"Clear your mind. Who cares? She's blowing you. A blowjob!"

♥ ♣ ♦ ♠

I eventually calmed down and was able to enjoy myself. Afterwards, she simply laid her head on my belly and we watched the reality show marathon that was droning on her TV. We laughed together at some of the sillier parts of the show, but mostly we just watched in silence. During the theme song for the next episode, she fell asleep with her head still resting on my shirtless stomach. I let her stay that way for two more episodes before waking her. She gave me a quick kiss on the cheek and I left for my own dorm.

CHAPTER 38

ICU: 1-3, Corvus: $8305

CHAPTER 39

Vic kept bugging me to come to the game that he was playing. I needed to work on a psychology assignment that was due the next day, so I'd said no several times. Apparently he was doing pretty well, taking nearly two grand from the game, and I was getting texts about all his big hands. Eventually he wasn't even asking me to join him; he was just describing his successful night whenever he had time between hands. Finally, he mentioned that there was a game going on at Coasters. Even though I tried to ignore his texts and write my paper, his discussion had gotten me wound up to play. When he mentioned the Coasters game, I finally convinced myself to abandon my paper and head over to the bar. One last look at my paper showed me that I was only one and a half pages short of the required length. I could definitely finish that before class time.

I lost my first buy-in to a torturous run of shitty cards. Mostly I just paid the blinds and had to fold when the pot was raised, but I also had the fun of dumping some money away on two small bluffs that failed. Attempting bluffs was fucking suicide with the crazy cast of characters around the table who weren't afraid to throw money around. The only person who was any good was a skinny guy who always wore a baseball cap that had a "Pizza Hut" logo on it. Needless to say, the poker table is not typically a place where you'll see high fashion. He was a boring player who hardly ever played hands and usually flipped over winners. I pretty much never got involved with him. All the other guys were regulars from the bar who usually gave their money away. On this particular night, at least early on, they were going wild, hitting crazy hands, and passing chips back and forth while I sat in frustration.

With my second buy-in, I won a couple of small pots and was up thirty or forty bucks on the buy-in. I thought maybe I would pick up some momentum, but four players all got involved in one huge pot, three of them in rough shape because they made stupid decisions. Naturally, one of the idiots hit two cards on the turn and river to make a flush. He took all of the money and our table was down to only three players. It was quickly decided that we should quit because it wasn't really a proper game so shorthanded.

♥ ♣ ♦ ♠

Brad, the guy who ran the game, was in the kitchen at the same time I was after the game broke up, smoking a cigarette. I joined him.

"Hey, Donkey Donny and I are going to a game in Haverston. It's a house game but it's organized and shit; they have a couple of nice tables and they even set out pretty good food. The guy who owns the house, Terry, actually owns a catering business, so he puts out some kick-ass grub. You interested?"

I took a puff and blew it out the side of my mouth. "Yea, definitely. I was about to go in the bathroom and give myself paper cuts on the wrist with the shitty cards I've been getting. A venue change might be nice."

"Well, I should let you know that this game is a little bit higher stakes than you normally play here. They play five and ten blinds. Is that okay?"

I had never actually played at that level before, but I had thought about trying sometime. Vic had recommended that I hold off on playing some of the larger games in the area because they get crazy. I realized it wasn't a great idea to play it when I was frustrated.

"Yea, it's no problem. I just gotta stop by my dorm room and get some more cash. Are you leaving right away?"

"Nope, I have to get these stragglers out of here before I can go, plus I have to go downstairs and talk to my brother. Just get back here as soon as you can and you, me, and Donny can all ride down together. I'll drive."

"Sounds good, I'll be back in a half hour or less." I said, zipping up my jacket.

♥ ♣ ♦ ♠

It was only an eight minute drive to campus, so I was there before I knew it. I paced quickly through the parking lot, scanned my card to unlock the door, and took the stairs three at a time up to our room. When I opened the door, Josh was standing in the middle of the room, tottering back and forth while he stared at himself in the mirror.

"Yo man!"

I laughed at his goofy ass grin, knowing he was fucked up already. "You seem like you're having a nice Friday already, what's goin' down tonight?"

"Oh man, lotsa good shit, dude. That big house over on Green Street is having a banger tonight. I was just there with Noah. I had probably five or six beers and two shots there. I bought a sack of weed from this guy who's in Delta Tau Delta. He invited me back to their place for the rest of the night. He said as long as I brought a few girls, he'd vouch for me. Kaitlyn and Steph said they'd go with me, so they're waiting back at the Green Street house. I just came back to the dorm to grab a shower and change quick. You wanna come to the party, dude? I'm sure it would be okay with this guy. His name is Ryan by the way."

I was tempted to cancel going to the poker game in Haverton and get fucked up with him, but the urge to play killed that almost right away. The game at the bar had been way too short. "Nah, I'm actually going to a pretty big money game in Haverton. The smaller game I was at broke up really quick tonight."

"Oh, sick. A bigger game than what you normally play? Damn. You already play way over my head!" He adjusted the collared shirt he was wearing underneath a black sweater, tugging it back and forth but not realizing he wasn't really doing anything.

"Damn, you're getting all dressed up. Lookin' sharp," I said, wondering again why I wasn't going with him.

"No shit, I know it!" He turned towards me with glassy but smiling eyes. "You sure you don't want to go to this party? There will be some seriously hot chicks at this place. I'm about to leave, but I'll wait a couple minutes if you want to get ready and come with."

"Appreciate it man, but I think I'll pass. Sounds like a blast though. Get two girls tonight to make up for me not being there. Maybe we can party next week sometime."

He nodded at himself in the mirror one more time, flicking a lock of hair. "Alright. I gotta tell you, though, I was already planning on getting two girls tonight, so I'll have to get three if I'm making up for you!" He laughed and punched me hard as hell on the bicep.

"Jesus, take it easy on the arm" I jokingly whined. "You haven't even had two girls in your life, much less two in one night."

He grinned his stupid grin again. "While that might be true, I can still dream big, baby. I'm tryin' to add some numbers to that total tonight!" He started walking towards the door. "Good luck at the game, man!" He stepped out the door and I yelled after him: "Same to you!"

♥ ♣ ♦ ♠

Driving back to the bar, I put all my windows down and lit a cigarette. I let my arm hang out the window. The fresh air felt pretty good, but it didn't blow away a little worry that was nagging me. I couldn't shake the thought that it was weird that I was choosing to go to a poker game instead of taking Josh up on the offer to go out and party with him. I had to wonder if I was letting the typical college student life pass me by just to go out and play cards with a bunch of degenerate gamblers, most of whom were at least twice my age. I felt almost stupid about it, but I continued on my way towards the bar.

When I arrived, Brad and Donny were already waiting in Brad's running SUV, listening to The Rolling Stones on his stereo. I parked my car and approached the truck, reaching out to tap on Donny's window. I heard the doors unlock before my knuckles even got to it, so I pulled the door open and slipped into the backseat, feeling a blast of freezing cold air conditioning hit my face. I could barely make out Donny's face in the glow of a single dome light, but I saw his eyes point up towards the rearview mirror. He greeted me and said, "Is this your first time playing 5/10? I've never seen you at a game before."

"Yeah, figured I'd give it a shot since the other game broke up."

"That's cool. The money moves a lot faster in a game like this, but you'll be okay."

Brad snorted and said loudly, "Wise goddamn advice from this guy. Most of the time it's a race between which will disappear first, his twelve-pack of shitty beer or his chip stack." Donny laughed and Brad gunned the engine, exiting the Coasters parking lot.

♥ ♣ ♦ ♠

We finally arrived to the game after what felt like a pretty long drive; probably forty-five minutes or so. The house was a nice one out in the country, set back far enough in the woods that you could barely see it at night except for some flood lights poking through the trees and leaves. We crawled up a windy stone drive-way. Brad parked the truck in the furthest available spot, and, even though nobody had said anything, announced, "I don't want to get parked in here." He pulled his cell phone out and punched in a couple words. "I let Terry know that we're here."

Brad had opened the door to let us in and Terry was standing near the door chewing on a chicken wing that didn't appear to have any more meat left on the bone. His mouth full, he nodded at the three of us as we walked in, then locked the door behind us. Terry had on a collared shirt that had several stains on the front. He had either spilled a bunch of different stuff on himself or he had been wearing the shirt for multiple days. I would put my money on both. He had on a pair of regular glasses and had a pair of sunglasses resting on the brim of his hat. After a painful looking swallow, he finally said to us: "Welcome fellas, 'sgood to see some fresh blood, we're kind of low tonight. Right now it's just me, Deurron, Micah, and Brandon." With each name he lazily pointed a finger towards the table. "Vic and some other guy were here, but he left a little while ago."

Hours later, I ended up in a big hand with Terry, facing a $645 bet from him. The hand had started very promising for me when I peeked at two black queens in front of me. I'd lost one $500 buy-in already, but had worked my next $500 into almost $900. $865, to be exact. I raised the ten dollar blind up to $45. It was a pretty big opening raise, but Terry had joined the game with a large stack of chips, well over a grand, and he was playing loose. Consequently, the rest of table had become a little bit crazier, so my raise wasn't really out of the ordinary for the circumstances. Everybody folded till it got back to Terry in the big blind. He cleaned his fingers with a napkin, then glanced at his cards. He immediately reached for his chips and threw in $110 worth, four $25 chips and two $5 chips. The action came back to me as I was the only one left in the hand. I thought for a moment before announcing a raise and pushing $220 towards the center of the table. The smart move was to raise even more to really put him to the test, but I pretty much assumed he was just going to fold since I was representing a very good hand with my betting. Instead, he quickly called and the dealer gathered all of the chips in a pile before laying out the first three community cards: the eight of diamonds, the nine of hearts, and the ten of clubs. Terry was first to act. With a repetitive stacking and re-stacking motion, he played with a few $100 chips. Eventually, he put the three chips back with the others in front of him and scrunched his face like a rabbit, pushing his sunglasses up with one finger, and said, "All in."

I truly wasn't expecting the move, although I probably should have been. Terry didn't play scared at all, so he wasn't afraid to move the money around. A bead of sweat dripped down his face, working its way down toward his already wet collar. I wish that meant something in relation to the hand, either excitement or fear, but it really just meant that a fat guy was sitting in a basement that had gotten warm because of some heated cooking dishes holding wings. Terry sweated whether he folded, was in a monster pot, or had fallen asleep at the table; It didn't matter.

I started to feel a pressure that was unfamiliar to me. Usually I had the ability to play for decent sums of money without feeling any real nervousness, but this was just enough to put me a little bit out of my comfort zone. I checked my cards again, seeing the same two queens. It was really a pretty good board for a pocket pair of queens, all undercards to my pair and an inside straight draw as a bonus. Still, it had me worried that I wasn't ready to call off all my money. It was possible that Terry was holding a pocket pair of eights, nines, or tens. He may have flopped a straight with queen-jack. It wouldn't have even surprised me if he had gotten involved in the hand with something like nine-ten or eight-nine. Terry was silent, as was the rest of the table.

Eventually, I convinced myself that I was beat and released my hand, flipping it over for Terry to see and announced, "Fold." in a clear voice.

Terry just said, "Wow," and flipped his own hand. He only had six-six for a bad pair and a crappy inside straight draw.

I shrugged my shoulders and tried to play off my frustration at my incorrect decision. Inside I was absolutely steaming. My temples pounded and my body temperature seemed to instantly spike. I hoped nobody noticed my anger and embarrassment.

Naturally, the rest of the night was a terrible run of shitty cards and my own foolish decisions as to what to do with them. I lost all my remaining chips from my second buy-in on a poorly timed bluff against Micah, who had an ace-high flush. My last stupid decision was to exchange the last two $100 bills in my pocket for chips. I figured I might double up a couple times and recoup some of my losses for the night. I didn't. Every other person had a massive stack compared to mine and just bullied me and carved me up until I was nearly drained.

As I stood up from my chair after losing my last few chips, my stomach was rumbling from eating over a dozen chicken wings and drinking at least a liter of pop. The gas and faint smell of wing sauce under my fingernails was the only thing I took away from the game.

Brad eventually drove Donny and I home. Brad smoked cigarettes, lighting new ones off the last one before he tossed the spent butt out of the crack in his window. Donny slept. I sat in silence, looking out the window into the darkness. We got back to Coasters and our two cars were the only ones left in the parking lot. I thanked Brad for the ride and said goodbye right before slamming the door shut.

Once in my car, I sat without starting the ignition, still annoyed at myself and the loss. I could feel the weird spasms in my face that came before crying, but I closed my eyes and mouth tightly to avoid it. I'd felt depression after poker losses before, but hadn't been experiencing them very hard in the last few months. I'd been floating along with a security blanket of money, but this loss was enough to remind me that it wasn't exactly my money to lose. I saw the other guys were gone and began smacking my steering wheel in frustration. When that didn't feel like enough, I started slapping my own temples with the palm of my hand, over and over, until it burned. After a dozen or so strikes, I rested my head on the steering wheel and tried to take deep breaths while fighting the urge to cry out loud. I started the car with my head still on the wheel. I let the car idle for a good five minutes before sitting up and starting back to campus with no music and the night air rushing in from all the open windows.

CHAPTER 40

The body draped like a blanket, buzzing from the soul slowly sneaking from its pores.

CHAPTER 41

ICU: 2-3, Corvus: $7105

CHAPTER 42

I took a healthy sip of my bottled water to soothe my sore throat. I did my best to give my full attention to Dr. Cirelli, who was discussing the requirements for the paper that she'd just assigned.

"As you're all aware, this is primarily a class about the structure of words and written works. Our focus is on some of the more technical stuff. Even so, it's impossible to write on a high level without having style. Style comes from practice and talent, but it also comes from passion. Having strong feelings about a subject very often improves a person's writing because they have a clarity that allows the creator to write naturally, in more of a speaking tone, which, in most circumstances, is the best way to convey an idea. This type of writing, as any other, still requires close editing, but it provides an amazing intellectual infrastructure for the piece being written."

I was interested in Dr. Cirelli's lecture, but I was more interested in my phone when I saw a text from Ramona:

> "Im bored in math class. What r u doing?"
> "In English Comp"
> "Ohh . . . who do you have?"
> "Cirelli, she's pretty cool"
> "Don't know her . . . Wanna meet in the library around 7 tonight?"
> "I can definitely do that."
> " ☺ "

If my text looked too eager, I didn't really care. I really wanted to see her. I put my phone back in my pocket and turned my full attention back to Dr. Cirelli. She was finishing her lecture while passing out a sheet of paper that held the criteria for our next paper. The class was almost over and people were starting to pack up their stuff. Over the rustling and snapping and zipping, she said loudly, "For this assignment, I'd like to see some emotional involvement. I want you to think of a situation where somebody acted unethically but didn't face immediate negative consequences. Maybe even reaped rewards from the behavior. This is pretty wide open; could be in the workplace, in class, whatever. Pick something that evokes some kind of emotion inside you, whether it be sadness, anger, or anything else. Discuss if the ends justified the means for the unethical person, both from his point of view and yours. Write about possible negative consequences that aren't immediate but might later appear. In the words of hip-hop philosophers . . . keep it real!" The students who were still listening laughed while exiting the classroom.

I suspected it could get annoying after a while, the way she clicked her pen around her mouth and teeth while intently reading. For the time being, it just seemed incredibly cute. She had her calculus textbook open and was poring over it, only looking up every once in a while. Despite working pretty hard, she hadn't made it past the page she'd started on when we got to the library. Her anxious tic of clicking and chewing her pen was evidence that she wasn't exactly enjoying the material she was trying to read. I didn't really care about the book I was reading. I'd already read the required chapter for English composition, and written a response, but it was the book I was using as an excuse to spend time with Ramona in the library.

I heard her pen drop onto her notebook, and I looked up to her eyes watching me. I dragged my finger along a sentence on the page of my textbook, pretending I was finishing reading a section. I lifted my finger from the page and looked back up at her again.

"I hate this shit, I'm tired of this semester." Ramona let out a long sigh and took a long gulp from her bottle of spring water.

I looked at her and asked, "Why are you still in college if you hate it so much? Why not just quit now while you're not in too deep?" I didn't want to seem like I was judging her, but I was actually interested in her answer. I didn't want to get too personal too quick and creep her out, but I had my own doubts about going to college and I wanted to see how she felt about going. I tried to change my tone a bit and sound less judgmental, "What's your major, again? You may have told me but I forget."

She closed her book and stuck her pen in her mouth, forcing the little clip on the side of the pen onto her bottom lip. It hung there, looking ridiculous, but she answered seriously, "I didn't say I hated college, I just hate most of the classes." After saying the words, she laughed a little bit. "Okay, maybe not most, but a lot of them. My major is liberal arts, whatever the fuck that means. I'll probably change it by the time I'm done with all my general education classes."

"What do you plan to be after school? I've heard of painters and graphic artists, but I don't think I've ever met someone with the job title of liberal artist."

Ramona laughed and I felt a little buzz inside my chest. I was relieved she didn't seem to be annoyed by my questioning, and hearing her laugh at something I said was even better. She replied, "Smartass, I said that I'd probably decide on a better major at some point. Listening to you talk, you sound like you must have everything all figured out Mr. Freshman. Is that true?"

I smiled and snorted a little laugh and said back, "Hardly, maybe that's why I'm asking. This is only my first semester, and I'm already not sure if I want to be here."

"Fair enough. Just give it some time. Once you meet more people, everything seems to get a little easier."

"Actually, maybe some of that is what freaks me out a little bit. I mean, I like to drink, and I'm fine with people getting crazy sometimes, but it just gets ridiculous. It seems like there are just so many people that are just here for the parties. Or here because they're in love with the football team. Again, I love watching sports and appreciate what athletes can do on the field, but the rah-rah-rah, support-the-team-like-a-religion bullshit is just foreign to me. It makes me feel a little out-of-place sometimes, and I'm not sure if I'm being stupid or those people just really shouldn't be here. It costs so much money, and it seems like so many are just paying for an all-inclusive four year vacation. Sometimes I think the classes are the thing that I worry about the least!"

I wasn't surprised that she was a little taken aback by my rant. I found myself comfortable with her, so I'd opened up a little more than I might to other people I didn't know all that well. Some of the things I was saying could easily be taken as an insult to Ramona. After all, she was probably a regular partier and attendee at football games. From what I knew about her so far, I seriously doubted she was the kind of mindless asshole that I was talking about. Still, she could easily have taken my rants as some kind of harsh judgment of her.

"Well aren't you just a bundle of freaking fun!" She laughed and threw her pen at me. "But seriously, I kinda get what you mean. It's so easy just to fall into the same patterns as everybody around you on campus." She went on, "But you can definitely find people that aren't as shitty as you think, they're out there. And academics do matter to a lot of people, even though it might not get as much attention as our football team most of the time. Trust me, you might have to sort through some jerks, but you shouldn't be too negative before you give things a chance."

Even though I liked that we were having a meaningful talk, I was starting to get uncomfortable. It sounds terrible, but I was much more comfortable when I was directing the conversation without being questioned. "I know, I get it. It hasn't even been that bad, I just worry too much." I pointed to her folder and said, "I think you need to get back to your calculus. I can see your last test peeking out of your folder, and the grade isn't exactly Dean's List material."

She held her middle finger up on one hand and grabbed her pen back with the other. With her pen she playfully doctored the "71%" on her test to a "97%." While finishing the "7" she said, "Hey, you should come out to a some more parties with me. Actually, I already know of one my friends and I are going to this Saturday. It'll be at the teek house over on Franklin."

"What the hell is 'teek'?"

She snickered and spelled out, "T.K.E. It's Tau Kappa Epsilon, one of the fraternities here. I have a friend in the frat; he lived in my dorm freshman year and he said I should come and bring a few people. You should come along with me to the party, they're decent guys."

I didn't have a lot of confidence that I'd consider all of the frat brothers "decent guys," but I was positively sure that I wanted to be in the direct vicinity of Ramona when Saturday rolled around. "I think I'd be up for that. Call or text me sometime before the weekend if I don't see you, you can let me know what's up."

"Okay! It'll be fun to get out with you!" She smiled, looked back at her book, and worked her pen back onto her lip. She struggled and scribbled for another twenty minutes while I pretended to read in between glances at the bit of cleavage showing above her top. When we left the library, we went separate ways because she was going to a friend's apartment while I was just going back to my room. After exchanging quick waves goodbye,

I couldn't help but grin when I turned around and started back. Even when I tripped over a section of the sidewalk that had risen above the other pieces, I still felt pretty good.

CHAPTER 43

Alone in a locker room, a young man intently stares at a tablet. The lined pages of the tablet are filled with scrawled handwriting. In block letters at the top, in pen, is written: WEEKLY SCHEDULE AND ASSIGNMENTS.

He has a satisfied smile on his face as he draws a line through several of the items written on the lined page.

After stuffing the tablet into a backpack, he takes a duffel bag out of the locker in front of him.

He puts on a bright, neon yellow pair of shoes, ties them tightly, and stands up. He turns to one side then the other, twisting at the torso and stretching his back. He removes the jersey he's wearing, rolls it into a ball, and tosses it towards a large metal basket that's already overflowing with dirty jerseys. Satisfied when his jersey rests on top of the others and doesn't fall out, he puts on a sleeveless grey t-shirt.

After jumping athletically into the air a few times, he turns out the locker room lights and exits.

The door shuts itself most of the way but gets caught on the frame. With one sinewy arm, the young man closes the door the rest of the way and hums a beat while he walks down the barren hallway.

CHAPTER 44

The dragging of a chair leg on the floor woke me up and my head snapped up. Just in case anybody was watching, I pretended I was cracking my neck. It was a pretty lame attempt to hide the fact that I'd been napping while the professor spoke at length about the Tet Offensive in the Vietnam War. What I was catching was actually pretty interesting, but I couldn't control myself from dozing. The warm air in the room was like a blanket, and the professor's voice was a low quiet monotone. When I tried to stay awake, my eyelids felt like concrete until I gave in and shut them. I hadn't even been out that late the night before. I was at the poker game above the Coasters, but it had broken up early and I couldn't find any other game.

I looked at the professor, who was still addressing the class but was looking at me through his tortoise-shell glasses that had slipped to the front of his nose. He was a youngish-looking forty-something who still tried to dress somewhat fashionably. He mostly succeeded in retaining a youthful look, but his hair was on the whiter side of gray and he had a small paunch of fat around his waist that would accompany him into old age. He probably worked out and went on bike rides while clad in spandex and did other upper-middle-classy type activities to stay in shape, but his metabolism was still slightly getting the best of him.

I pretended to write something important in my notebook as an excuse to look down, but I sensed he was still looking at me. He announced that he was going to start the movie that he'd promised to show us. I heard him struggling with the DVD case, so I figured it was safe to look up again. He let out a restrained grunt, finally popping the case open. He poked his index finger and stood with it for a few seconds before sliding it into the player underneath the television.

A few minutes into the documentary, I felt Professor Jefferies standing at my right shoulder. He leaned down near my ear and whispered, "Please stay after class for a couple minutes to discuss something." I nodded and continued facing forward, watching the screen where three soldiers were smoking marijuana from the barrel of a shotgun.

♥ ♣ ♦ ♠

"What did he say to you?"

I rolled a dirty hacky-sack around in my hands, hearing the beads inside lightly grind against each other. I laughed and looked up to Josh drumming his pen on his desk, waiting for my response. "He just said that he's noticed I'm always sleeping in his class, and that I should go to the doctor if I'm not feeling well." We both laughed. "Obviously he knows that I don't have a medical issue, he's just being a smart ass. I told him that I've just had more work than I expected lately and that I'll try to do better with it."

"Did he punish you or something? I don't even know what a professor does to punish people for things like that. What's he gonna do? He didn't dock you points or some shit, did he?"

"No, actually he showed my last writing assignment that we had, the ten-pager I was working on last week about that Vietnam novel we had to read. I got an A on it and he asked me why I didn't try hard in class like I did on the paper."

"Hm, I would have thought he'd just leave you alone if your grade is okay." He scanned the page of the open book on his desk with his pen, searching for the spot where he had stopped reading.

"He seemed much more offended than I would have guessed. The funny thing is that I actually like the class, I just can't stay awake to save my life. I'm not trying to be a dick on purpose, I just can't help it. It makes sense, it's probably shitty to have to teach when some guy is snoring through your lesson."

Josh gave up on his page again, looking up to say dryly, "Yea, everybody knows you can't help being a dick."

"You know what I meant, ass!" I laughed and changed the topic, "You wanna go shoot basketball or something?"

"Are we betting $.50 a shot again? I need some money to buy beer this weekend. Your money had me drunk three nights in a row after last time we played basketball!"

I scooped the basketball off of the floor and tossed it at him, knowing he wasn't prepared, but he still caught it after it lightly thumped his stomach. "I'll be taking that money back, and more, tonight, pussy." I was pretty sure I wouldn't be taking anything from him, but I didn't care. $.50 a game wasn't even a concern after what I'd dropped at Terry's. Losing a few dollars to Josh might even feel kind of good. It might feel more normal than losing over $1000 at a game with a bunch of near strangers who I never spent time with outside of playing cards.

CHAPTER 45

ICU: 2-4, Corvus: $7096

CHAPTER 46

It was a good time to answer a call from my uncle since nobody was in the outside corridor where I was smoking a cigarette. I held the phone up to my ear and said, "Hey."

My uncle spoke very quickly, "We're going to meet at Sally's Liplicker Diner on Monday, October 20th at 2:00 p.m. Just you and I, obviously. I want our last meeting before the game to be in person. I'll have the stuff you're going to need. You can call me if there's some kind of problem with that time, but I expect you can rearrange things to make it. Remember, it's much harder for me to arrange time. Your aunt just pulled in the driveway, so I have to get off the phone right away. I'll see you there if I don't talk to you. Bye."

I was happy the phone call was short—I was always happy when my uncle was brief. I was about ready to leave for a game when the phone had rung. Vic let me know about the game, which was in a small city about a half hour from campus. I was going alone, but Vic said he was going to show up a little bit later. He called the guy that runs the game and let him know I'd be coming so he'd let me in.

The game was held in a building connected to a body shop: just one open room with concrete floors, an old couch, and a refrigerator that buzzed loudly. This was definitely a game of true degenerates. One guy playing, Jim, was a guy who dealt at another game. I'd heard Brad tell a story about Jim one night at Coasters. Jim and another guy had gone to an 'Off Track Betting' kiosk that was in a strip mall before the mayor put his sights on it. He drove them out with threats about zoning and the frequent drug use around the place. The bad shit was probably true, but it was nothing that any local politician cared to get rid of until they needed to get some good publicity.

Anyway, Jim and this guy who gave him a ride to the O.T.B. were gambling all day on horses that they didn't know anything about, running at shitty tracks in places they could have never located on a map. Jim is steadily draining money by making huge bets and chasing his losses. Not long before the place is about to close for the night, Jim hits an unbelievable super trifecta that pays him huge odds. He ends up winning $1600 and they leave.

Jim is the kind of guy who, if he's awake, pretty much needs action or he goes crazy. The whole ride home, the other guy and Jim are celebrating. Jim has his money in two stacks, and he's using them like drumsticks on the dashboard. The music is cranked and they're smoking cigarettes while ashes fly around them like tiny clouds of mosquitoes. Jim tells the other dude that he needs to take a leak and get some more cigarettes.

Both are in a bit of hurry, as they're on their way to a poker game to do a little more gambling, and now they have ammo because of the late score at the O.T.B. When they pull into a convenience store parking lot, Jim tells the other dude that he'll be quick, so he doesn't even need to shut the car off and come in with him. The guy doesn't need anything, so he agrees, putting the car in park. He sees Jim go to the counter first, getting his cigarettes and having a brief discussion with the young lady at the counter. He smiles, grabs his smokes, and goes into the bathroom. A short time later, he comes out of the store, hops into the Pontiac Grand Am, and they're on their way again.

Right before they come to the next convenience store, Jim says that now he's feeling a little sick to his stomach and directs the guy to stop and let him take a shit at the next store. The guy is getting a little annoyed, but pulls in the lot anyway. Oddly, Jim stops at the counter to purchase something. After a longer period of time in the bathroom, Jim gets back into the car, still sweating and seeming a little uncomfortable.

They end up stopping at nearly every convenience store that they see on the way to the poker game, the driver getting irritated and suspicious, but not asking too many questions because Jim seems genuinely sick. They finally get to the poker game and are preparing to buy chips so they can play. Jim pulls the guy aside and asks him if he can borrow a few hundred dollars. Long story short, Jim didn't have a stomach ache; he had blown through every penny of the $1600 playing $25 scratch-off lottery tickets in the bathrooms at the convenience stores and was now flat broke. The other guy lets him borrow enough cash for one buy-in, which he loses in 45 minutes. He makes $235 in tips dealing for nine hours straight, plays for two hours and loses it, then goes home to sleep. Jim and the other guy haven't talked about it since.

That story was a good representation of the average player in the body shop game. I wasn't sure how I compared to them. I still thought of myself as different, but I was starting to find myself at games pretty frequently. I'd go to a game, and for the first five minutes find myself worrying about all the things I was ignoring by being there. I'd start listing my assignments, or start fretting that I should be preparing to set up Raven, or even think that I should have called Ramona to ask her if she wanted to see a movie or something. I still had the T.K.E. party to look forward to, but I couldn't help feeling like I could be really pursuing something with her. All of those thoughts always disappeared very quickly once I got involved in some hands.

A large brown guy of a non-descript ethnicity dealt the body shop game. His oily skin had the color and appearance of the crust on a piece of pumpernickel bread. With his pumpernickel fingers, he occasionally pressed a button on his cell phone through his pants and talked to people through the Bluetooth that's hanging on his mole-covered ears. Although he's having side conversations, his attention towards the game never waned and he almost never made a mistake.

"Eleven bucks to call, young man." He pointed to me and then picked up his phone conversation where he had left off.

"I'm gonna fold and go have a cigarette. Just put my blinds in if it gets around to me again."

The dealer scooped up the cards that I had thrown in the middle and nodded to me silently. I stood up and bent backwards, stretching my back. I had only been sitting at the table for about forty minutes, but my back was sore from playing the night before. Even though it wasn't very exciting, I had sat for about ten hours until it broke up sometime in the morning. I had also slowly got drunk on Jack Daniels and Coke that somebody else had brought; and the aftermath of that wasn't helping my discomfort. I slid my pack of cigarettes from my pocket and moved to the small kitchen area that was sort of set apart from the rest of the room. There was an air vent hanging from the ceiling in this area, so it was the designated smoking spot. The vent could barely seize in air because nobody cleaned it, but it was better than nothing, I guess.

A much older gentleman who I knew as Gary from playing with him before, was already puffing on a long hundred cigarette, blowing nasty, cheap smoke straight into the vent. He stared upward, watching his own lazy smoke curl up towards the ceiling. "Fucking napkins," he said, not really making it clear if he was really talking to me.

"What about napkins?" I asked, still unsure if he even gave a shit about my presence.

"I might as well be using my cards as fucking napkins as bad as they've been all night. These fucking clowns, you gotta have something because they just call you down like monkeys. I don't know what the hell kind of cards these guys play anymore. Fucking television and shit. They don't understand that the game isn't about constant pissing contests. It's a bore; much more exciting to actually think about what you're doing and not act like a chimpanzee throwing chips across the table."

It was more words than the guy had ever said to me in the three times I had played with him combined. I cleared my throat after a moment and said "Yea, even though I'm younger, I actually like . . ."

My conversation was cut-off by a powerful, disgusting, hacking cough from the old man. He held up his hand to signal me to wait. I did so, awkwardly waiting while he repeated a cadence of "Gleeeeeeegh, hech, hech, blehhh!" several times. Finally he seemed to be finished, spitting once into the tiny aluminum sink. He apologized before taking a long slug of spring water.

I continued, "even though a lot of the younger guys like to play like nuts, I actually prefer a little slower game, myself. I like to keep it moving pretty fast, but you won't really see me going crazy over and over again like some of the dudes that play regularly in these games."

He spoke while staring at his cigarette burning in the ashtray, "Yes, I noticed that. You still play too fast for me. You should think a little more, take your time. I'm not saying you're bad at playing or anything, don't get me wrong. Just nonsense from an old shit that's been playing for probably three times longer than you've been alive."

"I'll remember that. I don't mind hearing advice from somebody that's been around since the cards were etched in rock." The joke was one that I had heard directed to Gary at games before. His gray-tinged pencil-thin mustache went up a little bit in the tiniest of smiles, and he sucked his cigarette down to his fingers.

"You're always with Victor, is that right?"

"Yea, I go to games alone sometimes, but typically Vic is with me. In fact, he'll be here in about ten minutes."

Gary blew the last bit of smoke from his nose, staring at the clock on the microwave. "I don't know about that motherfucker, I've heard some shit and seen some shit with that guy. Something rubs me the wrong way about him."

"Aw, he isn't so bad. He might run off at the mouth at times, but he's been a pretty good guy to me since I've known him."

"Well, I guess that's for you to figure out. We can't go around making judgments for other people, God knows that. If I worried myself trying to figure out these lunatics, I'd have dug my own fucking grave about fifty years ago. I'm sure you're a smart guy, so I'll leave it up to you to figure out who's your friend and who ain't. I don't mean to talk bad about your friend."

"No worries, I wonder about him myself sometimes, but he hasn't done anything to me personally."

I figured Vic must have talked too much shit to the old guy or stiffed him on money or something when he was wasted. I laughed a little bit to myself and stubbed out my spent cigarette. Almost on cue, Vic entered the room and shouted the word "Sickos!" He grinned at the players he knew and dipped his head lightly to the two players he didn't know.

I turned to Gary and said lightly "Let's go take that asshole's money." Gary shrugged his bony shoulders and smiled the same thin, knowing smile while we both made our way back to the table.

♥ ♣ ♦ ♠

Eleven hours later, Vic was stuck about $600 and I was up only about 60 bucks. It had been a long, dragging game with nobody leaving except for one guy who'd left not too long after Vic had arrived. Vic had been involved in what seemed like nearly every hand, throwing his chips around like confetti and riding an up and down rollercoaster. I had okay hands, but hadn't really done much because I usually avoided playing with Vic if I could. I had taken the last forty bucks or so from the guy who'd left early, but had just picked up a few pots here and there. Gary literally was taking naps at the table and only playing about ten percent of the hands he was dealt. It almost seemed like he had a cigarette for every hand he played, as he stood up every twenty-five minutes to smoke.

Vic thought he was hiding his annoyance at losing, but he wasn't really. His constant banter was similar to how he normally spoke, but I could hear the little bite of anger in his voice. It may have even been too subtle for others to notice, but I could hear it. Based on his stories, he had lost much more than $600 on other occasions, especially with some sports betting he'd done. Still, even Vic wasn't immune from getting a little heated at a cold run of cards.

He'd been sitting at the table, not playing, since the last time he busted. Without a word, he stood up from the table and walked towards the door where everybody was supposed to enter or exit. Beside it was a large roll-up door that opened to the small dock where I assumed car parts were delivered; or had been when the body shop was actually in business. With an unlit cigarette between his lips, Vic approached the roll-up door. There was some dusty junk piled in front of it, so it probably hadn't been opened in a while. Vic yanked at the bottom of the door before realizing there was a locking mechanism that he had to disengage. He popped it and the door screeched at first, but flew up quickly when the chain-driven pulley caught. The sun was shining brightly and Vic stared straight into it with one hand resting above his eyebrows.

The guy dealing the game stood up and his Bluetooth popped off of his earlobe and bounced onto the table. "Jesus Christ, dumbass, what the fuck are you doing?"

Vic looked back at him with no emotion and lit his cigarette.

The dealer continued: "You know, the cops generally leave us alone, but that won't last if we put our fuckin' card game on display for everybody that drives by. This game isn't really the best kept secret in town already."

Vic said, "It fucking stinks in here between the cigarette smoke and you fat-asses eating Cheetos and farting all night. Plus, Gary always has that goddamn mothball smell hovering around him. I'm just trying to air the place out for God's sake. Nobody's doing detective work on an illegal gambling thing at fucking six in the morning, fool. Ease up Ravvy, this ain't exactly fucking mafia business here, it's a goddamn two-five game."

"I don't give a shit, I run this game and I'd be held accountable for raking this game. I don't feel like advertising this shit, even if you think it'd be a petty issue with the cops. Which it wouldn't be, at least not with some of them. Shut that door."

Vic turned back towards the sun and held his arms wide, proclaiming loudly: "Daybreak, gentlemen!"

CHAPTER 47

Coming off of the high where nothing else matters but the risk and the constant chaotic calculations. The waves and valleys of feeling like a genius and a shmuck while the action is still alive . . . followed by the inevitable emptiness when it's over. The tiny stabs of devastation poking you while the saner part of you struggles to keep the dark part from taking over. This is loss. This is stupidity. This is high. This is low. This is survival. This is the process of realizing some terrible truths inside you. This is comradery amongst the defective. This is massive chunks of time lost. This is depression. This is scrambling to pick up the pieces when you suddenly have to care about a dollar more than you cared about 100 only fifteen minutes ago. This is the figurative punch in the gut that will have you hunched over ready to give up. This is not the stuff of fun and games even though it is cloaked as such. This is not a Kenny Rogers song. This is about people with particularly debilitating weaknesses and afflictions, yet intangible perseverance -albeit sick and misguided- to stick around till the next day and do it all over again.

CHAPTER 48

ICU: 2-5, Corvus: $7156

CHAPTER 49

"So, are you feeling pretty comfortable with the material in your classes? Have you been good about showing up and staying current with everything? Just going is a big part of the battle." I'd heard this mini-speech from my dad before, but I let him go on with it anyway. It made sense, and I was actually following the advice pretty well. I'd missed very few classes during the semester. All but two of my missed classes were due to my observing Raven. I was pretty sure he wouldn't want to hear about my classroom naps, so I just let him know that I was keeping up and showing up. "Even your worst day of class is better than not going at all," He cleared his throat, "Make it easier on yourself, ya know?"

"You're right, it helps just to go and get all the papers and stuff that professors hand out, if nothing else."

"Right, I'm glad you agree. To be honest, I was pretty crappy at going to class for some parts of college, and they always ended up being my worst semesters. Caught up to me when it came time to apply for graduate school, too." I knew he'd wanted to be a college professor when he was younger, but had never ended up continuing his education. I'd never actually heard him say that it had anything to do with his grades in undergraduate. I'd always figured he'd just decided to start a family and changed his plans. "I could still have gone somewhere, but I got a little discouraged when I was turned down from some of the places that I really wanted to go to." There was a slight pause and I could hear his breathing, slow and steady, before he changed the subject. "So what's going on as far as tests and papers coming up for the mid-term?"

I gave him a quick rundown of my classes. While I did, I half daydreamed, remembering when my dad and I used to go to the grocery store on Sunday nights when I was little. My mom hated going to the store, so she always made a list and then Dad and I would pick the stuff up. He'd let me stand in the big basket part of the cart, like a miniature ship-captain, until the boxes of cereal and pasta and bags of produce piled up enough that there wasn't any room for my tiny body. He'd always let me pick whatever I wanted as a treat. I'd ignore the ice cream and candy, opting instead for a particular brand of cherry cough drops. They came in a box about the size of an index card, probably 24 or so in each box. I'd have three or four lozenges eaten before we even got home from the store. Even though they were pretty sweet and tasty for cough drops, it was still a strange choice for a kid. It had never really struck me how weird it was until I started daydreaming while talking to my Dad.

"That sounds good, bud. Good luck with everything."

"Thanks. Hey, what brand were those cough drops you used to buy me?"

He let out a boisterous belly laugh and answered, "Luden's. Wild Cherry flavor, or something. We probably weren't supposed to let you eat those damn things like candy. What the heck made you think of that?"

I had no idea what had made me think about them, so I just said, "Uh, I saw some guy with cough drops in class and started telling him about getting them as a treat when I was a kid, haha."

"That's funny. Alright buddy, I'll let you go. Mom says hello and she loves you."

"Love you, and tell Mom I said the same. I'll talk to you closer to fall break." We both said goodbye and I let him end the call first.

I yanked off my hat and tossed it towards the corner of my bed, trying to ring the little post that stuck up above the mattress. It spun around a few times before falling to the tiled floor. I left it there and slid into my bed on top of the covers. The air in the room was cool but comfortable, a bit of a breeze sneaking in the slightly cracked-open window.

"I don't even know how you make it to class. Dude, you're always out late. I've barely seen you throughout the semester."

I leaned on my left elbow, looking lazily at Josh. "Sorry man, I didn't know I was supposed to provide you with my daily sched- ule." I hadn't meant it to sound nasty, but there was a clear hint of annoyance in my voice that I hoped Josh wouldn't pick up on.

"Didn't mean anything by it. I'm just sayin', we live in the same room and I barely even see you. We don't have to be best friends, but you barely even let me know when you're gonna be around."

This time, I had a genuinely angry reaction to his words. I sat up in my bad and put my sneakered feet on the floor. I stared at him while I started seething inside. I wasn't exactly sure what was causing him to make comments to me, but it felt like some kind of accusation. "What the hell man, we just played basketball the other night. Do I have to answer to you about my everyday life? I have a life outside this dorm, and maybe it's more complicated than you understand. You know, you don't have to be close pals with every fucking person you meet."

He shook his head at me. "Relax, man, I'm not trying to pry into your life. I don't really care that much. I'm a little pissed from the other night. You said you would be back to the dorm around one in the morning. I told you that I forgot my key when I visited my hometown. I went to Steve's apartment to work on a group project. You locked the door when you left, and it was still locked when I got back at quarter after one. You weren't here and didn't answer my call or text. I had to wake up the freakin' RA to open the door up for me. You never did answer me. Bullshit, man."

I instantly felt bad, but I was still feeling defensive enough that I didn't want to say sorry. I laid back in the bed and stared at the ceiling, letting the silence build up tension in the room. Both of us were surprised when the door popped open. Standing in the doorway was the half-naked figure of Chad from down the hall, wrapped only in a green terry towel. He was constantly strutting around the hallway in a towel, or just boxer briefs, because he had the physique for it and because he was a dipshit.

"You guys wanna come along to get some pizza? We're leaving in about ten minutes."

Josh said he would go, but I said no thanks. I wasn't quite ready to apologize to him, so it would obviously be too weird to go and share a pizza with him.

CHAPTER 50

I stepped out of the screen door on the backside of the Tau Kappa Epsilon house, tripping over the beat-up rug lying right outside the door. The rug was grotesquely flowered, an obvious freebie from somebody's mother's kitchen. I was really starting to get the spins so I reached a hand out to steady myself. Unfortunately, my hand found the jagged remaining leaves of a dying holly bush. I yelled out and then sucked the little drop of blood from my palm and spit out into the yard in a high arc. I pulled my cigarettes from my pocket, opened the top, and counted them with one eye closed. Seven left. I struggled to pull one out between the nails of my thumb and index finger. I finally got it out, lit it, and blew a stream of smoke into the air.

I walked around the house to the skinny strip of grass that separated the T.K.E. house and the dwelling next door. After I zipped up I held up my beer bottle to see how full it was. I felt like my eyes were crossing without my permission. I'd met Ramona at the party and it seemed to be going pretty well. We talked for a little, I met some of her friends, and we played a couple drinking games together. I had to learn the rules as I went since I didn't know the games. That meant I had ended up drinking more than anybody else that was playing. Ramona was growing more attractive to me every time I saw her—on both a physical and a personality level. I was hoping we'd end up back in her dorm room again. I thought about stories I had heard of guys who had drunk so much that they couldn't get their dicks hard. What a terrible thing that would be if I messed up like that. I turned my almost-full bottle upside down and let the amber liquid and white suds splash onto the spot where I had just pissed. I didn't think I'd have that problem, but I wasn't going to risk it by drinking any more.

I went back inside to the blaring music and screaming conversations. I steadied myself on the nearest chair, trying to keep my equilibrium.

I looked in the living room to see if Ramona was in there. That was where we had been before she left to use the bathroom upstairs. I opened a door in the living room but it turned out to just be a closet. I poked my head around the wall, looking into the kitchen. There were a few people doing shots together but they didn't see me. No Ramona. I passed by a couple making out and went into the living room. It smelled strongly of beer and weed.

Cries went up from around the beer-pong table. I didn't see her among the people cheering. I did see Jen. She was much more animated than when I'd met her at the poker game in the dorm.

"Hey Corvus! What's up?!"

"I'm actually looking for Ramona, have you seen her in the last couple of minutes by any chance?"

"Ummm no, I saw her, like, forty-five minutes ago. I don't know where she is now, though. Sorry."

"No problem, Jen. Thanks anyway."

"Well, Jess and I are going to Jamie's to hang out. I think you met them when they were still here. Last time I talked to Ramona she said she's staying here."

"Thanks, I think I'll look around for her a little more. I'll see you in English on Monday."

"Alright, see ya in class if I don't see ya around. Bye Corvus!" She gave me a little wave and I returned it, still wondering where the hell Ramona was. I went to the open basement door and carefully stepped down the rickety wooden stairs.

I looked over to the faded-green couch and loveseat in the very far corner of the basement that became visible after a few people moved around. I found Ramona. She was on the lap of a guy I didn't know. He was an okay looking guy with a chiseled jaw that had patches of pimples on either side. He looked to be older, at least a junior. He had his left hand firmly attached to her ass cheek, and his right hand acting as a rest for Ramona's neck. She was giggling, the bitch. Not twenty minutes had gone by and she seemed to have totally forgotten I was even at the party. I couldn't believe it. I pounded up the basement steps quickly. When I reached the ground floor, I went straight for the front door. I left and started back to my dorm without saying anything else to anybody.

♥ ♣ ♦ ♠

I could feel my cell phone vibrate in my pocket. I thought about just ignoring it; I didn't really feel like talking to anybody. I had the foolish thought that it might be Ramona calling to apologize for leading me on and then hooking up with another guy. Immediately after having the thought I knew it was stupid. I didn't even need to look at my phone to know that. I pulled it out anyway to see who it was. It turned out that it was Vic, asking if I wanted to come to a party that he was at. I had gotten texts before from him when he was drunk at a party. He was the kind of guy that, once he was wasted, felt like everybody he knows should be right there with him drinking and hanging out. He would usually wait to text or call till he'd already been at a party for several hours, but once he had a steady buzz he was on the phone with anybody who'd answer. At least twice he'd sent me a text that was a mass text to a dozen or so people. I knew because people would reply and I'd get random texts for an hour or two. This particular time, his text was only to me.

I sat down on a big electrical box of some kind, needing a moment to calm down a little bit. I was still feeling all of the alcohol that I'd had, and was starting to sweat. I was shaken up by the situation with Ramona as well. I'd obviously expected too much from her, or at least expected something too soon. I completely misread her intentions.

Between the big loss at Terry's poker game and the bullshit with Ramona, I wasn't exactly riding high in spirits. The loss had shaken me because I started thinking about the time I was spending playing cards, and how much money I was putting at risk on any given night. I'd already gotten into the habit of skipping shit with Josh and the other guys to play. Although I hadn't forgotten or decided not to do any assignments, I could feel that I was neglecting the work enough that I definitely wasn't getting my best results. There was also, of course, the matter of my uncle and the plan. I still wasn't totally sure if I was capable of going through with it. Since I wasn't able to talk to anybody about it, time was just passing. With each day I didn't do anything, my situation grew more complicated. Aside from the first day of watching him, I hadn't done anything else to learn about Raven's regular activity. I was losing money I hadn't earned yet. On top of that, my nights spent playing poker took up all of the time I should have been using to find out more about Raven. My uncle said I could abandon the plan at any time, but he expected me to pay the money back in full. I hadn't had to talk to him for a while, but the time was soon coming that I'd have to. The game itself was approaching very quickly.

I tried to shake off everything. I looked at my cell phone again, noticing that Vic had accidentally sent the same message twice. I saw the lights of a campus security guard a few hundred yards away, and I stood up and started walking as casually as possible. The small SUV passed without even slowing down, and I exhaled audibly. It wasn't like I was doing anything wrong, but I didn't need to add some kind of stupid underage drinking or drunk in public charge to my list of concerns. I stopped in the middle of the sidewalk and texted an answer back to Vic.

CHAPTER 51

I'd started innocently enough, ranting about Ramona and Terry's house to Vic. Before I knew it, I was telling Vic all about my uncle in between slugs of beer. It was nearly 2:30 a.m., and there were only a few stragglers left at the house. I didn't know whose house it was, but I assumed Vic did. When I first got there, a whole crew of drunk kids were getting ready to leave. A bunch of them were shouting about going to a diner, presumably the 24-hour place that was closest to campus. After that, Vic and I were left alone in the living room.

"Jesus Christ man! Let me get all of this straight. So your uncle already gave you some of the dough to do this deed for him, and you have a plan and everything to set up Raven and his roommate with this shit. I thought you didn't even get along with your uncle?"

I held my plastic cup of beer to my forehead to combat the sleepiness that was slowly creeping up on me. "I don't, really. I mean, we don't argue or fight, but I really can't stand him most of the time. He seemed so much nicer when I was a kid."

"Yeah, maybe he wasn't such a dick when he was younger, but maybe you're just better at recognizing his flaws now. Kids do tend to look at grown-ups in a better light than they might deserve. I used to think my Dad was the coolest. Then I hit high school and realized he was banging a waitress at the family restaurant down the street. My Mom never knew, but I heard him talking to the waitress on the phone one day when he didn't know I was in the house. Let's just say they weren't fuckin' talking about scrambled eggs and bacon."

I put my cup on the table and stretched my back. "Damn, so your Mom never found out?"

"Oh she did, but she stayed with him and they fixed it by going to church together every Sunday. Dad used that free pass to find an even younger ho to sleep with. Picked up a nice little coke habit, too. He got hit by a car one night and picked up a big-ass lump sum of money. Miraculously, he was stone-cold sober that night, which is why he got a bunch of money for his injuries. That was his last sober night for a long time."

I shook my head, feeling a strange smile on my lips that wasn't from being amused, but from being dumbfounded by his story. I felt a little jolt of energy just from taking a short break from downing any alcohol.

"Enough about that jackass, back to this shit with your uncle. You don't have to tell me anything else, I know that shit is your business." He lowered his voice even though it was empty in the house except for one guy snoring in his bedroom. "If you don't mind telling me, though, how much is he going to pay you to help take care of this?"

I considered shutting up about it and playing it off like it was actually just something my uncle had said that I was just exaggerating. I realized, though, that Vic had slowly become the best friend I had at college. We spent hours upon hours together at poker games each week. Most of that was just spent playing, but we talked a lot too. The interaction we had just driving to games or taking breaks to smoke was easily three times as much communication as I'd had with Jeremy during the semester. It was clear that Josh and I weren't as close as I might have thought, judging by his frustration with how it was to live with in the same dorm with me. Vic wasn't the type to run to any kind of authority figure to turn me in—his line of work didn't exactly allow for much interaction with cops or school administrators.

I grabbed a shot glass that was sitting on the coffee table. I'd seen a girl drink a sip of it and almost spit back up the little bit that she had drank. I knew it wasn't gross, didn't have cigarette ash in it or anything, so I tipped it up and finished what was inside. "Eight grand, plus another seven if his contract gets renewed. Sounds kinda nuts, but he's up for a huge deal if he can turn the program around. I don't know, maybe that doesn't seem that high to you, you've seen all kinds of money gambling and taking bets."

Vic turned his head and looked at me from the corner of his eyes with a smirk carving a dimple on his cheek. "Bull-fucking-shit, dude. I've seen some money, but that doesn't mean that shit's a joke. That's some real cash. And you're saying he fronted you the eight already?"

"Yea, I guess to make sure I know he isn't fucking around. Probably a way to keep me from backing out too. If I took the money already, it's a whole lot harder to pull outta the whole thing."

Vic exclaimed loudly, "Man, that is insane!" His voice cracked a little bit, and he coughed and got quiet again. He whispered, "So what's the deal, are you definitely gonna go through with it?"

I immediately felt tension in my neck and back after he asked the question, and my cheeks were flushed after the liquor. "I'm not sure, man, but I know I gotta fucking figure it out. I'm down over a grand playing cards with the money. If I back out, I'm gonna have to figure out how to get that back. Now I'm all messed up in the head with this Ramona bullshit tonight."

Vic took his flat brim off and wiped a tiny bit of sweat from the top of his forehead, saying, "You need to put that chick on the back burner—or accept that she's already put you there. You have more important things to deal with. Anyway, there's more fish in the sea and all that jazz. You're at a college with girls everywhere. Unless you were planning on some kind of serious relationship with that girl, I'd recommend putting your fishing line back in the sea. Anyway, you shouldn't worry about that shit until you deal with this football game."

I thought about the reality of setting up a young man to potentially have his life ruined. Discussing it out loud seemed to make it more real. I could keep pointing out that my uncle was an asshole. I could tell myself that I hated his pushy attitude. The truth was that I would be a piece of shit if helped him set Raven up. I wasn't any better than my uncle. The fact that I had even taken the money and been considering being involved was enough. I had also been justifying my actions with my anger at the cost of going to college. No matter how much the cost of tuition bothered me, I was certainly not the only person who had to deal with the problem.

"I mean, there might be other options besides just going through with the plan," Vic said, staring down at a cigarette that had little tabs of tobacco spilling from the tip. He was pushing the strands back in with the point of a gel pen. Satisfied with his repair, he looked up and stuck the cigarette in his mouth.

I squinted and asked, "What do you mean? I see it as pretty black and white. My uncle doesn't seem interested in negotiating any halfway deals with this thing."

He motioned towards the door and said, "Let's burn one on the porch while we talk about it."

♥ ♣ ♦ ♠

Watching my cigarette burn unevenly into a canoe shape at the end, I snatched my lighter from my pocket and lit the other side to attempt to even it out. When I was satisfied it was burning evenly, I put away my lighter and tucked my left arm underneath the opposite armpit. It was after three in the morning, so it was really starting to get cold out. I was still feeling the effects of all the booze I'd had, but it wasn't enough to warm me up or distract me from the bite in the air. I looked over at Vic and he was messing with a huge maple leaf that sorta looked like a catcher's mitt in the dark. He was peeling strips of the leaf, delicately ripping the pieces from the veins and letting them fly away in the light wind that had kicked up. He held his own cigarette between his lips, not really smoking but letting a puff fly from the corner of his mouth every few minutes. It was probably the quietest and most reflective I'd ever seen him, and it actually made me anxious. Vic practically thought all of his thoughts out loud, so it was weird to see him just sitting and thinking without babbling something.

Finally looking up and seeming to come back to Earth, Vic looked over at me and said, "Seriously, have you thought about the different ways you might approach this shit?"

"I really don't know what you mean, so I guess I'd have to say no, I haven't considered my options." With the last word, I made little air quotes. Scoffing at my corny gesture, Vic lit a new cigarette with his old one.

"You have the two obvious options to choose from. You can go along with your uncle, just follow his lead and set this guy up and hopefully everything goes as planned. Of course, you can also just get the fuck outta this right now and forget it ever happened. I actually recommend the second if you don't have a stomach for this kind of shit. This is really gonna require some nuts, and timing, and good fortune to not get caught. You gotta know that this won't be taken lightly if the authorities find out. Do you really want to get yourself in some deep shit this early in your life? I'm talking some messy, three foot deep kind of shit, boss. I've pretty much avoided any legal problems, but I've seen plenty of dudes get in holes that they can't ever dig out of. Your uncle might be pissed at you for not having all the money, but he'll be too worried about his own ass to try to get you in trouble. He'd work something out with you."

I'd expected Vic to just support me being involved with the scheme, so it caught me off guard that he was saying anything that might steer me away from being involved. While his warnings were a bit of a surprise, I had a feeling the venturous side of Vic that I was more familiar with was about to come out. Sure enough, Vic took a deep breath and opened his mouth to speak with just the hint of slyness emanating from his face.

"Then there are the other options, if you decide you'd like to take a little risk." I stared at him without a word and he continued to speak. "Hear me out. Let's say, hypothetically, you turn this around on him a bit. Maybe you could take the money you already have and use it to make some money, then return that dough to your uncle and not owe him shit."

"No doubt about it, that'd be great, but I can't risk that kind of money playing in a card game or something. Too much risk I'll catch a bad run of cards and get unlucky." I took a quick drag on my cigarette and added, "I'm already down a fucking grand on money that's not technically mine."

"No, no, not cards. I think you have a spot where you have a little knowledge that gives you an edge that makes it worth taking a risk."

I wasn't exactly following him, and my blank stare probably gave it away.

He continued, "What I mean is, don't set Raven up. Bet most of the money you have left *against* your uncle's team. He already told you straight up that ICU is gonna have trouble with Middenburg, especially if Raven is playing. Add to that the fact that your uncle will be, at least in some ways, tailoring his game plan with the thought that Raven won't be involved. He won't be as prepared as he could be if Raven ends up playing."

Oddly, Vic was starting to make sense. Still, I immediately thought of complications in carrying out the new plan. "Dude, who would even take that kind of action around here? Even with the people you know, I don't know if we could make a bet that big."

"No, we wouldn't do it around here. For that kind of money, I'd be too afraid that a local guy wouldn't have the cash to pay out. If you ever even got it, it would take forever. No, what we would do is make those bets in Vegas."

I took notice to the fact that he was now saying 'we' as he talked.

Vic went on, "We'll spread the bets around a couple different sportsbooks to keep the bets low and avoid any kind of tax bullshit. We'll just pick the ones that are offering the best moneylines." He was clearly starting to get excited, his speech getting faster and louder. "I'm not gonna lie, I'm trying to get a plane ticket to Vegas outta this. I'll place the bets and you can hold the betting slips until the game is over and we collect. I won't take a cut or anything, a free trip to Vegas is enough for me. I'll get you an I.D. so that you can go into casinos, but I should definitely make the bets under my name since I'm over twenty-one. With that kind of money, we have to be legit so there aren't any problems getting the winnings."

The prospect of gaining a large chunk of money without having to rely on my uncle was very attractive. Even though it was his cash that would get me started, any money that I won would be completely mine. He'd just think I backed out of the plan at the last minute. There would be nothing that he could ever hold over my head. There was a considerable amount of risk involved in betting all the money, but a very tempting reward if it worked.

"Don't make a decision tonight. It's just an idea. Do what's right for you, man. In the end, it's your decision. You gotta make some crazy decisions in your life, and you gotta own them." He seemed to kind of forget that we were even talking about an insane plan to go to Vegas and put way too much money on the line on a single football game. "Believe it or not, I would like to be different from what I am now. Someday I'd like to finish this fucking degree and get the fuck outta here. I want the job, the career actually, the whole thing. Maybe spend more than a month with the same girl." He looked at me with a grin and added, "I think I can be like those people that actually get outta school on time and get normal gigs—it'll just take me a little longer."

Vic's last statement threw me for a loop because I'd never seen him so vulnerable. I almost felt like giving him a hug for some strange reason; instead, I just put my hand on his shoulder. After a few seconds I pulled my hand back and we both stood up without words. It was odd that we'd moved from talking about my uncle and coming up with a new plan to bet against him, to ending with Vic emotionally opening up about his own life.

We started walking side-by-side down the alley that led to his apartment and my residence hall. The skeleton of the leaf that Vic had picked apart moved along the gravel, pushed by the slow but steady wind. Any parties that were kicking before had ended, so the scratching sound of the leaf seemed loud against the silent air.

CHAPTER 52

From high above, a hawk's perspective, there is a monochromatic sea moving in a frenzied fashion. The sea is made up of bodies that are young and bounding with energy. The faces on the figures are turned towards the green field below, with only brief glances away from the action on the turf. In between wild, primal screams, there are more reserved murmurs of a less barbaric nature. The quiet discussions center around one particular shoulder-padded chess piece.

Amazement and awe overcome impulsive shouts and shrieks. The player on the field has the rare deftness, power, and intelligence that can actually turn otherwise shallow people into reflective philosophers. When intangible skill is on display, it hints at magic. There are a lot of things that kill faith, so it is a welcome burst of unexplainable metaphysical energy. A bone-crunching tackle demonstrates a rare combination of raw mass and speed. The avoidance of a tackle, without even being able to physically see the tackler coming, points to a more mysterious nature that is intriguing and even magical.

The bodies in the bleachers, in head-shaking amazement, talk about the person beneath the pads and helmet:

"I hear he's a good guy too."

"Dude came from a rough place but he's never gonna look back to that garbage."

"Had a 4.0 GPA in high school and runs a 4.5 forty yard dash. Ain't that some shit?"

"Heard the kid is already doing volunteer work in his downtime. Not many freshmen are that mature. Hell, most grownups aren't even that selfless."

"He does it the right way. He's quick and evasive, but he also isn't afraid to get gritty out there. That's what I like to see."

"I hope everything goes right for him; he could be really special."

Among the throng, a young man stands watching it all. He focuses on the revered player very closely, only breaking his

concentration to cheer along with the crowd during especially excit-
ing moments. The young man watches the player both on the field
and on the sideline, examining his movements and behaviors.
Unexpected purity and clarity has the ability to turn tides.

CHAPTER 53

ICU: 3-5, Corvus: $6929

CHAPTER 54

Im in.

I waited anxiously to see how Vic would respond to my text. Despite Vic's warnings to really think about taking the trip to Vegas to make the bets, I knew that he wouldn't have proposed it if he didn't really want to do it. Vic loved action even more than I did, and was even up there with some of the more compulsive gamblers at the poker games. I was pretty sure that once I gave the go, he'd be ready to roll with it.

"Niceee. Ill take care of the planning. Ive been there, so I know my way around a little bit."

"Sounds good man. I totally thought it through and Im good to go."

"K dude, not gonna lie, Im pretty excited about it hahaha."

"Lol, Im nervous, but I can handle having that money on the line."

"I guess we'll see haha. Like I said, I got everything. Just do what you need to do this week so you're ready to fly out FRIDAY morning."

"Got it. Ill be ready."

"Cool, Ill get back to you about the exact time of the flight and shit."

"Ok"

After punching the last two letters on my phone, I looked up into the flooding streetlight that just barely reached my car. When my eyes adjusted, I could see the shiny exterior of the diner. My dad always talked about the cool "art deco" style of the classic diner buildings. It didn't do much for me when we saw one, but he always gushed like it was an amazing piece of fine art rather than an old place that served cheeseburgers and weak coffee. I wasn't familiar with this particular place until my uncle had suggested we meet at it to discuss final plans and exchange the pre-packaged contraband. I had purposely texted Vic right before meeting my uncle on my way home for fall break. I thought talking to Vic right before would give some extra courage to blatantly lie to my uncle. I was gonna have to really lay it on.

When I started walking towards the front of Sally's Liplicker Diner, I immediately heard a door close. Another set of feet started crunching in the small limestone pebbles that filled the parking lot, but I didn't turn to look at the person.

"Hey." It was my uncle's voice. He said, "I thought that was you, but I figured I'd just wait in the truck until you got out."

"Sorry, I was just finishing a text conversation with a friend. I didn't even see your SUV or I would have gotten out sooner."

"No problem, let's head in."

I resisted the urge to make a comment along the lines of "Nah, let's just chill out here and order our food takeout." I had to keep my head in the game of lying to him. I couldn't screw it up now that I'd given Vic the okay. Vic was probably already online booking tickets and making reservations for us. I was freaked out to go through with it, but another part of me was absolutely buzzing to get the bets made and wait in anticipation for a payday that could be the beginning of my financial independence.

We sat in a booth that was directly below a print of an oil painting that looked a bit out of place. It was held in a tacky gold frame, the thin plating peeling in several spots. Despite the frame, the image was a calming landscape that featured a man with a mustache working on the beach. I looked at the words beneath the print and read out loud, "Sifting Sand, 1891." In the corner of the print was the name "Guillaumin." I wasn't sure how to say the name. Looking around the restaurant, I saw that every booth had a painting above it. The paintings were all visible because there were only three other people in the dining room. I couldn't make out any intricate details on the other paintings. The three people were all elderly men by themselves and all seated far enough away that we could comfortably speak without anybody hearing our conversation. If we spoke quietly, it was virtually a guarantee that nobody would even hear a single word. I looked back at my uncle and he was already fixated on the menu.

"You guys wanna start with some drinks?" It was hard to peg the waitress's age, but it was probably somewhere between forty-eight and sixty. I could see a pack of Virginia Slims poking out from her faded black denim pocket. She waited with her pad in hand and a purple pen poised directly above it in her other hand.

Her pink shirt was still bright but the embroidered letters on her chest spelling out 'Judith' had several loose threads that gave away how many times it had been through the wash. Her tanned, leathery arms contrasted with the color of her sleeves. She had long fingernails that were painted a dark burgundy. Two of her nails were starting to crack a little, both on her right hand. The index finger and the pinky finger. I wondered if she was able to go to some place where friendly Asian girls paid attention to her and painted her nails for her. I hoped so.

My uncle answered, "Yes ma'am, I'd like a coffee and a Coke."

"Just coffee for me, please."

She finished writing the drink order and said, "I'll be back shortly, unless you're also ready to order your food."

My uncle spoke again, "We're ready. Let me get a Diner Special Burger with fries instead of chips."

I hadn't actually been ready to order. In fact, I hadn't even had a chance to open my menu. I didn't complain though, because I usually ordered the same thing whenever I went to diners. "I'd like a turkey club, chips are fine." I grabbed the menu that my uncle was still holding and handed them both to the waitress. She thanked me and I smiled back at her. At the same time, I was running through what I was going to say to my uncle. I watched the waitress walk away, grabbing an empty plate from another table as she paced quickly towards the kitchen. While we waited, we both sat looking at our phones. I scrolled through my text conversation with Vic several times. I could see Uncle Pete was going through his e-mails.

Once we had our drinks and food, my uncle laced his fingers together in front of him. He wrinkled his brow while sipping from the straw that was in his glass of Coke. He spoke in an uncharacteristically restrained voice and said, "So let's run through this and get every detail on lock down. It will be in our best interest to not talk after this, including the day of the game. Especially that day, actually."

"Well, as you would guess, he has a very strict schedule as a player. He pretty much does the exact same thing every week. On Monday nights, which is his only true weeknight that isn't spoken for by the team, he's always stayed in his apartment. But that doesn't matter since I'll only need to get into his apartment later in the week." I felt a little sick, but I also had an odd sense of pride in my confident introduction. "We're very fortunate regarding his standard Friday night before an away game. Like the rest of the team, he has to stay in a special dorm area that's only for the players so they avoid any partying or stupid behavior the night before away games. They practice, eat dinner, and then go immediately to the dorms with no down time. Well, technically they have some time if they finish eating fast, but all the players pack a bag to stay in the team rooms. Nobody that I've seen, including Raven, ever goes back to their regular place for any reason." It was true that the team stayed in the special dorms the night before away games, but I'd added the last part on my own. Around campus, I'd heard about the special dorms but I'd never actually watched the players there. I paused and looked hard at him.

"Good so far." He chewed a fry gingerly. "Keep going."

I finished chewing my own bite of turkey club and finished the last half of the water glass that the waitress had brought with my coffee. I hadn't asked for it, but I was grateful she'd brought it for me. "I'm done with classes early in the afternoon. Just to be sure, I'm going to wait for Raven to go to practice. He usually stays on campus in the library and then gets a ride straight to the stadium for team meeting and practice, but I'll wait until I'm sure he's gone before going anywhere close to his apartment."

I saw our waitress on her way to our table, so I stopped talking and plucked two chips from my plate. After politely letting her know that we didn't need anything else for the time being, I put the chips in my mouth and crunched them loudly. After swallowing, I continued where I'd left off. "So when all is clear, I'll make my way to his apartment. There are only a couple of other people in his building and they're all students. From what I've seen, all of them stay on campus an hour or two later than I do. By the way, getting into Raven's apartment won't be difficult. He keeps a key under his welcome mat. He didn't at first but he locked himself out once when I was watching him. He had to call his landlord to let him in. Landlord wasn't real happy about it." The key thing was another fabrication that I'd thought up. "Anyway, that's another thing that makes this a lot easier. Not much else to say other than that. I figure I'll pick some spot to stash everything, make it look believable that they're hiding it, but not make it too hard to find with a little searching. I figure I'll leave some blunt wrappers and a little bag of weed on their coffee table or something. I even got an old cell phone to put with the other stuff. They have these donation boxes where you can toss your old phone. They give 'em to old people for emergencies because you can still dial 911 on cell phones even if it isn't in service. I yanked one from one of those boxes. Since I didn't buy it, there's no chance it could be traced back to me. It'll be dead, so the cops will have to find a charger for it. I figure that will just add a little more confusion to everything."

"And what about the roommate? Have you been watching Figueroa as well?"

For a moment, the question caught me off guard. I hadn't, in fact, thought at all about Figueroa. Honestly, I had sort of forgotten about him. I only paused a moment before recovering and responding, "Oh, yes. That's another thing kind of working in our favor. He and Raven basically have the same schedule. I'm sure that was done on purpose to make things easier for them. The only difference is that Figueroa stays on campus a little bit earlier on Mondays to get extra tutoring. So he won't be a problem for us."

He looked at me, clearly impressed, but I couldn't help but feel like he was a little skeptical. For a second, I worried I was laying it on too thick. He spoke for the first time in several minutes. "You sound like you have everything pretty well figured out. I have to admit I'm pleasantly surprised by how thorough you're being." I had a sudden urge to yank out one of his long gray nose hairs with my thumb and index finger, just to watch his reaction to the sharp jolt of pain. "On my end, I'll keep it short and sweet here. Our acquaintance at the Middenburg PD is still on the same page as us. Rest assured, the police will be at that apartment that morning. You take care of your part and everything should fall into place. For now, I'll pay this check and then we can get outta here. I'll give you the shit out in the parking lot when there aren't any cars around."

I waited by my car while Uncle Pete went to his truck. He returned with several thick books, all of them older hardcover editions with worn spines. The cover of the top one was totally worn except for the name "Rene Descartes". He went to the passenger door, waited for me to unlock it, then opened the door and slid inside. I got in the driver's side.

I remarked, "Picked up some reading material, huh?"

He looked down at the books and shrugged. "Got 'em at a book sale in the library on campus. Don't even know what the hell they are. Good way as any to hide shit without drawing attention."

I looked at the books incredulously and asked, "Wow, do people really use this trick in real life?"

"Don't knock it till you try it. I know it seems stupid, but it's better than just stuffing everything in a backpack and having it visible if somebody opens it. One more level of protection can't hurt. I used to sneak booze this way when I was younger than you."

I grabbed the books from him and sat them on my lap.

He awkwardly shook my hand and said, "Good luck." Without another word he left the car and walked to his own truck. He started the engine and left immediately.

I pretended to type on my phone again, waving my hand quickly as he drove away. I sighed deeply when he was able to pull out of the diner parking lot. I rolled my windows down, pulled a cigarette from the pack that was in the center console, and stuck it in the corner of my mouth. I flipped open the top book and thumbed through the pages until I reached pages that had a rectangle cut out of the middle. The little hiding spot was about six inches by six inches and was about two inches deep. Stuffed inside were dozens and dozens of tightly packed bags containing pills and powder. I stared for a moment and then quickly closed the book. I put them in the empty backpack that I had brought and put the bag in the backseat. I turned the ignition, put the car in gear, and left the parking lot.

In less than a mile, there were reflections of flashing lights bouncing off my rearview mirror. I thought I might throw up my inner organs onto the dashboard. The cop was directly behind me with his siren on blast and lights swirling like a two color rave party. I didn't even reach for the books. I was entirely too scared to think of doing anything but getting my car off the road and onto the shoulder. I nearly started to cry in the process. Once pulled over, I put it in park and closed my eyes with no idea of what to do other than await my fate. Even though I know it was just an innocent-looking backpack, it might as well have been marked with a neon sign that said 'DRUGS HERE!' the way my heart was beating against my ribs.

And then, the beautiful sound of a police car rushing past my open window. I opened my eyes and saw the dead taillight of a car on the shoulder a few hundred yards in front of me. Then the entire rear of that car was blocked by the cruiser. I laughed and let out a shrill scream of relief. I put the car in gear again and gassed it just enough to get moving at a clip of five miles per hour under the speed limit. In my rearview mirror I watched the officer saunter to the side of the other car without so much as a glance towards mine.

CHAPTER 55

*Whether it be vice, work, or hobby, the most damaging conse-
quence of an obsession is measured in lost time. Time not being
used to advance the self and the mind, and time that will be owed
to others, but is impossible to pay back. It's cliché and dreamy-
sounding, but money and trivial material things that are lost really
can be found again. Sometimes, a consuming obsession can even
bring about temporary joy in the form of money and material gain,
providing justification for these activities and behaviors. Of course,
this passes, and that is when it becomes more apparent that this
compulsive preoccupation is detrimental. It is easy to begin listing
the tangible things lost as evidence to a problem. Too often ignored
is the time that begins to disappear in larger pieces and with more
frequency. This is the non-tangible loss that is at the heart of de-
generative behavior.*

CHAPTER 56

ICU: 4-5, Corvus: $7072

CHAPTER 57

Fall break had been pretty boring, and I'd been pretty distant with my parents. I'd just told them that I had a lot to prepare for with midterms coming along, that I was doing well but had some papers and tests coming up that were a big part of my grade. That pretty much kept them from bothering me, and I mostly spent time in my room reading non-school books. I'd gone out once to see a crappy action movie with Harrison. I'd hoped to see Jeremy at some point, but his family was away on a family get-together at his Grandpa's cabin.

Four days back from fall break, I was making an effort to spend some time with Josh and some of the other people from our dorm. Not partying or anything, just some hanging out. This included playing a pool tournament consisting of two-person teams. Everybody decided that the teams should just be room-mates. Several guys mentioned that this might make it harder for some, as it would be all-guy and all-girl teams. Although said in a polite way, this received a wave of protest from the girls on our floor. One girl, I didn't know her name, stated confidently that she'd been taught pool at a young age and was probably better than most of the guys playing. As it turned out, the girls did hold their own. Josh and I got third place, our team straddled on either side by girl teams. Fourth place was two girls that I didn't know, and the second place team was the team with the very confident girl. She was a very good shot and would have won if her partner had been capable of doing something other than scratching. They lost in the championship to Kevin and his roommate Antwan. They'd beaten us, and when they did, Josh put his head down and goofily presented his cue like a knight giving up his sword. She smacked him playfully on the shoulder and he let out a child-ish squeal, eliciting laughter around the common room.

I felt like I was just watching all of the people around me rather than participating in the social interaction. The others seemed in-credibly comfortable and congruent with the college atmosphere.

I knew it couldn't all be real, but even if they were only half-faking, it was still more adjusted than I was with everything. I watched them float around the room, talking and playing in all fluid motions. It was funny how, even with really relaxed attire, there was clearly attention paid to every piece of clothing. From perfectly angled hats and strategically messy ponytails the whole way down to calculatedly un-hip slippers and colorful flip flops, it seemed incredibly obvious. While I wondered why this was the way they interacted, I also wondered why the hell I cared about it. It wasn't really my business anyway. Besides, I probably did some of the same things to fit in. We're all just so fucking silly, really.

I felt my pocket vibrating and I pulled out my phone. It was Vic calling. He had quite impeccable timing when it came to tearing me away from things. I didn't answer the call, but I did say goodbye to everybody in the common room so I could leave and dial him back where there was less commotion.

Josh offered me a celebratory high-five and said simply, "Nice bronze medal, dude."

For a second, I didn't know what he meant because I was already thinking about Vic. I quickly realized Josh was talking about the pool tournament. I gave him a delayed return five that didn't connect quite right.

Josh didn't seem to notice the awkwardness. He smiled back and said, "Later, dude!"

I waved back at Josh with my phone still in my hand, then turned around and made my way outside to call Vic back.

♥ ♣ ♦ ♠

Vic answered after the second ring. "What's up, man?"

"How's it going? Did you make some plans for us?"

"Yup. We're flying out Friday at noon. I was hoping to leave earlier, but I have a couple things to take care of in the morning. We'll be arriving in Vegas around 4:30. We have reservations at the Tropicana. That's about it, really. Any questions?"

"Not that I can think of right now."

"Cool, I'm actually making a pick-up for a guy that owes and I just got to the bar where I'm meeting him. I gotta go."

"Thanks for making the arrangements. I'll talk to you later in the week."

CHAPTER 58

The days before Vegas went by quickly, partly because I was doing my best to stay caught up with schoolwork. Two days before the trip, I took an early midterm test for Psychology. I was pretty sure I'd passed, but not with flying colors. Probably a C or something. I also had to finish my paper for English, the one about some ethical situation. Although I should have been chock full of inner turmoil about ethics and values in my current situation, I ended up just writing the paper about being on the debate team in high school. I discussed seeing the top person on our team accidentally coming across a copy of the questions at one of our debates, which was obviously not allowed. Questions were supposed to be a surprise to us, although we were given several general topics about which to prepare. I detailed how our MVP went to the bathroom with the questions and made quick outlines in a notebook to frame our answers before returning the copy back to the spot where he'd found it. We, of course, went on to dominate and the event started our run to the regional championship, becoming another bullet point on our star's high school resume.

I had never been on a debate team. My high school didn't even have one. For some reason it was easier to write about a hypothetical situation and feign guilt and anger at something that didn't really happen. It was easier to shape everything about the story in a way that was conducive to writing a paper rather than take real facts and fit them into the assignment criteria. It was way faster and ended up sounding pretty damn good. We were able to turn the paper in online on our class website and it was due the night before the Vegas adventure. I attached the file in the proper spot on the website with sixteen minutes to spare. Afterwards, with nobody in our room, I stared at the bag that I'd already packed. I looked back at a text that Vic had sent me earlier in the day.

"10 am at the bus stop near the drugstore a block off the square. Lets do this."

CHAPTER 59

I stepped out of the airport doors and an extreme heat hugged my body. I'd expected it to be hot, but it was still jarring after being used to the cool weather we were having back in Indiana. When the air hit me, I let out a whoosh of air that ended in a quick, sharp whistle. I dropped the bag I was carrying on my shoulder immediately and stood up straight to collect myself.

"Hot as hell, isn't it?" Vic laughed and stood watching me, not dropping any of his bags. "It stays hot pretty far into the fall."

"Crazy for this time of year, man. What's the temperature here, anyway?"

Vic pulled out his phone and squinted at the screen. "Says it's 89 here. 39 at home!" He laughed, picked my bag up by the stiff canvas strap, and dropped it onto my shoulder. My shoulder dipped down from the weight before I readjusted it.

"How are we going to get to the hotel?"

Vic was scanning his eyes around and said from the side of his mouth, "We'll just get a taxi right to the Tropicana."

He finally saw the sign that had 'Taxi Waiting Area' written on it. He started walking quickly towards the sign with me in tow. We took a place in line behind about six other people who were also waiting between the retractable nylon line barriers. Finally feeling like I could relax for a little, I started thinking about the main reason we were here. Thinking about that made my head start reeling again, and the heat didn't help with the spinning feeling. I blinked a few times and conjured up the feeling of a nice, heavy-weight clay chip in my hands, imagining the sound it would make as I tapped it against the other chips lying in a healthy stack in front of me. It conjured a small smile that lasted the entire ride in the old Ford Crown Victoria.

♥♣♦♠

We stepped out of the elevator onto the seventeenth floor of the Tropicana Hotel and Resort. I immediately smelled the stench of old cigarettes. Not helping the unpleasant odor was a stagnant, warm air, strategically manufactured to make people want to get the hell out of the hallways and into the casino.

When we opened the door to our room, Vic went in first and then turned back to look at me. I was certain my expression gave away how unimpressed I was. The room had a smell from the 70s, fake gold lamps from the 80s, and a TV from the 90s.

My eyes finally met with Vic's. I said dryly, "Jesus, how did you manage to get us the high roller room?"

Vic burst out laughing, running his finger over a delicate layer of dust on the edge of the television. He held his dirty index finger right between my eyes with his slick smile riding up one side of his lips. "They can dress this town up with lights and pretty colors, but the foundation is still the grime!" He wiped his finger on my shirt collar, leaving a light smudge.

I rolled my eyes. "I was just messing with you, but don't act like this cheap room is some kind of great symbol. Let's get out of here and go gamble."

♥ ♣ ♦ ♠

It was hard to tell which gave me more vertigo, the heat when I left the airport or the dizzying display of the casino floor. The heat was impressive, but the casino was definitely like nothing I had ever seen in my life. The carpet was a tacky blend of about a thousand different colors swirled all together in some kind of pattern that seemed to go on for miles. The machines, from the slots to the video poker and even the ATMs, were a show of blinking and flashing and glowing and shining. There was noise coming from every possible direction. A loud murmur floated around highlighted by blips and bloops and the occasional ring of a bell going off (inevitably followed by a shriek of temporary joy).

"What do you want to play first, my man? It's pretty much all here, any game you want to play can be found. How about some blackjack? Always a good, smooth start to a Vegas trip."

I just nodded back at him, most of my confidence shot by the realization of just how inexperienced and naïve I was about gambling in a real casino.

♥ ♣ ♦ ♠

We started our evening by playing blackjack at the Tropicana. We settled down at the half-circle table that was felted in black with purple and gold accents. A little plastic sign read: 'MIN BET: $25, MAX BET: $1000'. I was nervous, so I figured that I would just do basically everything that Vic did. When he laid $200 in cash on the felt in front of him, I did the same. The gold-vested dealer, who was previously not dealing to anybody else, gave us a huge smile and exchanged matching stacks of chips for the cash that we'd put down.

Vic smiled back and said, "We expect only the best from you this evening."

The dealer nodded and replied, "Absolutely, good luck gentleman."

Neither of us dipped down below $100 in the two hours we stayed at the same blackjack table, and we left up. We won $325, with Vic winning $225 and me an even $100. We also had a par-ticularly attentive waitress who made sure we had a fresh bottle of beer every twenty minutes. It probably helped that Vic tipped her $5 with all but one or two of the beers. At Vic's suggestion, we left the Tropicana and made our way to the MGM Grand. The evening air actually felt pretty good. The sun was still up, but it wasn't beating on us like it had been when we got off the plane. We crossed a big cement bridge that straddled the strip, and I stood at the middle of it, taking in the scene as far as I could see. Vic pointed a few things out while I half-listened and stared at the gaudy limos, excited people, and extravagant buildings. After a few minutes we continued on towards the MGM.

Following Vic, we weaved in and out of the crowd. The whole scene was half fascinating to me and half depressing. I thought about what Josh might be doing back in our dorm room. He probably wasn't there, probably getting hammered at some party that only a few freshmen would even be invited to. Maybe he was just taking a relaxed night playing basketball in the gym with Kevin and Shane from our hallway. I was jerked back to reality when I lost sight of Vic for a second. I stood on my tiptoes and saw his backwards flatbrim with a big 'C' on it. I dashed until I was beside him again. Before I knew it, we were walking past a massive glass cage that held a lion taking a nap on a giant stone. I stared at the impressive fake habitat for a while, but Vic never even glanced over.

After we'd passed the cage, Vic asked, "What do you wanna play here?"

"I don't know, are we gonna play any poker?"

"Nah, that's not the best thing to play to waste a little time. We're just gonna have a little more fun so you can see another casino floor, then it's time to get to business."

"Uh, how about roulette then?" I had never played anything other than poker or blackjack, even in a video game, so I didn't even know what I wanted to play.

"That'll work. That's a good game to play quick, and I only wanna play for an hour so."

"Cool with me. I just gotta take a piss and then I'll meet you at the table."

He was already walking towards a table and simply nodded his head to acknowledge that he'd heard me. I departed, looking at the signs hanging from the ceiling to find one that pointed towards a restroom.

On the way back, I got lost because all of the rows of slot machines looked exactly the same. Everything just seemed to go in one giant circle. As I paced briskly, I got in a state of mildly annoyed panic. It occurred to me that Vic and I weren't so much having a great time as we were just scratching an itch with our gambling. I started to feel a little bit sick so I stood beside an empty row of video poker machines to calm myself down from the combination of anxiety and fullness from beer. I was also able to light a cigarette since it was a special section where smoking was allowed.

I couldn't help watching the cocktail waitresses that floated around looking tucked, squeezed, plucked, and hair sprayed. Even the obviously veteran waitresses with crow's feet and leathery skin caused a stir inside me; turning me on but also kind of frightening me. I examined one near me and could see the faint outline of her nipples protruding from her red and gold glitter top that hugged her boobs. My eyes moved to the deep valley of cleavage that was somewhere between tan and sunburnt; somewhat rough but still sexy. She looked like she smoked cigarettes after she banged somebody. My eyes moved up from her chest and I realized that she definitely saw me staring. I sheepishly looked away. I knew that she probably had hundreds of guys leering at her every day, but I still felt embarrassed. The first thing I saw when I looked away was what appeared to be a bachelorette party of smoking hot '10s.' A pair of young women led the group, drunk and arm-in-arm. One wore a 'BACHELORETTE' sash, while the other wore one that said 'MAID OF HONOR' on it. They wore skirts that were so tight that the fabric seemed to disappear under the curves of their asses. My head followed them as they stumbled on their heels on the tricky marble floor, and I realized that they were passing the roulette table where Vic was sitting.

I hadn't exactly expected the trip with Vic to be a huge party like we were rock stars or something. Still, something felt off compared to other people around the city. Like the clan of young hot women I'd just seen, most other people seemed to be in a state of revel and celebration. Vic and I had basically done nothing but head straight to the tables. I don't know if I'd even have wanted it any other way, it was just very obvious that we weren't really part of the festivities. I put my cigarette out in an ashtray in front of the nearest slot machine and made my way back to Vic.

I got the gist of the game after a few spins and some instruction from Vic. We watched the white pill spin around the wheel and screamed out numbers and colors like lunatics for an entire hour. It was exciting, but we both lost what we'd won at the Trop playing blackjack. In fact, I lost another forty on top of that. It was okay though, especially because the other people at the table were nice to us and we talked about where we were from and other stuff. I still hated losing, but it wasn't as bad when I could commiserate with the other people who were losing. We had to fib a little bit about my age and left out exactly why we'd come to Vegas. We just said that we were taking a break from school and spending some extra money that we'd won picking football games in a contest with our buddies. Small talk was a lot easier with Vic assisting me. He had no problems socializing with strangers. The hour passed quickly, and we cashed out what we had left on the table and made our way to the MGM sportsbook.

As I expected, I got a little shaky now that we were actually going to go through with it. I'd been fingering the envelope of cash all day in my front pocket, making sure every few minutes that it was still there. This time, I pulled the whole envelope out and handed it to Vic, leaving a stamp of moisture from my fingertips.

He snatched it out of my hand quickly and put it in his own pants pocket.

Vic said slowly, "Relax, man. Nobody is going to bother us. You're okay, right?"

"It's alright, I'm good to go. I think it would be best if I just wait outside the sportsbook. You take care of the bet and I'll just watch from outside."

"Whatever you're more comfortable with, it *is* your money." He looked at me one last time and waited for me to nod in confirmation. I did, and he started towards the sportsbook.

While I sat at a penny video poker machine, I watched Vic stare at the complicated board of numbers, then disappear from my view towards the back of the lounge-area. Seconds later, my phone rang and I immediately picked up Vic's call with a little concern. I stood up from the machine even though I had credits left, and walked towards a quieter area of the casino floor. "What's up, something wrong?"

"Nothing wrong, I just wanted to check with you one more time now that I know what the actual moneyline is. You're looking at -110 to bet on Middenburg to win. Is that okay with you?"

I thought carefully about the numbers. -110 meant that I'd have to bet $110 to win $100, a total payment of $210 back to me. Betting $6000 would mean I could pay back Uncle Pete in full and have almost $3500 left. No debt for my uncle to bother me about and a head start towards paying for college. "That's fine, man, go ahead with it."

Vic answered very seriously, "Okay, just tell me in words that you understand how the moneyline works. I don't mean to be a dick, I just want everything to be crystal clear before you put this money on the line."

"I, Corvus, do declare that I understand how a moneyline bet works. Now please make the bet before I piss myself in nervousness and wimp out."

Vic ended the call without a word. Less than twenty minutes later I had a betting slip in my hand with the correct date, the time he'd place the bet, and large font at the bottom that said: 'RISK $2000.00 to WIN $1818.18, Middenburg University vs. Indiana Central University, 1:00 p.m.'

We made the same bet at The Mirage.

Then we made the final one at Bellagio.

By ten o'clock I had $6000 on a college football game. About $5950 more than I've ever bet on a single sports game in my life.

CHAPTER 60

I recognized the Fremont Casino (although I had never known its name). Across Fremont Street, the 4 Queens Casino was even more recognizable with its rounded, bulging awning that was jam-packed with lightbulbs. But Vic wasn't interested in going to any more casinos for the night. We ended up at a bar that he said was one of his favorite spots in Las Vegas, a place that his own uncle had introduced him to in downtown Las Vegas. It was called The Ruffled Wing, and it was on a side alley off of Fremont Street. I was a little more worried about going to a bar underage because it was a more intimate, but Vic assured me that I wouldn't have an issue. Sure enough, when we entered, the bartender only asked us what we'd like to drink. It appeared I wouldn't even need to use my fake I.D. in Vegas. Vic ordered a beer and a shot of Irish whiskey for each us without asking if that's what I wanted. When they arrived, he lifted the shot and said, "All the luck in the world, buddy." He downed his shot, barely waiting for me to lift mine.

We spoke again about his family, but it quickly shifted to mine. It was rare for him to ask questions about me, so I felt almost flattered that he was interested in hearing more about me and my life. I told him more about the dynamic between my dad and Uncle Pete, giving as many details as I could remember. I also told Vic about my friends back home, the things that Jeremy and I did for fun. And about our poker games.

"That's really cool you have a group of friends who play cards like that. You should hang on to buddies like that if you're lucky enough to have them," Vic remarked.

"Yeah, my friends don't play for as much money as the games you and I play, but it's definitely more fun with them. I don't mind most of the people at the games around campus, but it's kinda weird to spend so much time with strangers. I hardly know anything about the people we play with."

Vic answered with a hint of sadness, "You have no idea. I had more friends when I first started going to school. Now I spend so much time around games and dealing with bettors, I don't really have any close friends."

"But you go to parties and seem to know a lot of people at Middenburg."

"Half the people I party with just know me because they bet. Even the ones that don't bet are just people I drink and hang out with. Partying with people doesn't mean you're real friends. In a lot of cases, people just like to have as many contacts in their phone as possible so they always have a party to go to. I'm not bitching, and there are some people that I care about in Middenburg. I'm just saying, if you have some close hometown friends, try not to lose 'em."

I nodded and chugged the last few ounces of beer in my pint glass.

♥ ♣ ♦ ♠

After talking and drinking for another few hours, Vic looked at me with a furrowed brow and asked, "So what are you going to do with all these winnings if you exit Las Vegas a winner?"

"I was thinking I would invest it in CD's or savings bonds or something at the bank. It might not make a ton of money right away, but it's safe and easy to hide from my parents until I can think of some way to explain where the money came from. I'm probably gonna cut down on the poker games and just sit on those investments."

Vic stared at me for a moment. "The planning is fine, but be careful about thinking this win will solve all your problems. I've been in spots before where I won some money and thought for sure I'd use it to change my life. Before I know it, it's used up and I'm still the same guy I've always been. For your sake, I hope you follow through with your plans. Just don't put so much of your hope into it that it breaks you if it doesn't quite work out." He stared into his empty glass, letting a full minute of silence go by. "Hey, let's get outta here. We'll get a cab and pick up some beer. We can order some pizza on the way back and just pass the hell out till tomorrow's excitement. Good?" Since it was Vic, I didn't even bother answering. He paid for our drinks with cash on the bar. We left when the bartender scooped up the money and Vic said, "No change, ma'am."

CHAPTER 61

The cheap alarm clock on the nightstand told me that it was 12:32 when I woke up. It was nearly time for possibly the most important football game I'd ever watch. Vic wasn't around, but I figured that he'd just run out to get something to eat. I decided to get a three or four minute shower and slip on some fresh clothes before the game came on. Vic and I had decided to watch the game in the room; I didn't really want to be around other people while I watched. Even so, a clean change of clothes would be nice after the previous long day. When I came out of the bathroom in the clean boxers, jeans, and t-shirt that I'd taken in, Vic was sitting on the edge of the bed with a grim look on his face. "Fuckin' terrible news man." He simply pointed at the ESPN broadcast playing loudly on the television. My heart hit the floor when I finally understood what the story was about.

"Holy shit, they have no chance without them. How did this happen?"

"I have no idea, I'm so sorry about this. I don't even know what to say."

"What the fuck, I can't sit on these wagers; I gotta do something. I'm screwed if I don't!"

"Do you have another six g's to bet on your uncle? I'm guessing not. I wish I could help but I don't have that kind of cash. I have a little back at school, but it's a drop in the bucket anyway. Besides, the line is all wonky now, and it's fifteen minutes until kickoff."

"You gotta have something to at least hedge some of this action! C'mon, you really don't have anything? Don't you know somebody that can send us money or something?"

"I'm really sorry, but the people that I work with wouldn't do that. I'm small potatoes, dude. Nobody is gonna send an assload of cash to the desert because of the unfortunate situation of some young guy that they don't know. I feel for you, man, I really do.

I just found this out when I saw it on a TV at the one bar downstairs. If I could do anything, I would."

I'd mostly stopped listening to him and was staring with bloodshot eyes at the screen. After fifteen minutes of listening to me whisper every variation of curse words that I knew, Vic silently got up and changed the channel to the game broadcast.

CHAPTER 62

"Glad you're tuning in folks! We should have an interesting game today; we have a nice fall chill in the air, and both teams are ready to go at it in this annual rivalry. Middenburg has had the advantage recently, going 8-2 in the last decade. The typically perennial power, ICU has seen a depressing decline in the last few years, leaving Coach Pete Crayton on the hot seat this year. There has been plenty of activity in the rumor mills that Crayton must pick up a few key wins this year if he has any hope of renewing his contract. As many of you already probably know, there has been a troubling news story that broke very early this morning involving two Middenburg players. Let's go to Michelle Sanders with more on that story."

"Thanks, Bill. Freshman running back James Raven and sophomore safety Jamal Figueroa from Middenburg will be absent from today's game. Both are currently being held at the Center City Police Station. Officers discovered a significant amount of narcotics in the apartment that the two shared that appeared to be packaged for resale. Police seized just under 40 grams of cocaine, 75 thirty-milligram Adderall tablets, two ounces of marijuana, and an undisclosed amount of oxycontin. We'll have more on this story as details are released."

"Thanks, Michelle. This has, of course, dominated the news and sports blog headlines today. A ton of information is arising, creating a storm of hearsay and passionate opinions. Nowhere is more abuzz than the ICU campus, and Jefferson Buckley Stadium, where today's game is being played. The tailgating and wild atmosphere, known for being one of the craziest in college football, has been ramped up even more than usual today. These fans have had to deal with some rough seasons in the last few years, and the arrests made last night have ICU fans smelling blood. While the circumstances are extremely troubling, there is still a game to be played today, and the mojo will almost certainly be on ICU's side to start this game. Let's take a quick commercial break and then we'll be back for the kickoff!"

CHAPTER 63

"Both teams are lined and ready to roll. Annnnnnnd, with the simultaneous roar of the wound-up crowd, the ball is up in the air off of Middenburg kicker Jefferey Lentze's foot and about to land in the waiting hands of ICU's speedy return man, D'onte Jackson. With that, we're off!"

Right as the game was starting, I got a text from Jeremy. He wondered if I wanted to bet five bucks on the game just for fun. He said he'd even take Uncle Pete's team if I wanted to bet on Middenburg. I dropped my phone into my suitcase and zipped it shut then buried my face into a pillow.

"Halfway through the first quarter, ICU has a tiny 3-0 lead due to a decent drive that was finished off with a thirty-eight-yard boot from junior kicker Frank Stells. Other than that, this matchup has been a tough defensive struggle with neither team getting anything significant going on offense. Already, it's obvious that Middenburg is sorely missing its young star, James Raven. They've netted only eleven rushing yards, six of which was from a Q-B scramble by Boone. Following the scoring drive, Middenburg has just had another three and out, and now has to kick. The snap is a good one and Salvock gets the punt off with no trouble. Jackson fields the high-flyer around the thirty-five. After going towards his own team's bench he changes his mind and stops on a dime to start toward the other side of the field. He doesn't look to have much room as the Middenburg punt team closes in on him. But wait! Jackson cuts inside at the hash marks and finds a seam amongst the bodies! He gets a block, avoids one tackler, and finds a little room! He's off like a shot and nobody is within five yards of him! He has some room before he reaches the sideline, and he takes full advantage of the space as he cranks off another fifteen yards! He's at the

Middenburg 45! 40! 35! Just when it looks like he's going to take it to the house, here comes Berman like a rocket! He's closing in on Jackson. He catches him around the twenty-eight yard-line! A fantastic play by Berman to save a touchdown, but ICU still has fantastic field position after the incredible return by Jackson! The ICU offense is on its way out to take over deep into Middenburg territory, and they look even more fired up than they've already been."

I wasn't hopeless, but I still had a terrible feeling about the game. Normally, I'd be happy to see a close game, even when I was betting on it. In this case, I hoped for all the ICU players to fall ill and force my uncle to put the cheerleaders in the huddle.

"On what has been Middenburg's first successful drive, they now find themselves facing fourth down and a foot on the ICU twelve-yard line. Normally, game strategy dictates that, especially in a close game, you kick the field goal here and take the easier points. Coach Williams must feel differently. He is opting to send out his offense to attempt the fourth down conversion. This is a dangerous decision, and one would have to guess that this is an attempt to really grab the momentum in this game. Apparently Williams isn't satisfied with a long, well-constructed drive and three points. The play clock is down to seven seconds, and in that amount of time we'll see if the fans will be calling Williams a genius or an idiot. Amidst the rush of sound that is the ICU fans, Middenburg sets up in an I-formation with Higgenbotham and Clark stacked behind the young quarterback, Boone. ICU stacks the box, obviously banking on a run play here despite the fact that Middenburg is missing its star runner. The safety, Jackson, is moving towards the line of scrimmage to further jam the middle. Boone takes the snap and exchanges the ball with Higgenbotham, who hits the line with great quickness. But it doesn't matter! ICU drops him a half yard behind where Middenburg needed to be! Oh, they're certainly missing Raven on this one. Higgenbotham has excellent speed, but he just doesn't have the mass that Raven does. Middenburg would have loved to use Raven's heavier frame to get that extra bit they needed to continue their drive. Instead, ICU will take over around their thirteen-yard line. The crowd is going absolutely bonkers as Coach Pete Crayton exchanges high-fives with his defenseman coming off the field! Despite the misstep by Middenburg, it's still only 10-0 in favor of ICU, although that last play may have been the early dagger in the minds of ICU fans!"

CHAPTER 64

"Welcome to halftime of this conference rivalry game in Indiana. As it stands, ICU is currently holding a 13-0 lead at half. After they stopped a Middenburg drive on fourth down, they marched it up the field but only managed a field goal on that possession. Middenburg is just incredibly out of sorts. They're missing Raven and Figuero physically, but it seems like even more of the team is absent mentally. Quite frankly, they're very fortunate to be in as good of shape, score-wise, as they are. There hasn't been an update on the two arrested players, as law enforcement is still trying to work out the mess and gather all the details. We'll give you an update if anything arises. Before we discuss the first half, let's check out some other scores from around the nation. What's going on out there, Pat?"

My halftime break consisted of smoking a stale menthol and the last ten sips of flat pop left in my cup from the night before, both consumed on the sidewalk in front of the Tropicana. I was far enough from the front door that security guards wouldn't shoo me away. A bleach blonde in a silver sequin dress asked me if she could have a sip of my drink. I told her she could have the rest and watched her Adam's apple move up and down twice before I turned around and started back to my hotel room. I could hear the click-clack of heels moving in the opposite direction.

CHAPTER 65

"After a first play for no gain, Middenburg sets up in shotgun formation for the second play of this half. Boone takes the snap cleanly and takes a three step drop. He looks immediately for his outlets near the first down markers, but quickly turns his attention upfield! Rarely used wideout Kenneth Martin has a step and a half on his man! Boone has enough time to set his feet securely and heaves it forty yards downfield . . . into the waiting arms of Martin! He's got it and it looks like he could take it to the house. The safety is gaining on him but he's running out of yards. He hits the red zone and it looks like nobody is going to get him! Wow, an eighty yard play on a gutsy call at their own twenty to get Middenburg right back in this game. Somehow, they were able to keep the score low in the first half, so one touchdown now has them within two field goals or another touchdown. And they have a fresh shot of momentum. With a missing star and a stagnant run game, they're going to have to rely on big plays to survive in this one, and they got just that from a Boone connection with Kenneth Martin. Stay tuned folks, we have a game here!"

I chewed on a leftover piece of cold room service pizza just to do something. I could barely get my teeth through the crust and the sauce was more like a film that could be peeled away like sunburned skin.

"After the big touchdown play by Middenburg, ICU accepts the kick for a short return to the 16, keeping the momentum on the side of M-U. ICU lines up to try to answer. On first and ten, ICU lines up with a single back and hands the ball off to him. It's Ron Barry, and he picks up a solid four yards on a nice second effort. The ball is officially spotted at the nineteen and a half yard line. On third and six, Barry gets the ball again on a screen pass to the weak side. He picks up eight yards and the first down for ICU! Middenburg expected a run to the other side of the field and enough space was created for Barry to work out an extra five yards after the pass to the get the first and a little bit more."

I went to the bathroom and took a piss, not caring to watch the steady progress of ICU. I washed and dried my hands slowly. I grabbed one of the wrapped plastic cups sitting beside the ice bucket. The ice had melted and one tiny bug was on the surface of the warm water, desperately batting its diminutive wings. I pinched it between my fingers and flicked it into the sink. I filled the cup halfway with water and drank it in one gulp before returning to the edge of the bed to continue watching.

"ICU is now in Middenburg territory at their twenty-four yard line. The snap goes off cleanly and quarterback Bukowski takes two steps to his left. ICU has a height mismatch in their favor on the left side and it looks like it could be a quick fade to see if the six foot seven Johnson can win the jump-ball. But no! Bukowski swiftly changes his vision and zips it to the tight-end Walters who is wide open at the back of the end-zone! Touchdown ICU! It will be a 20-7 ballgame if ICU is able to hit the extra point!"

Earlier in the game, Vic had been throwing in the occasional positive remark to try to cheer me up. Now he just sat with a disappearing twelve pack of light beer beside him, not offering any words to me since there weren't any that would do any good.

"Folks, ICU is showing to be the dominant team in this game, aided greatly by the holes in Middenburg's squad today. The score is now 27-10 after a Middenburg fumble that ICU turned into a long grinding drive that exploited several short passes up the middle where Figueroa would normally be taking care of business. ICU capitalized on that drive with another touchdown, this one taken in on a keeper by Bukowski. Middenburg could only answer with a field goal before the end of the third quarter. Even that drive was peppered with near interceptions and a fumble that they were lucky enough to recover. A pass interference call got them into field goal range before they stalled out and took their three points. Again, it's 27-10 as the teams flip sides for the last time in this game."

I couldn't stand to watch the rest of the game so I took the elevator down to the casino and parked myself in front of a slot machine. I tapped the same button over and over, watching fifty dollars disappear one dollar at a time. After a half hour, the little red glowing number was below fifteen. Then ten. Five. Four.

"Three, two, one, and that's all she wrote folks! ICU is gonna have bragging rights in this conference rivalry until next year's matchup! Coach Pete Crayton is gonna be mighty happy to have this win under his belt. This one might take him off the hot seat and save his job, although only time will tell what happens with that situation. Stay tuned after for a postgame breakdown with the guys back at the studio!"

CHAPTER 66

ICU: 5-5, Corvus: $190

CHAPTER 67

Alone, save for a few stragglers and a couple members of the library staff, a young man sits at one of the many computer desks placed around the first floor. His desk is only three away from the checkout area where the head librarian is tidying up a few things and organizing some returns in preparation for the next day. She presses her stubby finger on the button of the intercom system and holds it in while saying gently, "Attention, please. The library will be closing in five minutes. Please check out immediately if you need to, log out of any computers you may be signed into, and exit the front door only."

A student member of the library staff appears at the bottom of the main staircase of the library and makes her way towards the head librarian. "All the other floors are empty, Ms. Gillen. Everybody is on the first floor or left."

"Thank you, Jill. I'll see you next Wednesday." After a brief wave, the librarian bobs her head while counting the three people still left in the library.

The young man, who is still seated at the computer, has a large pair of headphones on, and is staring intently at the monitor in front of him. A news video is playing, and the screen changes from a blond reporter to a blue background. In the center of the screen, the young man is suddenly looking at a mirror image. His face is on the screen with white letters underneath that spell 'James Raven.' Feeling the eyes of the librarian, and being aware of the nearing closing-time, he pauses the video with two minutes left. He pulls the headphone plug from the jack on the front of the computer tower, folds them up, and packs them inside his backpack. After zipping up his bag, he presses play on the video again, letting it play out loud since nobody is around.

"This bizarre story has not been completely pieced together, but the original suspects have been released without being charged. Raven and Figueroa have been cleared of all

wrongdoing. Police found sufficient evidence that the students' residence was broken into in the very early morning on Saturday. Detectives have developed a timeline for what they believe happened at the apartment from Friday afternoon to Saturday morning, based on several witnesses they interviewed. On Friday afternoon, an employee for a heating and air-conditioning company completed a service call at the apartment. This was arranged by Raven and Figueroa's landlord after the two complained of inconsistent heating in the apartment. The employee was in both the basement and the living room to complete the work, then left around five o'clock p.m. The landlord stopped by around midnight to collect rent checks from a lockbox outside the apartment complex, but did not enter the residence. Between six and six-thirty the following morning, a neighbor was out walking her dog and noticed dark smoke exiting an exhaust pipe outside the apartment. When she received no answer at the door of the apartment, she called the police. When they arrived and also got no answer at the door, they retrieved the landlord's phone number from a resident of another apartment in the building. The landlord and the police entered the apartment and immediately saw packaged narcotics on a coffee table in the living room. The landlord informed the police that Raven and Figueroa are on campus preparing for an away football game. An officer is sent to detain Raven and Figueroa before the bus leaves for the game. He took them to the police station where they are put in a holding cell. At approximately eight o'clock a.m., the heating and air-conditioning employee is contacted by the landlord and summoned to the apartment to examine the furnace. He discovered that he had a setting wrong on the furnace that was causing an excessive level of fuel to be burning. While in the basement, he pointed out to the police a broken window that he claimed was intact when he was at the apartment the previous day. Police questioned him further regarding the state of the apartment. He noted that the apartment appeared to be significantly messier than the day before. They asked him if he noticed the narcotics on the table in the living room the first time he was in the apartment. He did not remember seeing anything suspicious on the table, and, in fact, believed that the table had been totally empty. Police closely examined all of the rooms in the apartment after talking to the employee. They now suspect that a low-level drug dealer -possibly a student who was acutely aware of the players' schedule- forcibly broke into the apartment with the intent to burglarize the residence. A video game system was unplugged from the television, several drawers in the bedroom had been rifled through, and two pairs of valuable collector's edition sneakers had been removed from a closet. Police suspect that the perpetrator was alarmed—possibly by the landlord collecting checks- and fled the scene, leaving behind drugs that he or she was carrying. The heating and air-conditioning employee is being questioned further but is cooperating completely with police and has no criminal record or history of drug use. Police will be interviewing nearby residents to determine if they saw anything strange at the apartment from Friday afternoon until early Saturday morning. Anyone with relevant information is encouraged to contact the police tip-line at 1-800-INFOLINE. As for Raven and Figueroa? Cleared legally, by the university, and by the N.C.A.A., both players are again active on the team and back to class as usual."

With the video coming to an end, he scrolls to the bottom of the video box and takes note of the time the video was posted and how many views it had. In less than a week, the video had been viewed 1,229,387 times. He shakes his head in amazement, closes the page, and logs out of the computer. Feeling a light hand on his shoulder, he turns his head back and up.

"All done and ready to go?" The librarian smiles at the young man, patting her hand on his shoulder in an almost motherly gesture.

"Yes, ma'am. Sorry if I'm holding you up." He tosses on a flat brim cap and slides his backpack onto his shoulders.

"No problem, dear. You have a good night, now."

He grins at her and responds, "I will, and same to you."

CHAPTER 68

ICU: 6-5, Corvus: $167

CHAPTER 69

Before leaving for Thanksgiving break, I'd passed off the baggies of narcotics to Vic so he could try to sell them. He wasn't much of a drug dealer, but he said he knew somebody who would take them all in one shot if we gave them to him cheap. That meant the recovered money, especially after giving Vic a cut of the money, wouldn't even begin to cover my Vegas loss. I was definitely okay with that since I wanted them gone as soon as possible. I just wanted to get through the rest of the semester avoiding any distractions. That included poker and parties. It felt like at least a small weight was off my shoulders when Vic took the backpack from me. I had emptied the bag of all my books. I'd sold two online that I wouldn't be needing the rest of the semester. They were replaced with the books from my uncle that still had the drugs hidden inside. Getting rid of them made me feel like I could at least calm down and coast through the rest of the semester, get some kind of low "C" average, and distance myself from the whole thing.

We sat down to Thanksgiving dinner a little later than we normally would, around 1:30, because it was only my parents and I. I was happy to hear that Uncle Pete wouldn't be showing up because he had team matters to attend to; whatever that meant. It was out of the ordinary that our extended family wasn't together for Thanksgiving. Grandpa Crayton had gone on some kind of golf vacation with some buddies he'd recently reunited with, and my aunt had planned her own vacation when she heard that he wouldn't be around for the holiday. She and my cousins were in New York City while Uncle Pete stayed home. I was curious what matters he had to attend to, but I was pretty sure he wouldn't be sharing that information with me. After he'd found a different accomplice to pull off the setup, I could absolutely say I had no idea what all he was doing behind closed doors. Since it was only my parents and I, mom had made a much smaller meal and didn't rush around to get it done at a certain time, which made for a really relaxing day.

I loaded up my plate with everything except the canned cranberry sauce that always looked to me like old Jell-O. My Mom looked at me with a smile, a bite of stuffing on the fork that was poised midway to her mouth, and said with mild excitement, "Guess what?"

"Turkeybutt."

Mom rolled her eyes at me and went on anyway, "Your dad is back in the bowling league. He bowled a 207, a 177, and a 195 his first week back! It was so fun to watch him again!"

I looked at Dad and said, "Holy cow, how long has it been? Fifteen years? Seventeen years?"

He finished his bite and answered, "Something like that. Way, way over a decade anyway. My bowling bag looked like an antique amongst the others. Felt great to bowl again, and I did pretty good."

"That awful bag was old and out of style when you played in the league before. I'm not surprised it looks a little out of place," Mom said with a giggle.

"Hey, as long as that bag carries the ball that rolls me 200 games, I don't really care if I win the fashion award."

While we all laughed, I suddenly had a flashback to when I had a birthday party at the bowling alley. Somebody had given me a pack of baseball cards and I'd gotten an Alex Rodriguez rookie card. I'd kind of recognized that it might be worth saving, so I'd put it a plastic sleeve when I got it home. That didn't really last though and I ended screwing up the corners of the card from messing with it all the time. Any value was lost and it just became another crappy card in my collection that I ended up selling for fifteen dollars when I needed gas money. The party at the bowling alley had been made up of a dozen or so of my elementary classmates. Probably half of them I hadn't spoken to since that party. A couple, like Jeremy, I still talked to today. I got good presents that day, but I still regretted not taking care of the rookie card. Buried somewhere in my closet was a real bowling pin with "Happy Birthday!!!" written on it in sharpie.

"That's really cool, Dad." It was nice to see my Dad doing something that seemed to make him genuinely happy. I only barely remembered when he had previously bowled in the league, but I do remember him talking about it fondly years later. "Glad you're bowling again. I expect to see that 300 game you always said you could get if you tried hard enough. You're getting pretty up there old man, before you know it your bones will be too weak to handle anything but a six pound ball."

Dad laughed loudly again and held up his glass of iced tea, saying, "I'll drink to that!"

After dinner, Dad and I did the dishes in a sort of satisfied silence. Every once in a while, we would get in each other's way by accident and exchange quiet, mumbled apologies. The TV was on in the living room and Mom was watching it intently, one foot in the kitchen and the other on the living room carpet. Dad kept nudging me and gesturing at her with his chin, snickering because she was so involved in the show that she dried the same dish for a solid ten minutes. She finally put it back in the cabinet while he and I grinned at each other.

CHAPTER 70

Between Thanksgiving naps and a full night of rest, I probably slept an amazing eleven hours. I was awake but still in bed when I heard a light knock on the door. I said, "C'mon in." My dad stepped in with the newspaper and cordless phone in his hand.

"Did you hear about your uncle?"

I looked up from my book, pulling the folded coupon I was using as a bookmark from my mouth and stuck it in the page I'd been reading. "No, what's up?" I thought for sure Uncle Pete had been caught and the whole story would be exposed. It's astounding how fast blood can start coursing through your body sometimes. My heart immediately started to hammer like a dose of high-powered drugs had been shot into my bloodstream. Maybe it was just my paranoia and hyper-sensitivity, but I felt like my anxiety was on obvious display.

My dad apparently didn't notice, because he continued, "Sources are saying that he's going to get the contract that he's been stressing about all year. I just talked to your aunt on the phone and she said the word in the athletic department is that they're going to offer a three-year deal. Aunt Sarah says it should be somewhere between $3,000,000 and $4,000,000 total. I watched the news after I talked to her and they said pretty much the same thing."

Once I realized Uncle Pete hadn't been caught and my blood pressure returned to normal, I was able to process what my father was saying. I responded, "I can't believe they're discussing it already. Last game is tomorrow. I thought it would be months after the football season before anything would happen."

"Nothing is official, but it certainly seems that something will be offered that will allow him to stay at ICU. I don't know how he pulls it off. He just always seems to find ways to get what he wants. I don't always understand it; I guess we're just different kinds of people is all. It takes all my energy to get a couple thousand a year raise. Some years I haven't even gotten that."

I shook my head and said quietly, "He finds a way."

My dad cleared his throat and said, "Don't tell your mother I told you this. Uncle Pete offered to lend us the money to pay your tuition. Actually, he offered it to me. As far as I know he never discussed it with your mother. He said he would only charge a little bit of interest to cover what he would have made on it if it was sitting in his savings account, which is peanuts compared to a regular school loan rate. I know you think about the money issue, and I'm glad you care about it. I hope you're not upset that I turned him down. You have to understand that loaning us that money is not nearly as loving as it seems. Part of it is my own pride, but it's not just that. He loaned your mother a couple thousand a few years ago when her car needed repairs. He was terrible. She paid it back to him long before the date they agreed upon, but it didn't matter. He was constantly making her feel bad about having to borrow money. He'd question us taking a vacation even when it was a just a cheap road trip to some state parks or something. He felt the need to offer me financial advice—in the most condescending ways possible, of course. Basically, he questioned my manhood and my ability to take care of our family. Anyway, that's that. Your mom and I are going out for the day, but we'll have dinner later. You aren't going out with any of your friends, are you?"

"Nope, I'll be sticking around tonight. I might hang out with Jeremy this afternoon, but I should be back around dinnertime." I thought for a few seconds and said to my dad, "Uncle Pete sure can be an asshole." I normally didn't swear in front of my Dad, but he just smiled and laughed again. Looking out the window, I caught a small glimpse of the far away river. It was just a glint and a sparkle barely peeking out from the horizon that mostly consisted of trees and rooftops. I suddenly wished I was eight years old again, when the heaviest weight on my mind was the struggle to get more than four skips with a stone on the surface of the water.

My dad turned to leave and said, "You ain't kiddin' buddy."

♥ ♣ ♦ ♠

Later, I met Jeremy near his house and we walked a half mile or so to the convenience store along Eighth Street. We got bottles of pop and stood outside sipping at them, for lack of anything better to do. I watched Jeremy and noticed a little grease stain on his index finger. It was probably from his job at a local hardware store that he'd gotten after he'd decided not to enroll in community college. He was good at fixing small engines like chainsaws and weed trimmers and stuff, which had helped him get the position at the store. "How's Harris & Sons treating you?"

"Pretty damn good, actually. Waking up early sucks, but it isn't much different than going to school every day. Plus, it's better than school because I get to do some stuff that's kind of interesting. I do a lot of bullshit like stocking shelves and putting price stickers on stuff, but every once and awhile they let me do some engine work. They hooked up with a tree-trimming company from Astonville, so they're regularly fixing their saws. The company has plenty of saws in rotation, so there's a little extra time to finish them. Because of that, they let me get some practice working on them."

"That's awesome, I'm glad to hear it's working out for you."

"I think I might save enough cash to get my own apartment by next summer. We'll see."

I still hadn't told a soul other than Vic about the situation with my uncle or going to Vegas or anything. I constantly felt compelled to tell somebody, especially a trustworthy person like Jeremy. Even with that in mind, what really bothered me was that I hadn't really had a decent conversation with Jeremy since the middle of summer. He seemed to be getting along fine, but it was still a dickish move on my part to pretty much ignore him the whole semester. "Hey, my bad for not really calling you or anything all semester."

Jeremy looked at me funny and replied, "Um, we're not dating, man. Seriously, you don't need to apologize."

We stood in silence watching a lone bird. A plastic fence separated the convenience store property and the small apartment complex adjacent to the store. The pear-sized bird was sitting on one of the plastic fence-posts, letting out a tweet every minute or so. I remembered a time when Jeremy shot a similar bird with a slingshot he'd gotten for his birthday. Jeremy had turned ten while I was still nine. He'd wanted a BB gun but had to settle for a slingshot because his mother didn't think he was ready for a gun yet. I remember that when the stone struck the bird and it fell, we ran like hell to see it up close. Jeremy was fascinated by it, but I was upset because I could see it was still breathing a little bit. I didn't know what to do so I picked it up and whipped it as hard as I could into the side of Jeremy's house to put it out of its misery. It made a disgusting crunching noise when it struck the brick and fell to the grass again. I'd cried the whole time, not really knowing why I was doing it. The death of a small bird wasn't usually a particularly upsetting occurrence for me, but it bothered me to see it perishing in such a dragged out way with struggled, desperate gasps.

Jeremy picked up a larger rock from the gravel that lined the curb in the store's parking lot. He tossed it sidearm at the bird but missed by about four inches. The rock struck the plastic and made an obnoxious cracking noise that made almost everybody at the gas pumps turn and look our way. Luckily, the rock hadn't pierced the cheap plastic post. Jeremy laughed and I said, "Some things never change." I didn't even know if it would make sense to him, since I'd only thought about the slingshot incident in my own head. He looked over at me and replied, "My aim is much better with a slingshot, though!" We both giggled and I punched him lightly in the kidney.

My phone vibrated in my pocket and I held up a finger to Jeremy. After accepting the call and putting my phone to my ear, I mouthed to Jeremy, "It's my uncle."

CHAPTER 71

ICU: 7-5, Corvus: $418

CHAPTER 72

A man who looks to be in his low or mid-twenties enters a darkly tinted SUV on a virtually deserted street.

After a half hour the passenger door opens and he is visible again.

The salt-and-pepper-haired driver shakes his head as he watches the young guy get further and further away.

The wind kicks up and causes the young man's below-knee length shorts to billow wildly. He tries to walk faster but his flip-flops prevent him from moving much quicker without tripping over them.

While the driver watches him, the young man lifts the lid of a dumpster along the street and tosses a paper tablet with a red cover inside.

Popping off the emergency brake, the driver throws on a visor with the letters "ICU" stitched on the front. Out loud he says, "Too fucking cold for shorts, even a pair that reaches down that far," and hits the gas pedal liberally. The revving engine causes the heat coming from vents to blast a tiny bit harder, and he falls back into a relaxed position while the grunting vehicle climbs the graded street that leads towards the major highway that will get him out of the town.

CHAPTER 73

I walked the whole way to my uncle's house. When I got to the end of his driveway, I started taking yard long strides while counting my steps. I watched my boots depress the snow a couple of inches with each step until I was totally consumed by the crunching and counting. So consumed, in fact, that I nearly ran into my uncle who was waiting in the driveway with a snow shovel in his hand.

"Whoa there!" He put up his beefy hand in the air but I stopped before his fingers touched my chest. "Sweet of you to help me out with snow removal."

"That was a nice touch calling my parents first, offering me good money to shovel snow."

"Well, I like to keep them aware of how willing I am to help you financially if you're willing to do a little work."

"That's very generous of you."

My uncle laughed and handed me the shovel. "You're lucky I'm in a good mood. If you haven't heard, the university is giving me my new contract after our team showed a little more promise this year. I'm good for another three years at least. 7-5 wasn't exactly a career season, but being over .500 and beating Middenburg restored a little faith in me."

"Welp, I better get working on this snow."

"So where's my money, shithead?"

"Nothing left."

He stared at me for a moment, his eyes dancing just slightly back and forth. "I guess that's where we're at now, huh? I figured you'd pull some chickenshit stuff or screw me over somehow. Way ahead of you. That's why I knew I should get a backup. My high school coach always told me that the best plays are the ones with backup options when the first fails."

"Fuck you and your old coach."

"Let me fucking tell you something. You may have a little inside info on me, but it doesn't really mean shit. Let's just say you'd have a very hard time proving I was involved in any way.

Plus, you're not exactly innocent in all of this. I don't know what you did with the money or if you're just planning to keep it, but between the drugs and still having that money, you're not gonna have an easy time of it if you were to approach the authorities. I know this, and I know the best thing for both of us is to just keep our mouths shut. Granted, I have more to lose, but I have a strong feeling that you don't want to deal with this bullshit." His eyes narrowed and he went on, "Here's the deal with all of this: I see what I need to do and I make moves. That's why I'll be putting my signature on multi-million dollar contracts while you spend the next decade in a bitchy little struggle to 'find yourself.' So, don't bother trying to screw with me any further."

I was silent, which was probably as much of a surrender as any response I might've given. It was hard to say exactly how I was feeling. I had some combination of guilt, anger, and regret. I knew what he was saying was true. Although my aversion toward my uncle was at an all-time high, I just wanted the whole experience behind me so I could move on—whatever that might mean for me.

Uncle Pete kicked the shovel hard out of my hand. It flipped once before landing a few yards away. He looked at it, then back at me, and said coolly, "You better get started on that shoveling. You're running out of light and you have a lot of work to do. I'd say about eight grand worth of work, in my estimation."

CHAPTER 74

In a haze of smoke and warm air, a collection of young men sit with goofy grins.

In old armchairs, sagging couches, and a few wooden chairs moved in from the kitchen, they've formed a very loose interpretation of a circle in the living room of the small house shared by four of the young men from the group.

The crew consists of young college football players, all of them with heavy arms and sinewy legs that provide false evidence that would lead one to believe the souls and minds inside are fully-formed men. There are a wide variety of personalities, dreams, and backgrounds all brought together in one room. The bond of being on a team together allows each to have an intricate understanding of at least one part of the lives of the others, even if it ends there.

It's the last week before they leave for a winter break away from each other. Their break will be short by regular students' definitions, but long for a group of young men who spend nearly every waking hour together.

There is one amongst them who seems a bit out of place, evidenced by his clumsy movements and uncomfortable glances. With all eyes on him, waiting in expectation, he doesn't disappoint. From his lungs and out through his pursed lips come the sputters and coughs of a person who has never had a full inhalation of smoke hit their lungs. Lighthearted laughs come from all directions while he continues to struggle with the smoke that causes a weird tickling and itch that can't be scratched. Still, he flashes them a smile in between coughs, confident that the others mean him no harm. He has a little sense of guilt, a little excitement, a little growing paranoia.

CHAPTER 75

I crunched loudly on a mouthful of Cheerios while I scanned the newspaper that I'd found on the kitchen table. I figured Dad probably grabbed it as soon as it had been delivered and read the entire thing before he and Mom left for the flea market that was open every Saturday. I flipped through the different sections, finally finding the sports section. On the bottom right corner there was a small article with the title: ***Raven again faces drug charges***. I couldn't believe what I read.

> Middenburg star running back James Raven is again making the news for something other than his running ability. Some believe that there might have been more to the story with his fall arrest, for which all charges were dropped. Police officers entered a party near the Middenburg campus last Friday due to several noise complaints from anonymous neighboring homes. Inside, several partygoers were found to be under the legal drinking age, and small amounts of marijuana were found around the dwelling. Among others, James Raven was searched and found to be in possession of marijuana and drug paraphernalia. Few other details have surfaced at this time, and the university athletic department has not commented on the matter.

I stood up from the table and grabbed my mom's laptop from the counter. She often kept it there when she planned to consult a website for a recipe. After signing in with her password, which I'd memorized long ago, I went to ESPN.com. I saw the name 'Raven' on the fourth line down on the SC Topics list. I clicked on it and started scanning the page that appeared. The story was almost word-for-word the same as the newspaper article I'd already read. Out of curiosity, I scrolled down to the comment section and read the most recent comments. Nearly all of them were awful, rude remarks ripping apart Raven's character. Some commenters referred back to his arrest during the football season, writing that he shouldn't have gotten off that time, and probably only did because he was such a high profile player. A few smug commenters were proud to say that they had been right about his guilt all along. Some called for expulsion, some for NCAA discipline, and others demanded serious jail time. I closed out the browser window and snapped the laptop shut.

I had mostly been able to push the whole mess with my uncle from my mind, but the article had it again gnawing at me. I felt a rush of guilt about being somehow involved in tarnishing James Raven's image forever, even if it was just from not blowing the whistle on my uncle and even if the major charges had all been dropped. I figured it was no coincidence that he had been caught at the party; he was obviously being watched closely. I also felt like a damn fool for losing all of the money that I had, even if I had been somewhat nudged into it by Vic. I felt terrible about lying to my parents about so many things, and I still couldn't quite figure out if I'd ever explain to them the truth about the whole thing. I folded the newspaper back up and pushed it away from my cereal bowl.

Beside the newspaper was a piece of mail addressed to me from Middenburg University. I sliced the top open with a butter knife, careful not to rip the contents. Pulling it out, I realized quickly that it was a reminder letter to register for spring classes, which I hadn't done yet. Accompanying the letter was a form that would allow me to register by paper and mail it back if I desired. I took both the letter and the entire newspaper, flipped the top of the garbage can open with my foot, and dropped them on top of some old fruit and an empty fried chicken bucket. I felt a rush of air come up at me with a sickening odor that slid into my nostrils.

♥♣♦♠

Not long after eating breakfast, I started walking toward the river, my feet scratching in the tiny bits of gravel, glass, and litter residing on the shoulder of the road. After a quarter mile or so, my sneaker unearthed a flat, smooth stone, flipping it forward until it stopped a few feet away. I knelt down and scooped it up, surprised that I had found such a stone so far away from the river. I stuck it in my pocket, and in the same motion, pulled out a cigarette pack with only one left inside. I lit the last cigarette, but the first draw stung my throat like the confusion and worry that was still stinging my brain from breakfast. I pinched the fiery cherry off the cigarette until it hit the ground, then pitched the rest of it behind me.

At the river I squished my way through the mud stew until I got to the water's edge, watching the lazy swirl of the current. I stood unmoving for a moment, closing one eye to the bright sun. I took the stone from my pocket and flung it sidearm slightly above the surface of the water. It finally touched down for good after skipping eight times. Probably three more skips than I had ever seen anybody throw. I laughed out loud because there was nobody around to witness the feat, and I'd probably never again find a stone so perfect, even if I looked really hard. The water that had been disrupted by the stone began to settle while the stone sunk down to join the other smooth orbs at rest on the riverbed. Plucked from the muck, free from the muddy bank, and clean again, at least for a while.

CHAPTER 76

ICU: 0-0, Corvus: $0.00

About the Author

Job Tyler Leach grew up on the banks of the Susquehanna River in the small town of Bainbridge. He now resides in East Petersburg, PA with his girlfriend Mika and their dog, Carlton. He graduated from Millersville University with a Bachelor of Arts in English and a minor in Sociology. He began writing in high school under the positive influence of an English and Creative Writing teacher. He now balances personal writing with full-time writing in the E-Commerce field. He has learned about several interesting and varied areas while writing in the digital environment including: restaurant equipment, fine hats, and car wash equipment.

Job enjoys reading a wide variety of genres including true crime, fiction, essay writing, classics, sports writing, and biographies. His favorite authors include John Updike, Chuck Klosterman, John Steinbeck, and Charles Bukowski. He also spends his time playing inconsistent golf, obsessing over fantasy sports trades, drinking good beers, playing drums in a band, and being perpetually frustrated at his dart game.

Job focuses his creative writing on novels and short fiction, but also occasionally plays around with poetry and drama. He enjoys updating his personal blog with reviews of whatever book he is reading at the time. *As the Raven Flies* is his first published novel.

28543315R00132

Made in the USA
Middletown, DE
20 December 2018